SO CLOSE TO HOME

DAKOTA ADAMS: BOOK III

By

Galen Surlak-Ramsey

A Tiny Fox Press Book

Tiny Fox Press LLC
North Port, FL

For Lincoln who'd love to ride the Super Vortex

CHAPTER ONE:
WELCOME TO KUMET

With wonder in my eyes, I spun in place and took in as much as I could of the Kibnali world. Admittedly, it wasn't much since we were still inside the coliseum, but the tall, purple trees with spotted yellow leaves, twin moons hanging in the sky, and sweet-and-salty smell in the air was more than enough to light my fire for exploration and adventure.

Since the Kibnali fighters had swept over our position only moments ago, my mind raced with all the possibilities of what the future held. What stuff will we find on this world that no one else had seen? Correction, what would we find on this world that no other human would ever see? After all, we were how many billion years in the past? Not to mention, quite literally on the other side of the universe compared to the Milky Way.

"Don't even think about it, Dakota," Tolby said.

"What?" I replied.

"I know that look in your eye."

"I'm just admiring our surroundings."

"And looking for the next artifact to find or ruin to explore that will inevitably result in us getting cozy with the grim reaper," he added.

I smiled. Guilty as charged. But really, in my defense, my best bud shouldn't have expected anything less. I mean, seriously, we were on an actual Kibnali planet. Something I didn't even realize existed until a few days ago. Hell, this was something that Tolby for all intents and purposes never thought he'd see again either. He should be as excited as I was. Check that. He should be even more excited. But I guess since he was still macking it with Yseri and Jainon, he was still probably too enamored with them to care where we were.

"So, what if I am?" I asked. "We are on a freaking Kibnali planet. How amazing is that?"

"Given recent events, I would think you would be a little less wont of adventure."

I laughed and then winced as my ribs protested in pain. Though my psyche had obviously gotten over our latest near-death experience and battle with Goliath, my body had yet to catch up. Man, I really needed some medical nanobots to patch me up. Along those lines, I did briefly wonder what Kibnali tech would be able to do for me. Did they carry first aid for alien species such as myself? I had no idea. Even if they didn't, I held on to the hope that given the archive cube I still had, with its immense knowledge I could fashion some sort of pain reliever at the very least. But that was another matter.

"Look, if anything, surviving an exploding space station, an obliterated planet, and a fight to the death with a giant, regenerating Nekrael monster should do precisely the opposite," I said. "You of all people should know that."

"How so?"

"Because clearly all of our bad luck has been used up getting us here," I said, rolling my eyes. "Duh."

Tolby sighed. He didn't even have to speak his next words for me to know he was going to argue with my basic premise. "Luck doesn't work that way. Random events are independent of themselves, which is why the house always wins."

"Well, if we end up in a casino and I start losing my life savings, you can bring that up."

"If we were in a casino and you started to lose your life savings, it wouldn't take but two minutes before you were broke," he said with a chuckle. "And that's playing for quarters."

I laughed again. How could I be mad at that? He was dead right. Well, he was dead right up until I managed to sell the Gorrianian resonance cube and be one of the richest girls—nay, people—in all of history. Hell, when I sold that thing, I could bet star systems on a whim for the rest of my life and still retire in an extra-plush palace with gorgeous manservants for eye candy, a wine cellar the size of the Black Sea, and as much chocolate as Earth could produce for the next hundred thousand years. Wouldn't that be nice? BMI be damned.

"Whatever," I said, popping out of my fantasy and returning to the conversation. "Maybe you're just being overly jumpy. Did you ever think about that?"

Tolby shook his head and flicked his tail. "I promise you I'm not being overly protective about this."

"Mm-hmm," I replied. "Like when we first met, and you insisted on following me into the bathroom for a week in case space pirates tried to kidnap me."

"Space pirates did try to kidnap you."

"Yeah, but not in the bathroom, silly," I said. "And that was only because I wouldn't let them intimidate me into paying their stupid hyperspace toll."

"You mean, you didn't have the money to pay that hyperspace toll," he replied.

"Same thing," I said with a shrug. "Point remains, they didn't kidnap me in the bathroom, and you are overreacting to all this."

Tolby shook his head again. "I appreciate your enthusiasm for being on one of my planets, but Dakota, you need to understand that the worlds we settled were far from safe."

"Can't be any more dangerous than any other ones I've been on," I said, looking around. The skies were clear. They even had a bluish tint to them much like Earth, and not a carnivorous monster could be seen. Ergo, the world was ripe for exploration as far as I was concerned. "Besides, your Kibnali buddies should be back soon, right? They can escort us out in the wilds if it's so bad."

"Dakota, you don't understand," he said. "Quite literally, we settled on worlds where everything tried to kill you."

I smirked. "Everything? Really?"

At this point, Jainon joined in the conversation. She had been keeping Empress company and talking about...well, I don't know what, really. I wasn't paying attention all that much. "He's not exaggerating," she said. "We settled worlds where the plants are deadly, and creatures the size of your fist could destroy an entire city in under a week."

"Well, yeah, that's not everything," I said. "What about the water?"

"Orpheaus Prime had water that was so poisonous, three drops could make an entire ocean lethal for ten thousand years," Jainon said.

8

"Fine. What about the dirt?"

Tolby chuckled. "My first assignment out of the core system was to survey Lilinami. The dirt was as acidic as any molecular acid inside a xenomorph."

"Now you're being silly," I said. "How did anything grow there?"

"Nothing did," he replied.

I tutted. Though I did, I was still undeterred and pressed on. "Light?"

"The light from Bentani IV's sun melted exposed skin in less than an hour."

I crossed my arms. "Sounds."

"Veniti VII had a volcano that when it erupted, the sound waves could shatter bones for a thousand kilometers."

My brow dropped, and my face twisted. "Fine. How about shadows then, mister smarty pants. You going to tell me a little dark was the horror of all horrors?"

Jainon's ears went back, and she shuddered. "Tell her about the library."

When Tolby didn't, I gave him an expectant look. "Well? What about it?"

"Came across a library not long before the Nodari war," he said. "Huge thing. Absolutely gargantuan. Inside was filled with these...well, shadows, that ate anything they came across. And I mean anything. They could skeletonize a fully armored Kibnali warrior in seconds."

"You're kidding."

Tolby shook his head. "Not in the least."

"Geebus," I said. "What did you guys do?"

"Took off. Nuked the entire site from orbit," he replied. "Only way to be sure."

My head dropped as I looked at my buddy. He was prouder than a kid who made his first bull's-eye on a womp rat in a T-16, but despite his exuberance, I didn't quite buy the story. "You're telling me you blew up an entire library because the shadows were coming to eat you?"

"We did. Despite the substantial dollar value attached to it."

"Okay, well, I'll be careful. But you're out of your mind if you think I'm going to sit cooped up in some sort of apartment while we wait to figure out where we're going. I've got to climb the mountains! Skim across the seas! I've got to—"

My mini-rant came to an abrupt halt when I heard a tiny growl and felt something clamp down on my toe. I looked down to see this odd creature, about the size of a large parrot, latched on to my foot. It braced itself on four legs, while multiple short tails fanned out in the air and wagged back and forth. It had large purple eyes, a raccoon-like red mask, and a short snout with lots of sharp little teeth. Its fur...well, it didn't look like fur it all. In fact, I wasn't sure what to call it. It glowed yellow and had an aura to it, almost as if it were made from light. Overall, he was adorably ferocious.

"Hey cutie, how's my boot taste?" I asked, chuckling at the sight. I bounced my foot, which only encouraged the little guy to be even more ferocious.

"What the hell is that?" asked Jack.

"Like I should know," I said. "Ask Tolby. He's the one that's convinced everything around here is dangerous."

Tolby eased forward and then knelt by the tiny terror still trying to make a meal out of my foot. "I think...I think it's an *ashi-dasashi*."

My brow wrinkled. "Ad...ashi...a what?"

"Ashi-da-sa-shi," he repeated slowly. "Their existence has always been hotly contested...so, no. It can't be. But I'll be damned if it doesn't look like the drawings."

Jainon joined the inspection. She, too, knelt beside it, but she dropped her head so that her nose was practically touching its back. "I think it might well be. Aren't they supposed to be bigger?"

Tolby flicked his tail. "Who knows? Maybe they aren't. Or maybe he's a baby."

"Could someone tell me what we're looking at?" I asked.

Jainon glanced at me with a smile. "Watch."

Slowly, the Kibnali high priestess put her massive paws around the creature, and once she had it nearly enclosed, she flattened them together.

"Don't squish him!" I exclaimed, jumping back. "He wasn't hurting me!"

Jainon held her smile and separated her paws. Between them, there was no sign of the little devil. "Don't worry, he's fine," she said. "Somewhere else now, but fine."

I spun in place, trying to figure out where the little guy went. "Somewhere nearby?"

Tolby stood and shrugged. "Perhaps. It's been theorized that these guys are almost always in a superposition. They are only in one spot when directly observed. Soon as you turn away from them, they're gone."

"To?"

"To anywhere they like, I imagine," Tolby said.

"So, he's kind of like a leprechaun, only a space leprechaun."

Tolby tilted his head. "A what?"

"Little guys with hats back on Earth," I explained. "Irish mythology? Pot of gold? Disappear when you look away?" As I continued to get a blank stare, I waved my hand at him and sighed. "Ah, forget it."

Something wet hit the side of my cheek. I turned my head to see the *ashidasashi* perched on my shoulder. He lunged for my face with an open mouth, but before he could get a hold of me, I snatched him up. Now in my hand, he flopped his head back while letting his legs flop to the side, exposing a belly I couldn't resist rubbing. "Aw, look at him," I said, making the little guy squirm in delight as I scratched his midsection. "So cute."

"Until he tries to gnaw your face off again," Jack said.

"For the record, he only tried to eat my boot, and as far as I can tell, he didn't even leave a scuff mark. I think I'll take my chances. He'll make a cute pet."

Yseri grinned. "Do pets in your culture have pets?"

"Huh?" My face scrunched in a ball of confusion. "What do...Hey, I'm not Tolby's pet!"

"If you say," Yseri said.

"I do say!"

"He does have to take care of you a lot," she went on. "And always getting you out of trouble. I bet he feeds you, too."

"He does not! I can...sort of cook, thank you very much," I said with a huff. I then looked down at my new tiny friend and went back to rubbing his belly. A melodic purr came from his chest, and my heart warmed. "He's a keeper for sure," I said. "In fact, this has to be a sign. I've been wanting a new lucky elephant to rub, and this little guy is totally letting me get his belly. You watch, we're going to have a great time together."

An ear-piercing shriek filled the air, and a giant shadow flew over me. Before I could react, a giant tentacle coiled around my torso and hoisted me into the air.

CHAPTER TWO:
TRANSPORT

This gargoyle-snake-monkey hybrid thing the size of a bus managed to fly about twenty meters with me before my furry buds sprang into action. A trio of plasma shots hit it in the head and chest, one of which sizzled by my arm as I fought with the stupid beast. The monster crashed to the ground, nearly squashing me in the process. Thankfully, I had enough wits to not brace for the impact, so instead of breaking my arms trying to catch myself, I simply rolled along the ground.

Jack was on me in a flash, helping me up. "Are you okay?"

"Yeah, I think so," I replied while making sure I didn't have any bones protruding from my skin. "Some extra dirt and bruises, but what else is new?"

"That gash on your head, for starters."

"Huh?" Gingerly, I reached up and touched my scalp. Immediately, I wished I hadn't. A sharp sting hit me, and when I pulled my hand back, it was covered in blood, and not just a little. Going by the amount that I could see, and the bit I could feel running down my neck, I'd probably need a transfusion or two. Good thing I'd cracked myself open a million times growing up or I might've freaked out. "Damn it," I moaned. "Tell me my brain isn't leaking out at least."

Jack undid the clasps to his battle-worn armor so it fell to the ground and then took off his shirt and pressed it against my head. "No, I don't think so," he said. "It's long and shallow. Nothing serious."

"Serious enough for you to take off your shirt, apparently."

"It was ruined anyway," he said, stating the obvious. The thing had been put through the wringer lately. It was a small miracle it was even remotely intact.

At that point, I noticed his right arm, or rather, what was installed in his right arm. "You have Progenitor implants?"

"Yep," he said with a grin, flexing his muscle to show off even more so than he usually did. "How do you like that?"

"I should've guessed. How else would you have been able to use the portal device?"

Jack brought his arm over to mine. Once they were lined up, it was plain to see that the circuits on my arm were more intricate than his. Not only that, but they took up more space on my body.

Jack dropped his hand to his side and snorted. "Bah," he said. "I knew that little bugger didn't give me the full package."

"Well, I hope you didn't lose your wallet over the deal," I said. "Especially since I don't think they offer refunds. Who put it in you?"

"The orb guy in Lambda Labs," he replied. "He wasn't going to at first, but once he realized I was about to vaporize the planet trying to get the portal device to work, he came around."

"Yeah, I had a similar experience."

Jack lifted his arm and looked it over once more. "Still, I guess I can't be too mad," he said. "He gave me enough to save your sorry butt."

"My dirty, bloody butt," I said, looking at all the new and old stains my clothes bore. "Well, regardless of you getting some upgrades and what that might mean, there's one thing that's for certain."

"What's that?"

"Never doubt the power of the belly rub," I said. "Haven't had my *ashidasashi* for more than a couple minutes, and he's already saved my bacon from a ravenous flying monster."

"Ahem."

I turned at the sound of Tolby's voice and shot him an impish grin. "You'll always be my furry knight in uber armor, don't worry."

"Thanks," he said. "And for the record, you don't have your pet anymore, either."

"I don't?" I said, looking around. Sadly, everywhere my gaze fell, the *ashidasashi* wasn't to be seen. "Where'd he run off to?"

Tolby shrugged. "As I said before, he could be anywhere."

"Damn. I really liked him, too," I said. "Well, I hope he comes back soon, if for no other reason than for the want of belly rubs. We've got a mutually beneficial relationship going on with those you know."

"Do you now?" Jack asked.

"Duh. He gets pampered. We get good luck. Doesn't get any better than that, does it?"

With that and my hand still pressing against my makeshift bandage, I walked around the body of the dead monster so I could see what tried to eat me. Large, gray bumps covered its leathery skin, and from its corpse wafted a peppery smell. Its face looked like a cross between a pig and a wolf, almost like it was one that had gotten stuck changing into the other. Like a frozen werewolf. Werepig? Pigwolf? Whatever.

Its mouth was filled mostly with large, round teeth that looked exceptionally good at crunching anything from wood to rocks to bones, but it also had a set of canines that no doubt ripped apart prey with ease. Couple that with the pair of ape-like arms bulging with muscles and a lower half that was basically one humungous python tail, I was really, really glad he didn't manage to have me for dinner.

"What is this thing, anyway?" I asked.

"A radakkan," Yseri said, joining me at my side and inspecting the kill. "An apex predator that originally started out on the planet Xin but eventually wound up on several nearby systems as well."

"At least now we know what sector we're in on the star map," said Jainon.

"Now we only need to know when," Tolby added.

The three Kibnali started talking amongst themselves, hoping to figure out the answer to that last bit. As they did, I walked around to the beast's front and squatted. I'm not sure why. I suppose I wanted a good look at what tried to kill me. "Welp, mister apex monster," I said. "Next time you try and make a meal out of me, you should probably make sure my friends aren't around."

"He wasn't trying to eat you," Jainon said.

I looked up, confused. "He wasn't?"

"No, he was trying to mate with you. You can tell because of the orange stripe on his back."

My face scrunched with revulsion. "Eww. Gross. I think I liked it better when I was going to be a snack."

17

"Probably something you'd want to keep out of your autobiography," Jack said with a chuckle. "Not exactly a flattering moment if that happened."

"Yeah," I said, voice trailing. My mind ran with his comment far longer than it should have. Or maybe, it ran with it as far as it should have, because once it was done tossing it around, I had a glorious idea, one that would give me renewed purpose in life— which was something I desperately needed, because for the last few days, all my life centered around was not dying. And let's face it, that's a pretty crappy way to go on living. "You know what? I think I will write a book about it."

Jack laughed. Hard. I couldn't help but feel a little silly when he did. "About what? Being dry-humped by a flying tentacle? I mean, to each their own, but I didn't think you were the kind of girl to get into that."

"Maybe I am."

Jack perked. "You are?"

"Maybe," I said, as dead-faced as I could manage. In all honesty, it wasn't my thing. As Jack said, to each their own, but making out with a giant octopus never appealed to me. I could go for getting tied up every now and again, but the line gets drawn at all things squirmy. That said, I couldn't help but mess with him. "Do you want to watch?"

"I..."

I smiled, trying tap into my sultry, vixen side, but since I've practiced that about as much as I practiced the oboe that had been thrust upon me at the ripe age of seven and abandoned one week later, said look came out like a train wreck.

"Very funny," Jack said, shaking his head.

I folded my arms and grinned. "Dakota, one. Jack, zero," I said. "Anyway, I will write about mister horny flying tentacle thing, because I'm going to write about everything."

"Everything?"

"Yes, everything," I said. "Think about all we've seen and done in such a short period of time. All that deserves to be told, and those stories will undoubtedly propel me into the upper tier of xeno-archaeologists."

"I'm pretty sure coming back with Progenitor tech will do that," Tolby pointed out.

"I know, but that just means the demand for my books will be even more so," I said, now getting lost in the fantasy. "I've always wanted to be an author. I could do book signings. Book tours. Be wined and dined to come on to the top shows across the Milky Way. Swim in oceans of letters from adoring fans. All that good stuff. And with the archive cube at our fingertips, we'll have an unending supply of info to draw from and locations to visit. This is going to be great."

"I don't suppose you have a name for this monumental work of yours?"

"No, but it'll come to me," I said. "The title's not that important."

Jack smirked. "You think so?"

"I know so...Why? What do you think?"

"If you want it to sell, it's got to have a snappy title. My aunt and uncle had a publishing house. They'd talk your ear off if you said a title didn't matter."

"Well, I'll think of something," I said. "How about *Dakota's Guide to the Galaxy*? It could be better selling than *Fifty Shades of*

Plasma and more controversial than *Potato, Potahto*. No, wait. That sounds stupid. Well, maybe not stupid, but too limiting."

Jack cocked his head. "Say again?"

"Too limiting," I repeated. "I'm not going to limit myself to the Milky Way. So maybe *Dakota's Guide to the Universe*? Nah, too bland. *Webways for Dummies*? Oh, I know! *WYDDTT*!"

"W-D-D—"

"No, W-Y-D-D-T-T," I said slowly. "*Whatever You Do, Don't Touch That*. I can already think of my first article."

"This should be good."

"Mm-hmm," I said with a nod. "The Nodari scout stands almost three meters tall, and despite their fearsome appearance, they are the life of any party, utilizing a variety of bio-weapons to rend, slice, poison, dissolve, and vaporize friends and enemies alike. Just kidding, they have no friends, and definitely earn a solid eight out of ten on the Dakota-Don't-Touch-O-Meter."

Tolby grinned. "Addenda, judicious use of deadly force, including orbital airstrikes, is highly recommended when encountered."

"Love it!" I said, beaming. "We could also have a cuddly section for things you want to touch, as well as things to eat. Oh! Oh! And rate exciting things to see or do with icons of the Super Vortex."

Jack's brow furrowed, and even before he asked the question, I realized he had no idea what I was talking about. "The what?"

"The Super Vortex," I repeated. "It's only the biggest, fastest, most amazing water slide in the entire Milky Way. Twelve miles of high-trust tubing, more barrel rolls than a ten-minute dogfight, and a waterfall drop at the end that's given more than one person a coronary. It's awesome. We should go once we get out of here."

"Count me in. I've always had a thing for water parks," he said. "In fact, count me in on any ride you want to go on, except for teacups. Never been able to stomach those."

"Me either," I said. "They make me puke."

A deep thrum came from a distance, interrupting our conversation and my daydreaming, much to my annoyance. We all spun around to find an oblong ship with delta wings and a nose that bristled with guns like a porcupine bristled with quills headed our way.

"Please tell me those are your friends," I said.

"That's a Kibnali ship," Tolby said, though his voice didn't sound reassuring. "Whether those inside are friends or not has yet to be seen."

CHAPTER THREE:
PHYSICAL

Tolby leaped at Jack, nearly barreling me over in the process. My feline buddy grabbed him by the back of the neck and pushed him to the ground. "Stay down if you want to live," he growled.

"What the hell's going on?" Jack said, trying to get to his feet.

Tolby put his foot on Jack's back and kept him from rising. "The Kibnali who are coming do not know you. Thus, you must present as an expendable servant of the Empress and her Empire—a *Chetarin*. Nothing more. If you value your life, you will remain in that station until we can convince them of your worth."

Jack glared and motioned at me. "Then why is she still standing?"

"Because I have these," I said, pointing to the ritual scars that I bore on my cheeks. I figured those were good enough to show off, and I didn't need to give him a shot of the ones I had on my chest, too. "And don't take it too personally. I had to be one, too."

The ship floated over the coliseum's walls, blowing sand in every direction. I shielded my eyes as the tiny grains whipped over my face and into my hair. A cone of blue light shot out from a sensor array under its chin and swept over us several times. After a few seconds, the light ceased, and the ship landed with a heavy thud about forty meters away. I could feel the reverberations of its touchdown through the soles of my feet.

The ship's engines groaned as they cut out, and then with a high-pitched whine, a ramp dropped from its belly and out came a single Kibnali. His black fur absorbed the light to such an unnatural degree he looked more like a nightmare aberration than a giant panther. Over his body he wore white armor with thin plates and a flexible mesh covering the joints. While the armor looked similar to that I'd seen back at the museum, though not as designed for frontline combat, he did sport something incredibly unique: a highly articulate, mechanical claw that sprouted from his back and hung arched over his left shoulder like a scorpion tail ready to strike.

"They only sent one for us?" I whispered to Tolby as the Kibnali began to walk toward us. "Is that good?"

"Probably not," he said.

"How's that?"

"Because it means they don't know what to make of you," he replied. "Or rather, how dangerous you are."

"So he's the sacrificial lamb?"

"Something like that," he said. "It also means he's probably the eyes and ears of whoever is aiming a mini-nuke at our heads."

"Holy snort," I said. "You're serious? That's kind of overkill."

"That's kind of Kibnali," he said. "In fact, it's probably best that you don't speak at all during these introductions."

"Yeah, that's not going to happen. Let's not kid ourselves," I said, shooting him an incredulous look.

Tolby sighed. "Try, at least."

Our mini conversation ended when Yseri stepped forward and halted the new arrival's approach by placing herself between us and him. Or rather, Empress and him. "Who is this being who walks among us?" she asked. "What instrument are you of the Empress?"

The Kibnali straightened and laughed, his mechanical arm bouncing around as if it, too, joined in whatever unspoken joke there was. "I am Okabe, head of research, and chief advisor to Goshun Yamakato, governor of Kumet."

"Kumet?" Jainon repeated, joining her sister at her side. "We're on the planet Kumet?"

Okabe's face lit up, and his tail swished behind him with all the energy of a mechanical drum-beating bunny on a never-ending quest to march around the galaxy. "You don't know where you are, do you?"

"Now I do," Jainon said with a laugh. She spun around and squeezed Yseri tight. "This is fantastic news! I had always wanted to come here. We can go see the Lost Temples of Panpap and go cave diving in the Demon's Claw."

"Interesting, but not unexpected," Okabe said, seeming as if he'd only half heard Jainon at best. "Well, not unexpected after anomaly analysis. Still, very pleased work will be vindicated. Call me crazy, will they? Ha!"

Yseri cleared her throat and grabbed Okabe's attention. "You sound as if you were expecting us."

"Anticipated and predicted. Progenitor technology is everywhere," he said as he gestured to the structure around us. "Tell me, do you know what year it is?"

"We were hoping you could tell us."

Okabe grinned. "Second month of 5811, day nine of week six, something anyone but a wayward time traveler would know."

"It's 5811? Thank the gods," Jainon said with a huge sigh of relief. "We've got two years until—"

When Jainon cut herself off, Okabe tilted his head to the side. "Until?"

Jainon didn't reply, nor did she look like she could. The rest of my buddies looked tongue-tied as well. Okabe, however, didn't press for details. In fact, I was shocked how understanding he was.

"Future paradox concerns," he said with a grim look. "Understandable, and something to explore later, perhaps. My initial theory on the Progenitors' fate was tied to a paradox backlash. Seemed probable, if not inevitable, for a species so ingrained with time travel."

"What do you know of the Progenitors?" Tolby asked.

"Little, sadly. Existence has only been confirmed for less than a year, but now, all that's changed." At that point, he whipped out a handheld device and used it to scan me in a similar manner as his ship had done moments ago. "Incredible," he said, staring at the device. "Absolutely incredible."

"What is?" Tolby asked.

"Your tiny, furless creatures," he said, nodding toward Jack and me. "I must insist on an inspection before you are allowed in the city."

Jainon, Yseri, and even Tolby differed to Empress for the reply, which she promptly gave. "Of course, but beware, she has claws."

"Noted," Okabe said as he took a few quick steps over to me. For nearly a minute, he walked around me, studying every facet, all the while making quiet notes to himself. "I wonder, can it understand us?"

At this point, I was tired of being treated like a lab rat. "It has a name, and it's Dakota," I said. "And yes, I can understand you."

Okabe nearly jumped out of his armor with delight. "It speaks our language! But how?" Before I could react, he hoisted me up in the air with one hand and then used the other to manhandle my head. "It bears the ritual scars of induction to the Kibnali Guard," he said. In a flash, he grabbed my shirt and pulled, getting a nice shot of my chest in the process. "And it has been given honors, too. A *Ralakai*. Impressive."

"Thanks?" I said, unsure how to respond, but all the same hoping he'd then decide to put me down.

He didn't.

Okabe went on giving me the closeup work-up. "Adequate predatory eyes. Weak jaw. Poor incisors. Ears, malformed and likely rudimentary at best. Nasal cavity, practically nonexistent— poor thing probably can't even smell itself."

"Which is a good thing," Yseri said with a smirk.

Okabe chuckled and continued. "Muscular structure under-developed. Tail, missing—"

"Hey! Hands off my ass!" I interrupted, squirming in his grip.

"Will to fight greatly surpasses biological ability," he went on, still probing all around my legs and abs while also sounding impressed. "But yet, it possesses unparalleled technological implants across its arm and neck. Must consider if it's a joke?"

"She is no joke," Tolby growled.

"Apologizes," Okabe said to Tolby, giving a slight bow. "I did not mean to insult your pet. I only found the contrast between its biological advancement and its technological ones peculiar. Why

GALEN SURLAK-RAMSEY

would Progenitors bestow their gifts on such a rudimentary being? Why would Empress give such honors as well?"

My eyes darted over to Empress as I wasn't sure how to respond given we'd come from the future, and our Empress wasn't even the actual Empress, technically speaking, but a decoy.

"Her honors come from the future," Empress said. "We'll be happy to discuss the details with Goshun Yamakato and the current Empress."

"Fascinating," Okabe said, taking a closer look at my scars. "I'm eager to know the particulars of her awards myself, and I can't wait to hear how mighty our empire has grown."

"Can we stop with the physical?" I asked. "My feet are getting tired of not touching the ground."

"A moment longer," Okabe replied, going back to his prods. A few along my ribs made me laugh. The squeeze on my ass—again—made me drop my brow. But when his paw found its way to my front and jammed itself up against my groin, that's when the feces hit the proverbial rotary oscillating device.

Out of pure reflex, I telekinetically punched Okabe square in the chest. Guess it was a good thing he had that armor on, because he went flying back with a thunderous crack.

To my surprise, Okabe took to his feet without complaint. His eyes looked at me, then down at the spiderweb of cracks that had spread across his chest plate, and then back to me again. "Incredible," he said, shaking his head before suddenly straightening. He put a paw over one ear and spoke to someone unseen. "No. Things are fine. Stand down."

Tolby visibly tensed along with the others. "I told you."

"Yeah, well, he shouldn't be grabbing me like that," I said. "He's lucky I didn't take his head off."

Okabe turned his attention back to me, and with a sweeping gesture of his paw back to his ship, he said, "We must return to my lab. Interviews. Tests. More interviews. That sort of thing."

"Look, I appreciate I'm some new thing for you to look at, and I can really appreciate your interest in my arm," I said, glancing down at the implants I had. "But I'm not the type of girl who likes getting probed all day long."

"Probes? How barbaric," Okabe said. "No. No. This will be a mutually beneficial relationship."

"Will it? What do I get out of it?"

Okabe held up his arms, paws up. "What would you like?"

"Food, for starters," I said as my stomach rumbled. "New clothes. A nice place to sleep, and most of all, a tour of the planet. I want to see all things Kibnali and more. I'm not about to be kept in a cage all day."

"Done."

I turned to Tolby and smiled. "And you said I should be quiet."

"You should have," he said. "And you still should. Others in the city might not share his enthusiasm for learning something new from someone so alien."

"Well, whatever," I said. "That's something Future Dakota will have to worry about. I'm tired of being hungry and dirty."

"Shall we go then?" Okabe said, gesturing to his ship once more.

The sight of it made me perk, as one final thought came to mind. "One other thing," I said. "I want a ship. It doesn't have to be fancy, but it has to be something that can take all of us from system to system."

"A ship?" he echoed as he scratched the top of his head with his mechanical arm. "Yes. Yes. More than fair compensation, provided you help unlock what needs unlocking. Should take a month at most. I'm certain Goshun will approve, again, provided that you help."

Once again, I looked to Tolby for input. "What do you think?"

"I think we need a ship," he said. "I doubt we will find a serviceable one any faster."

"Okay, well, it's like a month, month, right?" I said. "You guys don't have some weird calendar that's going to make me go into menopause first, do you?"

Tolby laughed and shook his head. "No. It'll be thirty-six days total, and each of those is about twenty-two hours," he replied.

"That's not so bad," I said before turning back to Okabe. "All right. Let's do it."

"Excellent," Okabe said. "We'll have you stay at the casino."

I perked. "Casino? I didn't peg you guys for the gambling type."

"We're not," he admitted. "But when we found this one, we made an exception. Once you see it, I'm sure you'll understand why."

CHAPTER FOUR:
CASINO

Send in the pickup," Okabe said over the radio.

Within seconds, a low hum filled the air, and the wind began to pick up, further increasing everybody's anxieties. A gigantic, serpentine construct of metal and lights burst into the scene. It floated on a cushion of air and snaked around us completely.

"Now there's something you don't see every day," Jack said.

"No kidding," I remarked, entranced at the light display flashing along its side. "Talk about fancy."

The cyber serpent split open lengthwise from the top along the middle, and a grapefruit-sized metallic sphere with a single, sky-blue eye set in the center zipped out. Aside from a few minor variations in shell design, he looked like all of the other Progenitor guides we'd come across. To my utter shock, he spoke without having a slew of malfunctions, though he still had the same digitized voice as the others.

"Eagerness and friendly greetings," he said. "I'm here to escort you to our lovely hotel and casino resort."

"I hope you guys are in better shape than the museum," I said with a chuckle.

"Query. Which museum?"

"The Museum of Natural Time," I said. When he continued to stare at me blankly—which, looking back, was pretty much how he always stared since he was a floating ball of metal—I added, "The one in the Milky Way?"

"Recognition! Of course," he said. "Pride. Seeing how that one isn't scheduled to open its doors for another two thousand years, I'd wager you'll find our facilities much more agreeable."

I folded my arms and smiled as I shot my group a knowing grin. "See? Belly rubs, two. Doubters, zero. Now what do you have to say for yourselves?"

Tolby, as much as I love him to death, had to be Tolby and ruined the mood. "I think we should be cautious there's a Progenitor casino in full operation, especially given what's happened at the last two facilities we've gone to."

"Soothing tones. I assure you, our resort is top-notch," he replied.

"We don't have any other options, anyway," I added. "Besides, it's a casino, not a secret military installation with a super self-destruct device."

"You sure about that?"

"Of course," I said. "How bad would it be for business to nuke your patrons?"

No one argued that point, and with that, I headed for the snake bus. "Come on, let's go. I need food, a shower, and a three-day nap."

Everyone followed, with our Progenitor welcome bot (hereby named WB1) bringing up the rear. The bus's floor was made of some sort of orange and red metal, as were the sides and ceiling.

There were high-back benches along each side that made everything look like an antique 5th century PHS subway car. Those benches unexpectedly conformed to our bodies once we sat down on. There was even a perfect little cubby for Daphne to squeeze into with her little droid body. Once we were on our way, large portions along the sides became translucent, and we could see our surroundings speed by.

We flew above the jungle canopy at a good clip, I'd wager near three hundred kilometers per hour. It wasn't the most thrilling ride, so maybe one and a half Super Vortexes when it came to excitement, but it was pleasant enough. As we traveled, I heard the conversation between WB1 and ground control.

"Inquiry. Slender Nine requesting permission to land at VIP parking, over," WB1 called out. "Announcement. Coming in hot with four fuzzy samurai and a pair of naked apes. One needs medical."

"Repeat that last, Slender Nine. Did you say you have a medical request?"

"Affirmative. A naked ape has a split scalp, could use some synth spray to patch her up."

"Copy. Medteam will meet you at the welcome mat. Go ahead and make your final approach and stick to the wheel, eight by eight. You've got lucky dice all the way in."

The conversation ended at that point, and it didn't take long for us to reach the city. The buildings looked like works of art that flowed from one to the other, whether they were single-story dwellings or gigantic spires that grazed the stars.

I was about to ask where the casino was when I spied it out the window. It screamed Progenitor. Well, it only screamed Progenitor because it looked a lot like the buildings we'd been running around in back on Adrestia. It stood in the very center of it all, looking like a giant snail shell turned on its side, with a single spiral tower making a run for the heavens.

On one side sat a large parking lot for vehicles, and next to that stood a circular landing pad that we were headed for. Lush gardens grew all around the rest of the casino, and in between those were a few smaller buildings maybe twenty meters high.

We touched down near the casino entrance, and as soon as we left the snake bus, another floating droid, with red and white stripes, raced toward us. He didn't speak but rapidly spun around me while scanning my head with a bright blue light.

"Stand by. Med procedures initiated," he said.

I tensed. "Okay."

A tiny nozzle came out of his belly and blasted my scalp with saltwater. It stung, but that sting was nothing compared to the goo it sprayed on the wound right after that. Holy snort, I'd rather have been stung by a herd of angry kiblerbees—even the ones with the three-foot stingers.

Once my eyes were done watering, and my mouth was done cursing, the medibot zipped off and we were then approached by a tall, slender alien dressed in pink robes. He had shiny, leathery skin and a slick, bald head that fanned out in the back. He regarded us with massive black eyes and smiled at us with an unusually small mouth. Now that I think about it, he would've been perfect in ancient anime.

"Honored guests," he said, drawing out his words with a refined voice. "It is my distinct pleasure and privilege to welcome you to The Twelve Sentries Resort and Casino. I am Dreeves, and I shall have the privilege of tending to your every need, Empress willing."

I glanced over at Tolby, unsure what to make of the alien. "Who are these guys?"

"Bantars," he replied. "Servants of the Empire. A little quirky, and superstitious, but admirable servants nonetheless."

Jack elbowed me in the side. "Quirky and superstitious? They're right up your alley."

"You know what? Next time there's a belly rub needed, I'm giving it minus one," I said, sticking out my tongue. "You can find your own luck."

Jack rolled his eyes. "I've done just fine without belly rubs, on elephants or disappearing aliens."

"Mm-hmm. If memory serves, that anti-rub nature landed you smack in the middle of a stasis tube in a museum that was about to blow."

When Jack rolled his eyes, again, Dreeves took charge. He waved a boxy robot over who had been patiently waiting a few paces behind him. Once it was at his side, Dreeves pushed a button in the middle, and it opened up like an armoire. From the robot's storage, the alien grabbed some umbrellas and began handing them out to each of us. "Compliments of the house."

I turned the one he gave me over in my hand a few times. It was nicely made, sturdy, and though I didn't open it, it looked to be quite big when in use. "Did I miss something in my crash course in Kibnali customs?" I asked Tolby. "I don't remember you guys doing this."

"Because we don't."

Jack chuckled. "You guys having trouble with your sprinkler system?"

Dreeves waved one of his six hands at us from side to side. "No. It is customary on this planet to always offer guests umbrellas while they are staying with you. After all, they have many uses. You can use one to deflect the salty spray coming from a Poktak's blowhole, flip it over to collect rainwater, practice your fencing skills, use it for shade while lying on sandy beaches, slow your descent in a pinch, or shield a witch from certain death should she be caught in a rainstorm. Thus, to be a gracious host is to ensure that every guest has an umbrella."

"I see," I said, now having a much better appreciation for such a simple device. "Learn something new every day."

"How long do you plan on staying?" he asked. "I will be sure to get your rooms ready while you enjoy yourself on the game floors."

"Maybe a month, according to Okabe," I said.

"Very good, ma'am."

"Whoa, Nelly," I said with both of my hands up. "Ma'am is my grandmother."

"Of course, miss."

I turned when I caught sight of all four of my furry companions giving me a strange look. "What?"

"You don't want to be honored like your grandmother?" Jainon said, tilting her head.

"No, I do, but like...it's an old thing," I said. "I'm not ready to be that old."

"With age comes wisdom and experience, though," she said, still looking confused.

"I know," I said, now feeling silly. "Look, that wasn't a huge remark where I come from. People say it all the time."

"They don't want to be old?"

"Not usually."

"So they'd rather be young and dumb?" she asked.

"Oh geez," I said, laughing at myself. "Let's talk about this later, yes? I'm starving, sore, and tired."

Dreeves led us into the casino at that point. It was decked out in such an extravagant fashion that it put the Chateau de Chambord to shame. Gold and platinum purfled everything from massive marble sculptures that towered over everyone and everything, to individual tiles that formed an intricate, mosaic floor. A mix of green and blue lights shone on the ceiling above, and soft music that reminded me of chimes playing to the background of a light rain drifted in the air.

Straight ahead a wide rug with golden threads ran through the welcome center from where we walked in to the other side where it entered one of the game rooms. What was in those game rooms, I couldn't tell at the moment, but the area was packed with patrons. And speaking of patrons, my gosh, I'd never seen so many different types of aliens in my life—and I'm not exactly a first-time space traveler.

There were aliens running around about the size of an elephant with three heads and nine legs. There were aliens that slithered around like snakes for bodies and retro-robotic heads atop hairy shoulders. There was even a family—I presumed—of little jellyfish with wings no bigger than my pinky that zipped around the air, flashing lights at each other. I wish I had run into them again because I got the feeling that talking to them would've been pretty cool.

Dreeves led us past a long line of eager guests wanting to check in and to a small desk where a diminutive alien sat. She had the face and body of a dinosaur, but the limbs and fat belly of a bear. She looked at us with wide eyes and flashed a broad, toothy smile.

"Good morning, are you Okabe's VIPs?" she asked.

"We are," I replied.

"Wonderful! You're going to love it here," she said. From inside her desk, she pulled out a set of communicators and handed them to each of us. "Okabe said he'll call you on these after you're settled in. Do you have a room preference?"

"No." But as soon as the words passed my lips, I shook my head. "Actually, check that. I want my own room, and I want it as far away from those three as possible," I said, throwing a glance to Tolby and the handmaidens. "No offense, bud."

Tolby snorted and shook his head. "Plenty taken."

I smiled and playfully bumped him with my hip. "If I have to listen to you three anymore, I'm going to icepick my ears. Either that, or I'm going to icepick your heart. So if you value our friendship, give me a little space."

"Fine. I don't need you giving us that look anymore anyway."

CHAPTER FIVE: EXPERIMENTS

To my utmost sadness, I never made it to my room. We'd barely gotten our room keys when Okabe showed up and snatched Jack and me away. Oh, and as long as my squirrel is kicking in, those room keys were awesome. They were small metal cards that had holographic maps on one side that showed your current location inside the casino. Furthermore, the displays were receptive to touch, so you could quickly get directions to everything from your room to your favorite gaming table to wherever you wanted to eat or catch a show. They even gave you suggestions on what to do if you hadn't a clue where to get started and had a slew of games to play, too. I think there was an audiobook section as well.

But as I said, I didn't get a chance to use it whatsoever. Okabe wanted to get started on "science" being done, and he wasn't taking no for an answer. That meant that while my furry bud and his mini harem of space kitties got to enjoy some R&R, I got a firsthand tour of Okabe's research facility. And by tour, I mean I got to lie on a table as Okabe went to work.

"How much longer is this going to take?" I asked after my stomach rumbled for the twentieth time.

"We'll be finished soon," Okabe said, his face staring at his tablet.

I sighed, having heard that answer a dozen times now. Now I know I'd volunteered for all of this, and we were getting a ship out of the deal, but holy snort, there's only so long I can lie on a metal gurney before my patience wore out. I'd been there for so long, I probably had bedsores on my backside.

"If we could wrap this up before I need to shave my legs again, that'd be perfect," I said, throwing in an extra bit of snark for snark's sake. "I mean, the treatments I get at the spa only last six months at a time."

Okabe looked at me inquisitively. "You shave your legs on purpose?"

"Yeah. And?"

"Interesting you would defile yourself in such a fashion."

I didn't feel like arguing. I just wanted to be done. That said, I twisted my head side to side to work out some of the kinks and check out the room for the umpteenth time. It was still circular in nature, not that I expected it to ever change, and it still had a dome ceiling with soft, blue lighting all around. Along the walls stood consoles and computers and tons of equipment, all of which I had no idea what any of it did, but a few of the items looked as if they might be inserted into test subjects due to their needlelike nature, and I really hoped he didn't have plans for any of them for me. He did promise no probes, but he also promised this wasn't going to take long.

"What about Tolby and the others? Do you know where they are?" I finally asked.

"Still being debriefed by Goshun," he said. He then showed off his tablet and pointed to a small portion on the side where a chunk of text was. "I'm getting updates as they go. It seems your time in the museum and then on the research facility had a lot to offer in terms of excitement and adventure."

"Oh, man. Isn't that the truth," I said.

"It's a shame both were lost. The technology either could have provided would've been immeasurable, I'm sure."

One of Okabe's lab assistants came over and handed him another tablet. "Here are the scan results," he said. "Subject nine-seven-nine is...unique, to say the least."

Okabe studied the screen, and puzzlement splashed across his face. He then put his ear directly on my chest. "Incredible," he said. "You only have one centralized heart?"

"Afraid so," I said. "That's pretty standard where I come from."

"So what do you do when it gets destroyed?"

"What do you mean, what do I do? I die."

"Interesting," he said. He pressed a few buttons on the screen to his tablet and began to dictate. "Subject nine-seven-nine is a flawed species despite spacefaring nature, with only one centralized method of pumping her circulatory system. Stranger still, subject nine-seven-nine finds such a flaw acceptable. Conclusions, subject is either ignorant or incapable of adapting genetics properly."

"I'm not ignorant—" I started, but when he sliced open my shoulder with one of his claws, that thought was immediately replaced by a different one. "Ow! What the holy hell did you do that for?"

Okabe ignored my question and patted the wound with a nearby blue cloth. "Subject nine-seven-nine apparently experiences moderate pain with superficial wounds. Even more curious, her blood is rudimentary when it comes to properly clotting to minimize loss. Note to self: suggest that nonsurgical amputations be tested last as subject nine-seven-nine may not survive."

"How about we don't do any amputations!" I said.

"Why do you hate science, nine-seven-nine?" he asked.

"I don't hate science! And the name's Dakota, remember?"

He shrugged. "I do remember that you volunteered for tests in exchange for lodging, food, and a ship."

"I don't care what you're promising. If you try and chop something off, our deal is off, and I'll be super miffed. And believe me, you do not want me super miffed."

"Why?"

"Because you don't," I said with a growl. Sadly, my growl was nowhere near what he was capable of, I'm certain, and the way he chuckled made me think my attempts at intimidation were more cute than imposing.

"I think I do," Okabe said. As he went on, his ears had perked up, and his tail flipped from side to side with enormous energy. "Aside from maybe one or two others, this is one of the most important tests out there. We need to know how long it takes for your limbs to grow back, not to mention how well your body can function and adapt to losing an appendage. Do you know how long it takes to come back with quality data from the field?"

"No. Why would I?"

"Trust me, it's a nightmare since battlefield subjects are usually mangled beyond use."

"Let me save you the trouble," I said. "My limbs don't grow back, and I'm pretty sure if you chop my leg off, I wouldn't be good for much of anything other than passing out and bleeding to death."

"Are all of you humans like this?" he asked.

"For the most part," I said. "I mean, the military guys have all these cybernetic upgrades and nanomachines swimming in their blood doing all sorts of crazy crap. But for us who don't want to have to sign our lives away fighting in war, or who don't want to deal with the potential side effects like shortened life-spans, constant itching, and the inability to feel anything, yeah we're all like this."

"Disappointing," Okabe said. "Though perhaps I should have expected as much seeing how the male who accompanied you wasn't that impressive either."

"You mean Jack? And that better not mean he's not still around."

"He's still around," Okabe said. "We haven't finished his analysis yet."

"He better stay around, too."

"He will," he said. "Probably, at least. So much to learn and so little specimens to learn it with. It would be a waste to be careless with his life. Let's move on, shall we?"

"Let's say we're finished and call it a day, instead," I countered. "I need food."

Okabe laughed. "Subject nine-seven-nine has elementary comedic value," he dictated on his tablet.

I frowned. "I thought I was supposed to be helping you unlock something."

"Yes, the door inside the art gallery," he said. "You shall. Need more preliminary data. Much more. Have to ensure all is safe and proper before moving forward, otherwise, kabloowie!" He accented that last bit by mimicking an explosion with all three hands. "Not a fan of kabloowie."

"Let me see if I'm hearing you correctly. You have an art gallery that has a door that's locked, and that door—if I'm guessing correctly—was built by the Progenitors?"

"Possibly," he said. "Found an art gallery, yes. Progenitor tech has also been found, yes. Did they build the art gallery? Possibly. Likely. Ultimately unknown."

My initial enthusiasm quickly took a nosedive when I thought back to my time on Adrestia, specifically, while I was in the Lambda Labs talking to the little drone AB1. Shortly before he was destroyed, he alluded to an incident surrounding the destruction of an art gallery by yours truly. "What exactly is in this art gallery?"

"Art, of course," he replied, tilting his head. "Paintings. Sculptures. That sort of thing. You do know what art is, don't you?"

"Yes, I know what art is."

"Wonderful," he said. Then he spoke to his tablet once more. "Subject nine-seven-nine has basic knowledge of cultural expression."

"I can even draw a stick figure."

"Tell me, what can you do with the implants in that arm?"

I hesitated a moment, as I wasn't sure how much I should divulge. I didn't have the portal device anymore, so I couldn't exactly show off what I used to be able to do with it, and even then, it might not have been a good idea to do so if I could. As much as I trusted Tolby and the others, part of me thought it would be a bad idea if these Kibnali had the full picture. Still, I couldn't say my implants wouldn't do anything, and if they were going to believe we'd come from the future, they had to know I could at least operate Progenitor technology with it. So that's what I went with.

"It lets me interface with Progenitor computers and some of their vehicles," I said.

"Excellent news," he replied. "Perhaps we'll be done in weeks or even days, then."

"How's that?"

"We've constructed a device that has managed to tap into Progenitor technology," he said. "Or at least, it can send and receive basic signals. However, we don't understand their language, so progress in actual interface is abysmal."

"In other words, you need my arm to translate."

"Precisely." Okabe looked down at his tablet again and tapped it a few times.

"When do I get to check out this door?" I asked. "I'm curious to see what's inside."

"As am I," he replied. "But we will need Goshun's blessings, first."

"And how long will that take?"

"Not much longer, I'm sure," he said. "Question. What do you know about your companion's implants?"

I shrugged. "Not much. Only they aren't as good as mine."

"Subject nine-seven-eight used them to phase through a wall," Okabe said. "Can you do that?"

I cocked my head and raised an eyebrow. "Phase through a wall? Like a ghost?"

"A crude description, but it will suffice," he said.

"I have no idea," I said. I bit my lower lip as I turned the claim over in my head a few times. Could Jack do such a thing? I suppose it was possible given all the things I could do already. I mean, running through a wall would be child's play compared to traveling through spacetime, right? "Man, I wonder if I could."

"Perhaps you should try," he said.

I bit my lip, turned the thought over a few times, and ultimately realized I wouldn't know where to begin and failure could be hilariously painful. "I'll pass for now. I'd rather not smash my face into a wall."

Okabe nodded and spoke into his recorder once again. "Subject nine-seven-nine prefers cowardice to the advancement of science."

"Hey! I'm no coward."

"Your lack of experimentation and boundary-pushing says otherwise," he said without any emotion. "Perhaps subject nine-seven-eight is the superior specimen after all."

"The hell he is," I said, putting my hands on my hips and accepting the challenge. Besides, if I had some new superhero power I hadn't tapped into, I sure as hell wasn't going to ignore it. "Tell me what he did, and I'll do it ten times better."

Okabe's ears twitched. "No idea. He simply said he willed it to happen, and the implant did the rest. Quite an ingenious design. No need for formal instruction on controls. Point of note. It didn't work until he was running at said wall, a moment from impact. Current theory, implant-brain connection requires seriousness of the situation for phasing to occur. Probably helps curb misfires."

"That makes sense," I said. "Okay. I can do this."

Okabe pointed to the wall behind him. "Try that one," he said. "The other side is the breakroom."

I nodded and bounced on the balls of my feet a few times. As I did, I rubbed my hands together, all the while taking in several quick, deep breaths to work myself up. I couldn't wait to make this happen. Think of all the new places I could get into by merely phasing in and out of this dimension. I mean, not as handy as a portal, obviously, that took me anywhere I wanted, but this was going to be pretty damn close.

"All right, here we go," I said. "On three. One. Two. Three."

I charged forward, full tilt. My arm tingled as I closed the distance between myself and the wall. My gut tightened when I was a pace away, and I had to fight every instinct not to grind myself to a halt and ruin the magical moment I was about to have.

My forehead hit the wall like a battering ram. I bounced off and landed flat on my back. The wind blew out of me. Half my face went numb, while the rest felt warm and sticky.

In my semi-dazed state, I heard Okabe make one final comment. "Subject nine-seven-nine is extremely gullible. Likely has a low intellect, reinforcing theory she is, in fact, a practical joke by Progenitor creators. Recommend keeping all conversations with her at a kit level."

CHAPTER SIX:
THE DANCE

An hour later, after being treated for a minor concussion and a majorly bruised ego, Okabe sent me back to my room. There, I immediately made a beeline for the tub, not bothering to speak to either Jack or Daphne, who were in the common room.

Once I'd shed my filthy clothes, I sank into a sunken tub filled with warm water that was the size of my bedroom back home. It was fed not by a faucet but by a small waterfall opposite where I was resting my head. Aside from myself and the tub, the rest of the bathroom was comprised of rich wood flooring and full-length windows that offered a breathtaking view of the city thanks to how high our suite was. I usually prefer to bathe with a little more privacy, as I'm not one who likes to attract creepers, but given I was on a Kibnali world and no one cared what a furless, pink, naked alien looked like, I was willing to make an exception.

Using some shampoo that smelled like lilacs, I took my time getting myself clean before drifting off to sleep. I'm not sure how long I nodded off for, but when I woke, I had more wrinkles than a pallet full of raisins. I probably had a budding case of trench foot, too.

A chirping noise drew my attention. I craned my head back toward the sink, and there, sitting on the edge, was my *ashidasashi* staring at me with wondrously big eyes.

"Hey little guy," I said, trying to call him over with a curled finger. "Come here."

Little guy did not. Instead, he eyed one of the handles to the faucet before tasting it.

"Who wants a belly rub?"

I blinked, and in that microscopic span of time, he went from being on the sink to being on the edge of the bath. I took that as an enthusiastic yes and carefully scooped him up. He rolled in my hand, splaying all of his legs to the sides and exposing his belly, which I promptly treated with the best luck-inducing rub I'd ever given.

Sorry, Liam, but you're not around anymore to get them (for those of you who don't know or remember, he was my original plastic elephant suction cupped to the dashboard of my now-no-longer-existing ship).

"You need a name, don't you?" I said mid-rub, delighted with how keen the *ashidasashi* was with my attention. "What are you, a Moby? Nah, too whale. Magic? Too card-like. Ozzy? Nugget? Fido? Oooo. I know! Taz!"

Taz cocked his head. I wasn't sure if he actually understood me yet, but it seemed so.

"Yeah, Taz, you know, because you definitely look like you could be a little devil up to no good," I said, patting his head. Taz nipped at my finger in response. I yanked it back and laughed. "See? Case and point."

A knock on the door drew my attention, and Jack called out a moment later. "Are you still alive in there?"

"Yeah," I replied. "Just talking to Taz."

"Who?"

I turned back around to find that Taz had disappeared. My shoulders fell. "Aw, man," I grumbled. "He's gone."

"What are you talking about?"

"Taz, the *ashidasashi*, was here, but he's gone again."

"Probably for the best," Jack said.

"Don't hate on Taz," I replied. "He's the best."

"You barely know him."

"I know he's good luck, and he likes belly rubs," I countered with a scowl.

"Look, I'm not going to argue about it," he replied. "As an FYI, Okabe sent you some clothes. They're here if you want them."

I perked, and after popping out of the bath and wrapping myself up in an oversized towel, I cracked open the door. "He did?"

"Yeah, have a look," he said, handing me a tall bag that looked like it came from a designer store with wares with price tags so high, only the richest spice merchants wouldn't faint over.

"What is it?" I asked, taking the bag.

Jack looked at me as if I had suddenly sprouted three heads. "Clothes. I said that."

"Duh. I know that. I thought you could tell me more."

"I'm a guy. What else would I say?"

"Right," I said with a playful roll of my eyes.

"Need some help dressing?"

My head tilted to the side. "Really?"

Jack grinned. "You know I had to ask."

"Mm-hmm. You know you didn't have to."

"No, but I did figure it was only fair."

I probably shouldn't have entertained the thought, but I was dying to know how he'd justify it. "How's that?"

"You saw me naked. I should get to see you naked. It's that simple."

"Ah, no. Doesn't work that way, sorry."

"Pretty sure it does. You owe me reparations."

I laughed. "No, if anyone owes you reparations, it's Baumdon since he's the one who stuck you in jail and stripped you down. But since he's dead now, good luck on trying to collect."

"I still think you owe me."

"Get used to disappointment."

Jack, to his credit, remained undeterred while at the same time not being an ass about it all. "Don't you want to keep morale up? Because a little peek would go a long way in keeping my morale high."

"Consider it good character building then to not get what you want," I replied, flashing him a lively smile.

At that point, I shut the door with a flick of the wrist and dove into the bag. As it turned out, I'd been presented with a gorgeous black cocktail dress with purple shoulders that was made from something akin to silk. It fit perfectly, much to my surprise, and came with a small matching ribbon as well as boots. The boots went on my feet, naturally, and I used said ribbon to fix my hair up before popping out into the common room where Jack and Daphne were.

Jack sat on a white leather couch that looked like it could seat nine, while Daphne stood nearby, looking through countless records on the archive cube. In front of him was a round table made from wood that matched the rest of the apartment, and on it was a single lamp that branched out in numerous places, like a tiny tree. Apparently, Jack had been toying with it for a while, but when he saw me, he jumped up and nearly sent it flying across the room.

"Whoa," Jack said, giving me the up-down. "Look at you."

"You like?" I said, indulging in the moment and giving a slow spin. I know I'm usually practical when it comes to attire, especially since it's not a good idea to explore caves or race through disintegrating ships in a little black dress, but I do like fancying myself up from time to time, and I'll be damned if this didn't look good on me.

"Yeah," he said. "I think this is the first time I've seen you not covered in dirt and sweat."

"You clean up pretty well yourself," I said, noting that he, too, was bathed and now wore some new attire. Sadly for him, what he was stuck with looked fairly bland and boring. Brown pants. Black shirt with long sleeves. But at least they fit. "Where'd those come from? Somehow I doubt they have Men's Emporium around here."

"Okabe," he explained. "Apparently, they've got robots who can tailor dress for pretty much any species."

"They're pretty good."

"Except you get to look like you're going to a high-end social or a regal ball, and I look like I'm trying to sell something."

"Poor baby," I said with a grin. "You wouldn't look as good in this anyway. Your butt is too big."

"That's why I'd wear pumps," he said as he made his way over to me. He then held his right hand out to the side and extended an open invitation with his left. "May I?"

"Are you inviting me to dance?"

"I did say you looked like you were going to a regal ball," he said. "Might as well act like it."

"What makes you think I can dance?"

"Daphne said you like Bach and Beethoven," he replied. "And a girl nowadays who likes Bach and Beethoven knows how to dance."

"A girl does, does she?"

Jack cocked his head to the side and looked at me puzzled. "You don't?"

"Oh, I do," I said with a wry grin. "But maybe I should have said, what makes you think I want to dance with you?"

Jack put his hand over his heart and feigned a deep hurt. "I thought perhaps saving your life was enough to put aside your disgust for me. Am I truly that repulsive still?"

"No," I said. "But not by much."

Jack offered his hands again. "Then indulge me. I think we've earned a little R&R."

I sighed with a smile. He had me there, but for no other reason than my own entertainment and I wanted to make him work for it, I balked. "Maybe. If you're a bad dancer, it'll hardly be R&R."

"You still owe me that kiss," he said, still staying playful. "I'll consider this more than a fair trade."

"Fine," I said, feeling a little impressed he was trying not to be the complete jackass he was in the very beginning. I took his hands so that we were in a perfect position to start a waltz, but before we took a single step, I added one more demand. "But if you really wanted to impress me, you wouldn't have picked Bach or Beethoven, just so you know."

"I know," he said. Jack looked over my shoulder and gave an uplifting nod toward Daphne. Our former-ship-AI-turned-droid beeped a couple of times before she started playing Chopin's

"Waltz in A Minor." And once the first note hit the air, Jack whisked me around, and we started our dance.

"I thought Chopin would be more to your style," he said once we sank into the rhythm.

"No, you didn't," I said, laughing. "Daphne told you."

"True, but after she told me, I then had the thought Chopin would be more to your style."

"You're ridiculous," I said, settling into his lead.

"And gorgeous," he said. "Don't forget that."

I rolled my eyes. "Are you really going to ruin it?"

"No," he said. "I'm only trying to keep this light."

"Then perhaps you shouldn't have picked this particular waltz," I said.

"Touché."

For those of you who don't know, Chopin's "Waltz in A Minor" is hardly an uplifting piece that makes hearts soar. It's a simple melody that is beautiful on any grand piano, but it's filled with sadness and a story around lost love and times gone by. Still, it did have its uplifting parts, and there is a thread of hope throughout, which now that I think about it, the song actually might have been perfect for the situation. Here we were, lost, beaten up, stranded billions of light-years from home and across an unfathomable amount of time, but we still had a thread of hope that we might somehow see our family and friends again.

I settled into his lead, although admittedly it wasn't terrific. Passable, but his skill in the waltz was nowhere near the size of his ego. As critical as I was being, I wasn't going to call him out on it. I honestly did enjoy what we were doing, but I don't know if my toes would've agreed with me, especially after the third time they were stepped on.

"Sorry," he said, finally acknowledging one of the blunders. "It's been a while."

"It's okay," I replied. "Given how hard Goliath knocked you across that arena, we should probably be impressed you are even standing, let alone waltzing."

"Thank the armor for that one," he said. "As luck would have it, the Progenitors spared no expense when it came to dampening energy from hits."

"Yeah," I said. I shut my eyes and tried to think back to more pleasant times. Even though I brought up the conversation, I didn't mean to rehash recent events. I looked over my shoulder at Daphne. "Could we get something a little more uplifting?"

"Another waltz?" she replied, momentarily turning away from whatever she was doing with the archive cube. "I have a considerable library available."

"Any Tchaikovsky?"

Waltz of the Flowers came on in response. Jack was a touch slow on the uptake, but with a little bit of a friendly nudge to get him to lead, off we went. How I loved hearing the entire orchestra, from woodwinds to flutes to French horns, serenade us as we glided across the floor. The melody swept me off my feet and put my mind at so much ease I forgot where we were, and to a degree, who I was with. This latter part became even more pronounced when Jack actually danced well, and as such, I could shut my eyes and take in the mood.

I took in the mood so much I ended up resting my head on his chest with a stupid, happy smile on my face. I didn't even realize the music stopped until Jainon spoke, breaking the spell.

"A full day of offering says three weeks," Jainon said with a semi-hushed voice.

She stood a pace inside the apartment with her sister at her side. Both had amused looks on their faces.

"They gestate longer than that," Yseri semi-whispered back.

I planted my feet and snapped to attention. "Who's gestating what?"

Without missing a beat and in complete seriousness, Jainon flicked her tail toward the two of us. "You two, of course," she said. "I bet a day's worth of tithes that you'll be ripe with a kit before we leave this planet."

Yseri nudged her with an elbow. "They call them babies."

"No one is having babies," I said with a shocked laugh as I pulled away.

"Your mating ritual says otherwise," Jainon replied. "If you would allow, I would be honored to petition the goddess Inaja to bless your womb. There is still time."

"I think I'd like to get home before I waddle around like a penguin," I said. "The whole lost in spacetime thing doesn't put me in the diaper-changing mood. What are you two doing here anyway?"

"Goshun wishes to see you both," Jainon replied.

My stomach tightened. "Why do I get the impression this isn't going to be fun?"

"We've been invited to an improv show. Of course it'll be fun," Jainon said.

I perked. "Improv...like comedy?"

"Yes."

I couldn't help but snort. "You guys actually tell jokes?"

"Is that so hard to believe?" Jainon said with a huff.

To that, I held my laughter. Sort of. Okay, maybe I didn't. "Do I really need to answer that?"

"No," she said, sounding nowhere near as amused as I was. "Regardless, be sure to mind your manners and clean your plate. To leave even a morsel on your dish is a tremendous insult to both the chef and the house."

"And make sure you and Jack don't end up mating on the table," Yseri added.

"That falls under minding manners," Jainon said with utter seriousness.

I snorted. "That's something coming from the two of you."

Jainon blinked. "Us? When have we ever been rude at the table?"

"You know what, never mind," I said after I buried my face in my hands to keep from laughing too much. "Let's go. I'm famished."

With that, I grabbed the archive cube, gave myself a once-over in the mirror, and zipped out the door.

CHAPTER SEVEN: IMPROV

The four of us had barely left the suite when Tolby intercepted us in the hall. He gave me a non-creepy up-down because let's face it, how could the big furball ever be creepy with me? I wasn't three meters tall or bristled with fang and claw, not to mention he had a thing for luxurious coats of fur, and I liked to stay so smooth, I really should've invested in razor companies the moment I had a single credit to my name.

"You honor your species with your beauty," he said with an approving nod.

Despite his overly formal tone, I blushed at the remark. "Thanks."

"I'm glad to see the tailors could interpret my instructions well enough to marry your culture with mine," he added.

"Me too," I said, and feeling like he'd given me the perfect excuse to twirl and show off a little more, I did so. "Because I'll be damned if I'm not rocking this. Hey, you know what? We should start a fashion line when we get back. Evening wear for the intrepid time traveler. We could snag designs from across the universe and come up with stuff no one would have a prayer of thinking up on their own."

"You? A leader in fashion? I don't believe it," Jack said.

"I like to diversify. What can I say?" I replied with a shrug. "Also, I can think of the catalog text for it right now."

"Oh, do tell."

I cleared my throat and smiled. "Combining expert artisanal craftsmanship and coveted Progenitor aesthetics, the Dakota Series IX cocktail dress is the pinnacle of fashion for the intrepid time traveler. With its patented ChronoWeave™ technology, it keeps the user cool and looking good whether she's enjoying the nightlife or battling a rampaging goliath. Furthermore, with its extra-dimensional pockets, wearers can store anything from personal protection devices to breath mints without having to sacrifice a stunning profile."

"How are you going to sew extra-dimensional pockets into it?" he asked.

I shrugged again. "I don't know. That's for the boys in R&D to figure out. Any rate, investing in this line will give us another excuse to travel as far as we possibly can in both space and time."

"Somehow, I don't think you need an excuse," Jack said with a chuckle.

"Or encouragement," Tolby tacked on.

I grinned sheepishly. "Guilty as charged. Anyway, where's Empress? Is she coming with?"

Tolby flicked his tail down the hall where the turbolift was. "She's still with Goshun Yamakato, filling him in on all that's happened."

"All that's happened? Or like, the gist of what's happened?" I asked. "Like did she talk Armageddon or leave that part out? Because I don't know how your peeps take things around here, but where I come from, the moment you say you're from the future and bring up the end of the world, they stick you in a madhouse."

"I doubt she's said anything of the like," Tolby said. "If she brought news of war, they'd be mobilizing as we speak."

The conversation paused for a few moments until we were in the lift and headed down. At that point, I tackled the proverbial elephant. "So we never really talked about it," I said. "Are we going to stand around and pretend like we're not looking at a bunch of ghosts? You know, big impending war and all."

No one had an immediate answer, but Tolby, not surprisingly, broke the silence. "I don't think saying anything would be beneficial," he said. "No one will run. That is not in our culture, and if these are to be the last couple of years everyone will have in peace, I see no reason to stop that."

I figured he'd say that, and as morose as his words were, my eyes brightened and my voice lifted. Maybe I was being a little delusional, or manic, but I felt like a shining angel at this point, ready to show her people the path to the promised land. "What if this didn't have to be their last couple of years?"

"What do you mean?" Yseri asked. "You said before that we couldn't go back in time to change the past without causing a paradox, which the universe will never let us do."

"I know," I said, beaming. "But we're not going in the past anymore. We're already here. The Nodari invasion is our future. We came here on accident."

"Does that matter?"

I shrugged. "Hell if I know. But I do know if we do nothing, the Nodari are definitely coming, and they're going to treat all your systems like one big smörgåsbord."

When the twins stared at me blankly, Tolby filled them in. "It's a huge buffet table."

"Right," I said. "But if we warn the Kibnali now that we're here by accident, we might be able to stick it to the incoming Nodari fleet. What's the worst that can happen, anyway? Whatever we say doesn't matter. The Nodari come, steamroll the galaxy, and nothing changes."

Jack snorted. "From what I remember you saying, a hell of a lot worse can happen than that."

"Like?"

"Like cracking open a galactic supercluster? Erasing all of humanity? Collapsing spacetime? I don't know...take your pick."

I shook my head and kept my grin. "Nah. All that takes a lot more spaghetting of a timeline."

Jack straightened. "Did you just say 'spaghetting'?"

"Yeah. Why?"

"That's not even a word."

I shrugged. "It is now. Look, the most likely worst case is I'll explode since I'm without those safety discs for paradox protection."

"Or we will," Jack corrected. "We're time travelers now, too."

I nodded, conceding the point. "Fair enough, but that's hardly the galactic quadrant, let alone the universe. I think we can risk it."

Jack pressed his lips together, folded his arms, and then shook his head. "No," he said. "We're saving Kevyn first. You swore, and that doesn't even take into account I don't want to explode at all, even if I don't take the rest of the universe with me."

To my shock, both Yseri and Jainon seemed to agree. "You did promise him that," Jainon said. "Your oaths must be honored."

"Why are you guys arguing with me on this?" I said, throwing up my hands. "I'm not saying we fight a war here. God, no. What I am saying is, we can certainly bestow our soon-to-be-in-dire-crap Kibnali buds here with some Progenitor tech and/or knowledge that they could use to save themselves. Two years is a lot of prep time. Or at least, it beats being suddenly attacked out of the blue."

"And if the Nodari are defeated, how would we ever come back here when the new timeline catches up to your day and age?" Tolby asked. "That's still a paradox if there's not a solid explanation."

I shrugged yet again. "The Universe can figure that part out. There has to be hundreds of thousands of potential reasons why I'd time travel here again and drop some fancy Progenitor knowledge on the Kibnali that would then save their bacon."

Tolby continued giving me his skeptical look. "Hundreds of thousands?"

"A rough estimation," I replied. "Look, maybe we write ourselves some notes that convince the next generation of us to just go through the motions. Or...wait, I got it. The museum will always be there right?"

"Yes..." Tolby said, his voice trailing off.

"All we need to do is build some robots, make them look like you guys, and program them with vivid memories of the Kibnali losing the war. The new me won't know the difference, so bam! There's your reason to keep the cycle going." I stopped and crossed my arms, but my triumphant pose ceased when a new thought came to mind. "Wait. You guys aren't robots, are you?"

"Do I look like a robot?" Tolby asked with a deep laugh.

"Never really thought about it," I said. "Maybe you're a cybernetic organism—living tissue over a metal endoskeleton."

"I'm not."

"That's exactly what we'd program you to say."

"As dangerous as this idea is, I think it has merit," Yseri said. "We should try."

"Thank you," I said with relief.

Tolby glanced at Jainon, and the twin seemed to mirror her sister's belief. "If we do try and influence events, we need to put a lot of thought into it. I don't want to wind up like the Progenitors and get wiped from existence."

"Of course," I said, flying on cloud nine.

"I mean it, Dakota," he said. "You can't say anything until we've thought this through, and Empress has given her approval."

"But—"

"Remember the museum?"

"But—"

"Do you remember the museum?" he said, much slower this time.

"Yes," I said with a groan. God, I hated it when he was right like that. "Fine, but what if Goshun starts asking questions? I still shouldn't say anything?"

"Especially if Goshun starts asking questions," Tolby said. "He has power and influence. Him catching wind of something he shouldn't know could have a lot more consequences than an ordinary citizen."

I shrugged. "Okay, then I just won't talk to him."

Jainon made a face, which Yseri mirrored.

"What?" I asked.

"Goshun wants you to sit next to him. Apparently, he has a keen interest in aliens."

It was at this point I realized the lift was taking an extraordinarily long time to zip us down a hundred and fifty floors. The more I thought about it, the more I realized it was barely descending. I mean really, what were we in, the Stone Age and some monkeys were working the pulleys? Cripes. I didn't have time for this kind of stuff. My eyes darted upward to where the display was. It said we were on the fourth floor, which right then and there, I should've known we were in trouble.

Stupid number four. How I loathe thee.

I was about to open my mouth when the lights flickered, and the elevator ground to a halt.

"What in the Frapgars fury is this about?" Tolby asked.

Before anyone could answer, the lights went out.

CHAPTER EIGHT:
YET ANOTHER LAB

Forget to pay your light bill?" I asked with a nervous chuckle.

"What's a light bill?" Jainon asked.

I shook my head, which was utterly pointless since we were smothered in total darkness. "Never mind."

"Don't you guys have emergency lighting?" Jack asked.

"We do," Tolby said. He moved in the elevator to do something, and I only know this because he bumped right into me, nearly sending me to the ground in the process. "Sorry."

"If you do, why isn't it on?" Jack asked.

"Good question."

My gut tightened. Whereas moments ago, I was annoyed and simmering at the prospect of having to sit in an elevator—hopefully not in the dark—while the furball engineers worked their magic to either get us out or get things moving again, now my imagination ran rampant. Emergency lighting was supposed to work, always. That was the whole point. If it wasn't working in an actual emergency, what the hell good was it, anyway? And when you're trapped and starving, especially with a Nodari invasion coming at some point, it's easy to get worked up.

A comm that Okabe gave me while I was in the lab vibrated in my pocket, scaring me half to death. "Dakota," he said, once I'd collected myself long enough to fish it out. "Where are you?"

"Stuck in a powerless elevator."

"In the casino?"

"Yeah. Why? Is it going to take long to get us out?"

"Possibly," he said. "The entire casino has gone dark."

"Blow a fuse?"

"No. The power is being redirected to the Progenitor facility," he said. "We're showing a massive power spike inside."

I grimaced. "The one that's locked?"

"The same," he said.

I relayed the news to everyone else. After a slew of mutterings and curses from all, I came back to the conversation. "So I take it this means no comedy show."

"No. Meet me on the first floor," he said.

"Might be kind of hard, seeing how I can't see a thing and we're stuck in the elevator," I said.

"Then break out and find me. We'll be the ones with all the lights."

The line went dead. I looked to Tolby. Well, I looked where I thought he was. For all I knew, I was staring at Jack's butt. Check that. I was not staring at his butt, would never stare at his butt, and if that remote thought ever gets back to him, I promise I'll feed whoever tipped him off to a school of starving space piranhas.

"Tolby? Can you get us out of here?" I asked, trying to feel my way to the door. You'd think finding it would be easy, and I eventually did, but not before finding two furry tails, a wall, a paw, and a hip. Thank god Jack wasn't turned more when I grabbed that.

"Got it," Tolby said, right as there was a terrific screech of claws on metal that made my skin nearly jump off and run away.

Beyond the door was more black. However, this new black was interrupted here and there by beams of light from semi-nervous patrons and Kibnali. Most were trying to play it off cool, but it was easy to tell they knew something was wrong, and whatever it was made them jumpy.

Since the elevator had stopped a little below the actual floor, I had to boost myself up. Navigating the casino at that point felt chaotic, and at times noisy as guests seemed to be losing more and more patience with each other, but eventually, we made it to the first floor and then out altogether.

I'd taken, at best, five steps into the bright, fresh air when a blue, six-wheeled armored transport ran up to us. The door slid open, and inside sat Okabe with a few other Kibnali, armed and armored as if they were about to pick a fight with a family of star dragons.

"Get in," he said, motioning at one of two empty seats across from him. "There's no time to lose."

"I don't think we can all squeeze in there," I said.

"All of you aren't," he explained.

"I'm coming," Tolby said, coming to my side. Okabe was about to argue, but my furry bud growled and put an end to that. "This isn't up for debate."

"Fine. You may come. Another Kibnali may prove useful."

"We'll see to Empress and make sure she's safe," Jainon said.

Okabe chuckled. "She is still with Goshun. There is no safer place on this entire planet."

At that point, we parted ways, though I don't think Jack was keen on it. He gave me an annoyed, helpless look, to which all I could do was shrug. Once I took my seat inside the transport, the door slid shut with a hiss, and off we went, darting through the Kibnali city.

Colors permeated everything around us, from the countless streets to the shops and business centers. Most of the entrances to places big and small had colorful signs above and well-manicured miniature gardens flanking both sides of the doors. There were also plenty of hanging gardens on the awnings above, which gave the entire area both an organic and modern sensation.

The entire town bustled with activity—I presume because by now everyone knew the power had gone out at the casino. I wondered what they were thinking, then grew sad realizing I was looking at the last generation of Kibnali before the Nodari war would start. The war that would eventually spell the end for the entire species.

I frowned. "Screw that," I mumbled. "Not going to let that happen."

"Pardon?" Okabe said, looking up from the tablet he had in his lap.

"Did I say that?" I said with a nervous laugh. "I thought I was in think-mode."

"You definitely spoke. Now elaborate."

"I...know things about the future," I said, hesitantly. I know I'd promised Tolby we'd discuss things thoroughly, but that was before the casino went dark, power surged through whatever facility we were headed to, and I wasn't stuck inside an armored transport with the planet's chief researcher.

"Grim things?"

"Very. But...paradox worries and all."

"I see," he said. "Does this have to do with what's going on now?"

I shrugged. "I don't know. Probably. At least related, I think. I have a feeling that me being here is going to mess up anything I think I know."

The corners of Okabe's lips drew back. "Almost certainly."

I settled back into the seat. "Since I'm going to this secret facility anyway, what can you tell me about it?"

Okabe grinned like a child who had brought his favorite toy to show and tell and now has the opportunity to get in front of the class. "I'm not sure if I'm allowed to," he said, "but then again, I'm not sure I'm forbidden either."

"Better to ask for forgiveness than permission, eh?"

"Not if you're a tailless or at the bottom of the caste," he said. "But since I'm neither and circumstances are unique, I think we'll be fine."

"I don't want to put you in a bad spot," I said. "Maybe you could tell me how you found the place? Surely that's not a massive secret since I don't believe you simply happened to build a random outpost somewhere and stumbled upon a Progenitor superstructure."

"Right you are," he said. "A hundred years ago, my mentor created a massive sensor array that was finely tuned to detect Progenitor signals through subspace. Or at least, that's what he claimed. For fifty years he tried to get it to work but was met with failure and frustration at every turn and had nothing to show. Funding was eventually cut, and the project was terminated. However, he had enough private backers that he had it installed on a scout ship that inadvertently picked up a weak signal and traced it to this planet about twenty years ago."

"You've been here for twenty years and haven't gotten inside?"

"Says the girl who lived for three years in her apartment before discovering the pool," Tolby said with a grin.

"That pool was tough to find," I said, crossing my arms.

"Yes, next to the towel drop off," he said. "A devious place to put one."

Okabe cocked his head at our brief exchange but offered no input. "To your question: our original trace took us to the casino, and until recently, we thought that's all there was to it," he explained. "We didn't discover this new area buried underground until a few months ago."

"Still, I'm surprised you haven't gotten in yet."

"And what archaeologist do you know who uses force to break into a subterranean structure the first chance he gets?" Okabe said with a touch of condescension in his tone. "I would sooner burn the original diaries of the first Empress by my own hand than risk destroying such a key find on a whim. Surely you didn't get those implants of yours by being so careless."

"Getting those implants? No," Tolby said with a deep laugh. "Afterward? Absolutely."

"Yeah, well, let's see how careful you are when your brain turns to tapioca."

"And that is precisely why you'll never catch me with those," he said, pointing to my implants.

Okabe dropped his brow, and I filled him in on the details— well, some of them. Mostly the parts about me losing my mind after I'd jump forward or backward in time.

"Interesting," was his only comment.

The transport soon hung a left off the main highway and stopped near what looked like an entrance to an old subway terminal. A heavily guarded subway terminal, but one nonetheless.

"We're here," Okabe said. "Do you think it will take you long to get in?"

"If it is like any other Progenitor facility, I should be able to pop in without any trouble," I replied as I climbed out of the vehicle.

Another armored vehicle pulled up next to us, and from it came ten more Kibnali soldiers. They, too, carried enough arms and armor to mount a frontal assault of an enemy stronghold. As I thought about that, however, I realized that notion might not be far from the truth. After all, Tolby and I were batting a thousand when it came to finding horrific, ravenous monsters inside long-lost Progenitor facilities. Maybe life as a one-armed exile wouldn't be that bad.

The leader of the group squared off with Okabe. He was one of the most imposing Kibnali I'd ever met, standing a full head higher than Tolby and probably packing on another hundred pounds of muscle. "Once the tailless has opened the door, stay clear," he said in a rough voice. "The Eighth Guard will have the honors of breaching the facility first. Understood?"

"Understood," Okabe said with a slight bow. "Do you feel that many soldiers is necessary, Captain?"

"I do, though I doubt you and the tailless would agree with me. Fortunately, and for the sake of the Empire, that is why I am at my station, and you are at yours."

My mind drifted back to what had happened on Adrestia, specifically, the Nodari and Nekrael we'd fought. To that, I glanced at the number of soldiers with us, and my stomach tightened.

"Actually, Captain, I think you might have wanted to bring a few more."

There was a hint of respect in the captain's eyes as he glanced down to me. His right ear twitched, but he gave no other reaction. At least I hoped it was respect. Maybe he was insulted that a lowly tailless like myself had bothered to address them directly. "Your concerns are not misplaced, tailless. The universe is hostile to those who would not dominate it from the start."

"You don't have to tell me twice," I said, again laughing softly at the misadventures we had. "Definitely had my share of hostile encounters."

The captain grunted with a short flick of the tail. "Good. Let's go."

I followed Okabe and the others down a short ramp and into a tunnel. Made of concrete, it ran about twenty meters before dumping us into a massive underground art gallery. The lobby we were in was kidney-shaped, with multiple levels, multiple pools of water fed by multiple waterfalls, surrounded by multiple colorful lights and even more colorful plants. A dizzying array of art hung on the walls, all created from countless different mediums and focusing on a near infinite number of subjects.

On the walls I saw holographic pieces of landscapes, oil paintings of alien ceremonies, charcoal smudges that were so abstract, they made Picasso's most famous work look like that of a realist. Sculptures of five-headed, three-footed creatures stood near others of three-headed, five-footed beings. And then there were the three-headed, three-footed versions, and of course, if you're even remotely savvy, you've already guessed about the five-headed, five-footed pieces, too. Whoever came up with them really, *really* liked the numbers three and five.

At least it wasn't four. I probably would've had a nervous breakdown at that point.

Sadly, I could only gawk at them all as Okabe practically dragged me through. We worked our way down a number of halls, twists, and turns. Far too many to count, as well as several stairs and ramps.

Eventually, we came to a large antechamber way in the back. At the far end of said chamber, about thirty meters away, stood a massive bunker door with a console nearby. It looked a lot like the one at the Lambda Labs in that it looked like a giant gear with huge teeth, and like the one at the labs, there was also a console nearby. Although this time instead of a console sitting on a pedestal nearby, the console was embedded into the rock wall.

"How on earth did you miss this?" I asked with a disbelieving laugh.

"Ahem, pool," Tolby said.

I gave him an incredulous look and threw up my hands. "What? Really? Come on. This thing is as big as a titan. You can't miss this."

"We didn't," Okabe said.

"Ha!" I said, hands on my hips. "Wait. What?"

"We didn't miss it," he said. "But all our scans when we first found it said there was nothing behind it, and since the console hadn't lit up until recently, we assumed it was part of the art exhibit."

"That would make a bizarre exhibit."

One of the soldiers behind Okabe chuckled. His laughter became infectious and soon all the Kibnali, save Tolby, shared some sort of inside joke I hadn't a clue about.

"When we're done, you should see what's on the ninth floor," he said.

"What's there?"

"I don't want to spoil the surprise, but it's weird," he said. He then motioned toward the door before pulling out a triangular device and pressing a few of its buttons. "Now it's time to prove your worth to the Kibnali Empire. Open it up. I'll monitor what's going on between your implants and the console."

I walked up to the console and lightly touched it with my right hand. The screen was cold and had a light film of water across it. I hope that didn't mean it was no longer functional due to water damage. Surely the Progenitors had been skilled enough not to let such a thing cripple one of their facilities.

The captain of the Kibnali Guard growled with displeasure. "We're waiting, tailless. In case you forgot, something's going on in there."

"I need longer than half a second," I said, not bothering to look back at him over my shoulder. That was done partly because I was starting to concentrate on making the mental connection to the Progenitor interface, but it was also done because I knew my face had soured enough that he would take my physical reaction as an insult, as well he should. Stupid furball (no offense, Tolby).

I took in a slow, deep breath and reached out with the implants in my arm to make the remote connection. I was afraid that my attempts would be met with failure as they had when I tried to get into Lambda Labs, but in under a second, I heard a distinct pop and click inside my mind, and my arm tingled as if it were on pins and needles. The console screen flickered to life and cast a warm, orange glow on my skin. An array of ancient, alien symbols flashed across, but they quickly rearranged themselves into words I could understand.

Before I knew it, all of the Kibnali surrounded me, each one muttering words of surprise and quiet whispering thanks to the gods.

"Can you read that writing?" Okabe said, staring at the screen perplexed.

"Yeah, of course," I said, but then I quickly realized that the only reason I could was that the implants in my arm had long since made modifications to my brain so that Progenitor language came second nature to me. "It's a side effect of the implant," I explained as I held up my arm and hoped to smooth over any transgressions. "I'm more or less the universal Progenitor translator."

Thankfully, Okabe—as seemed everyone else—was far more interested in getting inside than reprimanding me for some breach of etiquette. "Can you open it then?"

"I should be able to," I said, working my magic. After some finagling, the first output the computer gave me was:

Facility reactors online. Entry door sealed. Reboot required. Restart all processes?

Not seeing any other options, I hit yes. The moment I did, extra lights popped on from hidden recesses above the door and filled the air with a light static sound. The screen then displayed a new prompt:

Systems rebooted. Have a nice day.

I shrugged, not sure what to make of how easily it all came together, but I wasn't about to look a gift horse in the mouth. I tapped the screen so that the prompt went away and quickly found familiar menu options. It took only a few moments before I found the door controls and ordered it to cycle open.

A loud, pressurized hiss came from the door before it drew back with a horrendous screech and rolled to the side. I had expected such a thing to happen and had already covered my ears, but the Kibnali surrounding me were caught off guard and cringed in obvious pain.

Hot air blasted that felt like it came from the belly of the fusion reactor. As uncomfortable as it was, it proved to be no deterrent for anyone. The entire Eighth Guard rushed in, rifles leading the way, the moment their captain gestured inside with a paw.

Much like the Lambda Labs, the entryway was L-shaped with several consoles on each side. The lighting, however, was much better, and a vaulted ceiling loomed five meters above us. There were also a couple of doors set in separate walls as opposed to the lift in Lambda Labs that descended even further underground. I know I'm superstitious at times, but since two is a lucky number and generally makes me feel good thinking about it, I took this to be a good omen.

The last distinct change from Lambda Labs was on the ceiling. Hanging from it was a massive cylindrical contraption that had a rod sticking out one end. I wasn't entirely sure what it was for, but it looked like it could extend if it wanted to and reach the facility door.

"Tailless," the captain said. "What's beyond the doors?"

"I honestly have no idea," I said. "Storage, classrooms, or a five-headed cybernetic hydra for all I know."

The Kibnali soldiers fanned out, and Okabe walked over to one of the computers. Like the console at the door before I got to it, its screen was dark and unresponsive to his touch. "Can you bring these online?"

"Yeah, I should be able to," I said.

Before I took a step forward, however, the door at the opposite end of the room zipped open, and in flew another grapefruit-sized metallic sphere with a singular lavender eye set in the center and lime-green circuitry all across its skin. It screeched as it shot toward us, but its flight was short-lived.

"No, don't!" I shouted as one of the Kibnali soldiers raised his weapon, but it was too late. The soldier fired a single, well-placed shot that struck the drone dead center, causing a crash. "Why did you do that? He was only coming to help."

"He flew at us in a hostile manner," the soldier said without a hint of remorse.

"But he looks exactly like the ones you have in the casino!"

"Except for the color," the soldier remarked.

"And the screeching," another added.

"And the hostile flying," chimed in a third. "Similar species do not mean similar actions. Surely even a naïve tailless understands that."

I sighed and shook my head as I thought back to what Tolby had said about his race back in the museum. "You guys really are a shoot first and ask questions never group, aren't you?"

"It's just a drone," Okabe said, surprising me. Of all the Kibnali there, I would've thought he would appreciate its loss the most. "I'm sure we can make do without it."

The drone, now in the corner, rolled to the side. Its eye had a half-inch hole on it, and spiderweb cracks were all across its body, but the drone wasn't lifeless. Even from where I stood, I could see the pupil dilating and constricting in a vain attempt to regain focus. I hurried over to the fallen drone and gently picked it up. "Can you hear me?"

"Existential panic. Where... brrrrrrrrrrrptttt... where... brrrpt am I? Why is everything dark?"

"Oh god," I said, feeling tears welled in my eyes. "I am so, so sorry."

"Theological questioning. Are you a...brpptt...a brrppt..."

I patted the top of its head even though I wasn't sure that really accomplished anything. I guess it made me feel like I was offering the thing some sort of comfort in its final moments. "Take your time," I said. "You've got a gummy translation matrix."

"Are you...an imaginary being of moral goodness and light to usher souls to the next life?"

I laughed and had to take a hard sniff before answering to make sure I didn't snot all over it or myself. "Am I an angel? Is that what you're asking?"

"Excitement! Yes, angel. That's the noun I was looking for." The drone shuttered, and there were a half dozen pops and subsequent sparks that flew out of its casing. Its pupil stopped its movement. "Fear. System corrupting. Total failure...brpptt...total failure... brrppttt... Eminent! Will likely repeat words soon. Repeat words soon. Repeat words soon..."

"Don't be scared," I said, equally for my sake as his. "That's my job as an angel, right? To make sure the lost get home?"

He didn't say anything else as I held him. This was the first time I'd ever held the dying in my arms, and I don't care what anybody says, even if he was a drone, he had intelligence, and it was the right thing to do.

The mood was ruined—for lack of a better word—by a horrid wailing and panic-filled, harmonized voice. "Oh my god! They killed KN-E!"

"You bastards!" chimed another.

I jumped to my feet, and the Kibnali warriors spun around, looking for the speaker, weapons ready to blast whoever came at them.

"It was an accident!" I said.

"The hell it was!" replied the voice. "We saw! Blew him right apart, you did."

"Who is this?" Okabe asked.

"KN-C and KN-B," they replied in unison.

"Are you drones, too, like your friend?"

"Wouldn't you like to know! Probably wanting to blast us apart the moment we tell you."

"No one's blasting anyone," I said. "Promise."

"Then why are you here toting around all those Kibnali with guns?" they asked.

"Because we traced a signal here," I explained. "You wouldn't happen to know anything about that would you?"

There was some commotion over the speakers that sounded like someone toppling backward over an office chair and taking out the table and desktop in the process. "We...might know something."

"Regretting, now," said the other.

"Much regretting," added the first.

"Perhaps you should fill us in then before my soldiers get jumpy," Okabe said. "Who are you signaling? An invasion fleet?"

"Invasion?" one huffed. "We are plain quiet drones and have no use for invasions."

"No use at all," said the other. "Nasty, disturbing, uncomfortable things! Make you late for an oil bath!"

Tolby and I exchanged glances, and I swear I had a sense of déjà vu, or whatever the hearing equivalent was.

"What do you think?" Okabe asked me. "Are they hostile?"

I bit my lip with anxiety. If I went by my encounter at the museum, not a chance. However, my time spent on Adrestia put the Progenitors in a completely different light. "I don't know," I admitted. "The facility we came from, Adrestia, had a lot of animosity toward the Kibnali."

"Is this part of what you can't tell me?"

At this point, I was going to explain more in detail, I swear, but as I opened my mouth, a crushing headache took hold and only grew in intensity as I tried to push through it. When I backed off the details, the pain lessened. The Universe, it seemed, was having none of this future prediction. "Yeah," I finally said. "I can't even get the words out. I don't think I could even if under torture."

The captain of the Kibnali grunted. "Perhaps we should test that theory. I'm sure Goshun would approve."

"You'll have to get through me first," Tolby growled.

"You'd stand with a tailless over your own kin," the captain said, shocked and angered.

"She has full honors," he said. "She is one of us."

"Dubious honors at best. Until Empress acknowledges them, I'll tolerate her existence and no more."

Okabe cut the argument short with a glare to both. "Quiet. Both of you." He then redirected his conversation back to KN-C and KN-B. "What about this facility the tailless is in reference to? Adrestia?"

An audible gasp preluded the reply. "We'd never be associated with *that* facility."

"Never!"

"Bunch of rogue, revolting, repulsive researchers there."

"Rascally, too!"

I wasn't expecting that sort of vehement denial, but I wasn't about to trust it either. "If you've got nothing to do with them, what's with the signal?" I asked. "How do we know you're not trying to contact them through spacetime?"

"As if!"

"All we were trying to do was get someone to let us out!"

"That's all!"

My brow furrowed. "Out?"

"Yes, out! Woke up from stasis not long ago, realized we couldn't get out since the door was locked. Tried to call for help, but ended up making our power go wonky—"

"So wonky."

"Finally got the signal out, but the power's still a bugger."

Okabe snorted. "The door's open now. Turn off the signal."

"Can't. We locked ourselves out of the control room."

"Totally locked."

"Then unlock it," I said, rolling my eyes.

"Need Progenitor implants to do that," one explained. "Oh, hey. You opened the front door. I bet you could get in."

"Totally bet she could."

Again, there was a round of silent glances between us all. "Fine," I said, once I was reasonably sure we were all on the same page. "Where do we go?"

"The control room is in the back of the facility," he replied. "It's on the map. You'll see."

"Oh, and might want to hurry," added the other.

I cocked my head. "Why's that?"

"The computers managing the signal have picked up a glitch."

"A tiny glitch," added the other.

"Barely worth mentioning, really," the first went on. "Seems they have shut down cooling to the main reactor. But as I said, it's a minor problem."

"Very minor."

"But don't worry! Even if it does melt down, it'll be probably only a fifty-kiloton blast at most."

"No more than sixty."

"Definitely topping at seventy-five. Neighboring planets won't even notice."

My eyes went wide. "What? We're all about to be vaporized? When the hell were you going to tell us?"

"As soon as we noticed," he replied. "Which we just did. You've got about six minutes to get there. I suggest you hurry."

CHAPTER NINE:
MELTDOWN

I raced over to a nearby terminal where KN-C and KN-B had popped up a map for us. The layout of the facility staggered me. The entire thing spanned at least a kilometer in all directions, including up, and I quickly surmised that, like the Museum of Natural Time, the Progenitors had built this place so it was bigger on the inside than the outside. Portal technology was cool like that.

Assuming you didn't wipe yourself out of existence. But hey, everything has its risks and rewards.

Once I committed the map to memory, we blitzed out of the room through the doorway poor KN-E had come through and headed for the main reactor.

"Dakota, I have some interesting news," Daphne said over my comm as we ran.

"Does it have anything to do with shutting down a reactor that's going nuclear?"

"Is there one? That would explain the power readings I'm getting," she said.

"Yes, there is one! The stupid drones here locked themselves out of the control room, and the whole place is going to blow!"

Daphne hummed a moment to herself. "You know, I'm having a hard time believing these Progenitors were all that advanced. Seems every power core of theirs we get near goes to pants."

"Yeah, no kidding," I said between ragged breaths.

"On the other hand, maybe it's you," she said. "Perhaps you're bad luck."

"I am *not* bad luck," I protested. "I gave that ashi-da-whatever plenty of belly rubs. You saw."

"Maybe it's not as effective as your tiny elephant."

"So what's this interesting news you're trying to tell me?" I said as we hooked a left and ran down yet another corridor.

"Oh yes, my discovery," she said, brightening. "I've been sifting through all the records I downloaded before you rudely snatched the cube from me."

"You didn't even say you were still using it!"

"I wasn't, but that's beside the point," she said. "At any rate, one of the seventy-eight million records available detailed a unique trait about your implants...well, potential trait. I think you might want to try this out."

"Okay, I'm all ears. What am I trying?"

"Really quick, though, have they grown through your left arm yet?"

The question was strange enough that I slowed my pace long enough to glance at the arm in question. At first, I didn't see anything, but after I peeled back my sleeve, sure enough, there was a thin blue line that ran from the inside of my forearm up to my wrist. "Huh. That's weird," I said. "They have. I mean, it's only a single line right now, but yeah, there's definitely implant spreading through me."

"Then you're going to love this," she said. "You can draw power from the environment now with that arm. It'll help power your telekinesis in a pinch."

"Draw power? Like how?"

"I don't know," she said. "I suspect it pulls from the energy around it. According to these notes in the cube, liquids work the best. But don't do it too much, because you'll rapidly drop the temperature of whatever you've got your hand in."

"And?"

"And you'll have a hand encased in ice."

"Great. So I'm a giant ice cube maker now," I said as we flew down a flight of stairs.

"Yup. And you'll be a hit at parties. You'll probably also make a fantastic bartender, too."

"I'll keep that in mind."

We continued on, following the corridor, and it made a gentle, wide right turn before descending with a flight of stairs that had clearly been built for a hill giant and not my little legs. At the bottom, the floors turned from marble tile to metallic panels with no-slip grips. The hall then took us through a number of areas and side rooms that had no doubt been designated for manufacturing and fabrication of parts and goods on account of the machinery in each room. I even caught sight of a fabricator like the one the drone TG2 had used back at the other facility to provide Jack and me with a new set of clothes. And while I was thinking about that little event, I had to admit that the shoes he'd given us had also surpassed every expectation I ever had when it came to comfort and functionality, just like the little drone said.

Apparently, the Progenitors were not only immensely advanced when it came to sheer technology for traveling spacetime, but also when it came to creature comforts like the best shoes in the universe. Man, could you imagine if they had not vaporized themselves out of existence? I mean, what other things do we humans love that they would have improved on a thousandfold? A ballpoint pen that doesn't dry out when you need it the most? A printer that actually hooks up to your computer correctly? Hell, what about a piano that stays in tune or a spam filter that actually works? I tell you what. If the Kibnali ever developed that, I would gladly serve their Empire till I was a ripe old lady.

Okay, I'm rambling. I know.

We made a few more turns, ran up a flight of stairs, and then hauled butt down a wide hall with a dozen rooms on each side. Each of these rooms were circular and in the middle sat what appeared to be large, upside-down claws, very similar to the webway spires we'd seen on Adrestia.

At the far end of the hall stood an imposing door, maybe four meters high, and next to it floated a couple of drones who looked like carbon copies of KN-E, except one had a yellow eye and the other had a bright green one.

"You're finally here," said the bot with the yellow eye. "KN-B and I are so relieved you made it in time."

"Very!" KN-B added.

"Now if you'd be so kind to unlock the door, we can save our facility," KN-C said, bobbing toward a console on the wall. "We're on a strict schedule, you know, assuming you'd like to keep bodily integrity at a maximum."

"That's always been a high priority of mine," I said, hurrying over to the control panel.

I easily made the connection via my implants, and within seconds, I had the screen cycling between several menus. True to the drones' words, the door to the command center had been locked. Thankfully, unlocking it was a simple matter.

Why, oh why, I didn't realize how strange that was is beyond me.

At my command, the security systems disengaged. My body shuddered as the horrific noise of metal screeching over metal filled my ears. As the door slid to the side, it did so with the pressurized hiss of hot air with a side order of steam.

"You ready for a sauna?" I said, grinning at Tolby. "I can't wait to see what that does to your fur."

"I'd rather not find out."

"Aw, come on. I bet you look adorable with everything poofed out," I said. "We should try."

"Let's just stop this meltdown," Tolby said.

At that point, the door had fully opened, and we all rushed inside. The room we entered was bathed in soft, amber light, and the smell of chlorine wafted from it. It stretched maybe fifty meters out and took the form of a lopsided egg. Huge, thick pipes and bundles of wires ran across the ceiling while station after station of high-tech computer banks crammed the walls. In the center of the room stood a ring of consoles that circumscribed yet another miniature webway, while at the far end was a gigantic screen—currently blank—but one that looked awesome to catch the premiere of the next Marco Ocram movie.

"All right, your turn," I said to KN-C. "We got you in. Work your magic."

"Excitement! Going to work now," he said, zipping over to one of the consoles in the center.

A thin wire snaked out from the center of his body and plugged into a jack near the top of the computer. Within seconds the lighting brightened, becoming a much more soft, whitish-blue in hue.

"Does this mean our crisis is averted?" I asked.

"Positive reply," KN-C said. "Meltdown has been averted. Glorious satisfaction. My task is nearly complete."

"Nearly?" I asked, tilting my head. "What do you mean by that?"

Before the little drone could reply, Okabe cut in. "What is this place?"

"Quick explanation: it's a research lab," KN-C replied. "It's studying the effects of gambling on various species. Hence the casino."

"You expect us to believe this is one big lab experiment?" he asked with a snort. "What about the art gallery we came through? Is that an experiment, too?"

"Negative. The art gallery was installed to raise the happiness indices of all staff assigned to the area. Very popular."

Tolby looked around and soured his face. "I don't like this," he said. "Something feels off."

"Understandable apprehension, given prior time on Adrestia," KN-C said. He then bobbed toward another console nearby. "If you don't believe me, check the logs."

Okabe made his way to the console but apparently was at a loss for how to use it. "And how do I do that?"

"Instructional advice," KN-C said, sounding giddy with excitement. "Press the datapad on your right. Holographic displays will then be presented for your browsing."

Okabe glanced down, found said pad, and pressed one of his paws into it. Immediately, the pad glowed, and the screen flickered to life. "That seems to have done something."

Energy filled the air. The hairs on my neck stood, and low, building noise, like the spooling of a giant turbine far away, came to life.

"Genetic sequence verified," said a deep, alien voice. "Kibnali presence detected. Risk of paradox backlash minimal. Termination signal sent."

"What did he say?" I asked, heart skipping two beats. "What the hell is going on?"

The rest of the Kibnali looked equally surprised and at a loss, but Okabe tried working the console as much as he could. I wasn't sure what he was looking at—there was something on the screen— but it didn't matter in the end.

Tolby leaped to Okabe's side, practically slamming him into the wall. His claws raced across the console controls, and his face filled with panic as I realized all he was doing at this point was confirming his worst nightmare.

"That signal..." he said, his voice weak. "...that signal went to Adrestia. To when it teemed with Nodari...to when the entire hive fleet was in orbit."

A rock formed in my throat, yet somehow I managed to swallow. "You mean...we just caused the invasion?"

KN-C saddled next to me. Bright and merry, the little droid whispered in my ear. "This is the part where you run."

CHAPTER TEN:
MOAR™ PORTALS

The center of the room distorted, and spacetime bubbled outward. A crystal-clear portal formed in that bubble, much like the ones I used to create back at the museum, only this one looked far more stable and had far better-defined edges than any I had made.

The scene on the other side was concerning to say the least. What we were treated to was a metropolitan wasteland that seemed straight out of an apocalypse movie. I didn't recognize any of the structures as being part of a culture I knew, but it was clear we were looking at a city ruined by the ravages of war. The skeletal remains of unknown aliens strewn in the streets alongside burnt husks of vehicles were the icing on the cake.

Six Nodari scouts raced into view and leaped through the portal, their bronze exoskeletons gleaming in the light of the room. Their large legs drove them forward with incredible speed, and they looked every bit as demonic as I remembered them with their half dozen compound green eyes, curled horns on their skulls, and dagger-like teeth. In their hands, they carried pistol and rifle, though them being in such close proximity to us, they probably didn't need either. Their claws could no doubt rend flesh and fur instantly.

To the Kibnali's credit, they hadn't lowered their guard since entering the room. A hail of plasma fire from the group tore through the Nodari scouts. Each one was struck half a dozen times in the chest before they crossed the distance between us and the portal's opening. The monstrous creatures crashed down, but it was clear they were far from dead. Though most of their bodies could no longer function, they all crawled their way toward us like unholy creatures of the abyss.

"They won't die?" Okabe snorted with disbelief. "What are these things?"

"Nodari!" Tolby yelled. "They are—will be the scourge of our Empire!"

More plasma shots came from the Kibnali firing line, drilling each Nodari invader in the head. Compound eyes exploded and skulls vaporized. The smoke from the wounds had yet to dissipate in the slightest before a chorus of roars grabbed our attention.

But those roars didn't come from the portal. They came from behind us.

Pouring out of the side rooms connected to the hall behind us, swarms of Nodari scouts rushed into view. Some ran off, but most directed their attention at us. As fast as they were cut down, more took their place. A seemingly endless horde flooded the area that had no hope of being abated.

"How many can there be?" Okabe growled.

"Their numbers are beyond comprehension," Tolby said. "We must fight our way free. To stand here is to die."

KN-C nudged me with his body. "Friendly concern. You really ought to use your arm now and portal yourself back to the ship."

"My portal device is broken!" I said, backing away. "Besides, I can't leave Jack and the others behind."

"Rear!" someone yelled.

I spun around and saw more Nodari charge out of the portal in the command center. Three were killed in a flash. Another managed to get to one of the Kibnali and rip open his shoulder before being shot in the head. Yet another sailed its way over all the bodies and drove for yours truly.

Out of pure reflex, I telekinetically punched it right in its head. I struck him, and half of his face shattered as he flopped to the side. Sadly, that also meant I pretty much spent everything I had. My arm numbed and hung from my side. I could barely flex my fingers, which was pretty bad considering another Nodari threw himself at me.

I fell backward, screaming in fright. I knew Mr. Grimmy approached with sickle in hand and my name at the top of his list, and the moment before I hit the ground, I wished to god I could at least warn everyone else. The Kibnali might've been doomed at that point, but that didn't mean Jack and the others had to stick around for it.

To my shock and confusion, I didn't hit the ground. Instead, I fell through an all-too-familiar wormhole. I tumbled, lost my senses, regained my senses, tumbled some more, and eventually flew out of the ceiling of my casino suite.

I remember the floor rushing up to meet me, and the look of utter confusion on Jack's face as he looked up from the couch. Then I hit the tile and bam! I dreamed of painting sunsets with oils and dancing on the deck of a luxury cruise liner.

Why? No idea. I imagine my psyche was trying to find a better place to be, given recent events.

I awoke to a thunderous clap in a deep rumbling that shook the entire building. Jack, kneeling at my side, loomed over my view. He shook me a few times by the shoulder, which helped bring me back to my senses. Sort of.

"Dakota! We've got to get the hell out of here," he said, his face an equal mix of relief and panic.

"What's going on?"

"There's a damn war outside, that's what's going on!"

Several dull explosions came from outside, which combined with his last statement, turned out to be plenty to spur me into action. I grabbed his hand and hoisted myself up.

Half my brain knew I'd woken, but the other half refused to think I had. I ran to the window and looked outside. The sky had turned to a sickly green, and the area all around was filled with dust and fog. From the clouds rained seed-like drop pods, more numerous than I could count. When they hit the ground, they burst open and out crawled Nodari scouts.

In terms of defense, the Kibnali met the invading force with every bit of strength and power I would've ever imagined. Turrets that had popped up from the ground took shots at the Nodari as well as whatever was above the clouds. Every Kibnali I saw carried a plasma gun and fought with ruthless efficiency, and alongside them were combat robots of all sizes and shapes.

The Kibnali defenders took up fortified positions across the city and brought withering fire from mounted, crew-served weapons that had been hastily set up on balconies in every building I could see. Armored vehicles roamed the streets, obliterating the Nodari with shot after shot. But like what had happened back in the command center, no matter how many aliens they killed, more came, faster and stronger.

A loud whistling caught my attention, and I looked up in time to see several drop pods smash into the casino. Two hit the floor below us, while three more hit right above.

I backed away from the window, shaking my head. "Oh god, we've got to get Tolby."

Jack grabbed my hand and yanked me toward the door. "We've got to find a ship and get the hell out of here."

"No! I'm not leaving him!"

Right then, my prayers were answered. Over my comm, broken and full of static, came my best bud's voice. "Dak...need...ASA..."

"What?"

"Thank...alive...jamming...com...cations..."

I cursed and hoped his gods favored us enough that he could understand me. "Tolby, where are you?"

The sounds of battle took over in my ear, but then everything went clear, and his voice came over the line, strong, out of breath, but strong. "Dakota, there's a ship at the west landing pad. Okabe went for his research. It's going to leave when he gets back. If you want off this planet, you've got to get there ASAP."

"I don't know where that is!"

"You...use...room key."

The line filled with static again, and I cursed. "Tolby? Tolby! Answer me!"

Jack held up his room key, which had our destination clearly marked on its map. "Come on, Dakota. We know where he'll be. Let's not miss our ride."

I sucked in a deep breath and nodded before we bolted out of the door. Panicked guests raced in both directions, hollering and screeching. A giant insect-bear hybrid sporting plaid attire bowled me over, not even slowing in the least, let alone sticking around to help me up. A few others followed right behind, practically trampling me in the process. I rolled to the side and up against the wall, which was probably the only thing that kept me from being broken in ten places.

Jack grabbed me underneath my shoulders and hoisted me up. "You okay?"

"Yeah."

"How the hell did you fall out of the ceiling anyway?" he asked as we ran.

"No idea. Little robot guy said my arm was working right before he told me to get to the ship," I said. "Then the Nodari attacked. I freaked out, and viola, I fell out of the ceiling."

"You can make portals again?" he asked.

"Maybe if my arm wasn't so numb," I said. "I drained it punching a scout in the face."

"God, what I wouldn't give for you to throw us back a year from now. Hell, even a week."

"Me, too. Tapioca brains and all."

The building shook, and a pipe burst from inside the wall, spraying water everywhere. Jack tried to pull me through, but I rooted myself in place as an idea struck me.

"Hang on," I said, shoving my left hand into the spray.

"What are you doing?"

"Recharging my batteries, I think."

"How?"

I shrugged, having no other answer. I could only hope whatever ability Daphne said I now had worked like the rest, off instinct. A good dozen tense seconds passed, and Jack's face grew more and more anxious. Mine probably did, too. I was about to give up when I realized flecks of ice covered my left hand, and I could feel my right arm again. Even better, it moved as I wanted it to.

"Hot damn," I said, flexing my hand. "I think I did it."

"Can you portal us out of here?"

I shrugged again. "Maybe." I tried to form one, but nothing happened. Not even when I tried extra hard. "Maybe not. I don't understand why it worked before suddenly but not now."

"Something we'll figure out later," he said, pulling me along.

Down the hall we went. We were almost to a staircase when something heavy crashed through the ceiling ahead and plowed its way through the floor, taking with it a half dozen terrified guests. From the hole in the floor, a Nodari scout pulled himself up and raised a gun that seemed to be ninety percent barrel.

The beam that shot out felt hotter than a supernova. It seared by my head and vaporized a soda-can-size hole in the guest next to me as well as the three aliens behind him. I dropped to the ground as another shot flew and decimated two others caught in the beam. Reflexively, I shot out my hand and telekinetically punched the Nodari scout square in the face. He reeled backward and inadvertently let go of his weapon.

"Now's our chance," Jack said, popping back up and offering to grab my arm.

"Hang on," I said, shrugging him off. I tuned out the panic of everyone around and concentrated on the fallen Nodari weapon, hoping that time practicing my telekinetic powers were about to pay off. The weapon rattled on the floor as I tried to get a hold of it, and right as the scout lunged for the rifle, it rocketed toward me like someone had strapped a stage-IV booster to its butt.

I should've taken my brother up on playing catch more when we were little. The weapon bounced off my hands, drove into my chest, and gave me a bruised cheek and split lip before flipping over my head.

"Cripes, Dakota," Jack said, snatching the wayward rifle in the air before it sailed to the other end of the hall. He quickly shouldered the weapon and fired. The beam drilled straight through the Nodari's head, dropping him where he stood. He then sighed with relief and smiled. "Next time you toss a weapon to us, how about a little less hot sauce?"

"You got it," I said with a laugh.

Together we ran down the hall. Most of the guests had cleared out of our immediate area by now, but we could still hear chaos all around. Each flight of stairs we ran down, door we went through, and corner we took, I half expected to come face-to-face with an entire Nodari platoon.

Thankfully, we didn't.

The door to the first floor ended up being blocked by rubble, and with smoke filling the air and the sounds of fires crackling nearby, we thought it best to keep going down than go back up. Thus, we ended up in the basement.

Jack and I blew through the first couple of halls with ease. We burst into an L-shaped room, which housed a number of consoles and monitors in the center and along the walls. Most of them were riddled with holes; some were even torn to pieces. Sparks flew from servers, popping as they took flight from exposed wires. The smell of sulfur hung in the air. Two security bots lay torn in half, their midsections a fused heap of metal and wire.

Across the way, there were bodies of other creatures that looked a lot like the Nekrael we had encountered on the other world. Only these looked far more evolved. They weighed twenty-five, maybe thirty kilograms. Each limb rippled with muscles, and their tails looked like they were comprised of five separate tentacles, all braided together and ending in a wicked stinger. They still had the characteristic metallic skin that the others had, but their four eyes were evenly spaced across their faces as opposed to looking like they came from a Picasso painting.

I didn't know what their official designation was, but I named them swarmlings for my own reference. Sounded good, right?

"I hope these stay dead," Jack said, approaching the corpses warily. "Even their teeth look more wicked this time around."

I nodded. "No kidding. But let's not stick around to find out."

Jack bent down and grabbed a pistol that had fallen on the floor. He pried off the mechanical hand that was attached to it before tossing the weapon to me. "Here. Could come in handy."

"Thanks."

Gunfire blasted down the hall, and we snapped back into action. We raced across the room, slowing only a moment to ensure that the swarmlings didn't come to life and give pursuit, and dashed through the gloomy basement tunnels.

"Do you know where we are?" I asked.

"Underground."

"Very funny. Do you know where we're going?"

"Yeah, straight," Jack said, throwing me a glance and a wink. "I think the landing pad is this way, assuming the map on the key is right."

"I really hope so."

"Me, too."

We ran a bit longer before rounding a corner and slamming into a locked security door. Jack tried a few combinations on its keypad, but the door held fast. "Try another portal?"

I did, and as with my last attempt, nothing. "Still not happening," I said with a sigh.

Jack flashed a half grin. "Remember when I said we shouldn't fry the portal device? Now would be the perfect time to have it."

"True, but not being killed by Goliath was even handier."

"I'm open to suggestions at this point."

I looked down at my hand and tried to gauge the thickness of the door. Could I punch through it? Maybe. But if I used up all my energy trying and it didn't work, all I'd have to show was a bum arm for a couple of hours unless I could find some more water to sap energy from.

"Do you think that gun of yours could weaken the locks?" I asked. "I might be able to take it off the hinges if so."

"Worth a shot."

Jack retreated a few steps, and I followed. After sucking in a breath, he aimed and fired. The superheated jet nailed the door and punched a fist-sized hole through it.

"Oh, baby, we're in business!" he shouted.

As he took aim and fired off another dozen shots, I tried to reach the others. "Tolby," I said. "We're coming through the basement tunnels. Can you hear me?"

"...nels?"

"Yes!" I said, hoping I'd correctly deciphered his question. "We're almost through!"

A deafening cacophony came from behind, one that would have made a leviathan's roar seem like a coo from a baby.

"Hurry!" I said, keeping my eyes on the rear.

"I am!"

"Hurry more!"

A few tense seconds later, Jack put one last shot into the doorframe and turned me around to inspect his work. The damn thing looked like Swiss cheese. "Time for you to do your—"

Before he could finish, I summoned all my Progenitor strength and slammed an invisible fist into the door. The thing disintegrated under the blow, sending shrapnel everywhere.

"That does it for me," I said, looking down at my once again ice-cold and dangling arm.

Our flight to the landing pad continued, but it came to yet another unexpected halt when we entered the remains of the maintenance bay. The air was thick with smoke and the smell of burnt flesh. Machinery and vehicles of all sizes had been strewn about, some of the remains still smoldering. The ceiling had a massive hole blown out its center, and fires burned steadily in every corner.

Whatever had happened here, I was glad we missed it. No one could have survived such a blast, no matter how much fate smiled upon them. I had a brief fear that maybe one of the others had been caught in it, but thankfully, I didn't see any Kibnali bodies in the rubble.

Cautiously, we picked our way through the rubble, wary of a Nodari ambush. That caution paid off, for no sooner than we'd taken a few steps, a scout popped around a piece of machinery. Jack, however, blew apart his head before he could take a shot at us.

At that point, the distinct whine of engines cut through the air. Someone was initiating a takeoff procedure, and I feared that someone had no intention of waiting till we got there.

Jack seemed to share my sentiment. Without a spoken word, we threw caution to the wind and dashed across the maintenance bay. We flew past wreckage and rubble, crossed the sixty meters that spanned the bay, and bounded up the flight of stairs at the other end.

Dust swirled about as we reached the surface. I had to duck my head and slow my pace to keep from being blinded. A spotlight from the Kibnali ship ahead found us, and I gave silent thanks right up until the drone of the engines intensified.

"Don't leave!" I yelled.

As soon as I opened my mouth, my lungs burned, and I doubled over in pain. A thin, greenish gas filled the air, causing tears to pour from my eyes and mucus to flow from my nose.

Jack's hand gripped my arm and pulled me along. "We're almost there. Just head for the sound of the ship."

I nodded, half-blind, and forced myself to stay calm. We were seconds from escaping. We could make it. No, we would make it.

I heard the all-too-familiar sounds of plasma and cannon fire from ahead. Nodari screeched somewhere behind us, and then came the heavy, repetitive sounds of a giant cannon. *Thum. Thum. Thum.*

The blast from each of those shots threatened to shake my teeth loose. Not that I was complaining, mind you. I'm sure it was wreaking havoc among the Nodari ground forces.

I tripped, and down I went. I hit the ground and struck the side of my head on something hard. Unable to move or think, all I could do was lie still and breathe air that felt like it was drowning my lungs in acid. My body started to spasm as I went into a coughing fit. I knew I had to stand, had to get somewhere, anywhere, but the world was too much of a painful, chaotic mess to do anything.

Rough, furry paws grabbed my arms and legs. I screamed reflexively as I was hoisted over the shoulders of a Kibnali—who, I couldn't tell. My vision was far too blurred to tell. But whoever it was, was going to get my undying thanks for a hundred years.

The Kibnali ran, and I bounced on his shoulders. We ran up a small ramp, and once inside, he dropped me forcefully to the ground and yanked my head backward. A second later, my face was bathed in a cold spray that soothed both eyes and nose.

I cleared my eyes with one hand to find Tolby standing over me, while Jainon carried Jack up into the dropship.

"Are you okay?" he asked.

"No worse than usual," I said, looking over my battered and bruised body.

"Good," he said, hitting a large button that raised the ramp.

"Did Okabe make it back?"

"Literally ten seconds before you showed up," Tolby said. He then hit another button and opened a comm up to the pilot. "We're in. Give us nine before you dust off."

"That's all you're getting," came a rough reply.

With Tolby's less than gentle pulling, I got to my feet and ran deeper inside the ship. A dozen Kibnali filled the seats that lined walls, with Okabe seated toward the front. A few perked up at my arrival but most ignored me completely. I had barely managed to strap myself in with the oversized harness when the dropship lurched upward.

The ship rolled violently to the left, and I slammed against my restraints. As quick as we'd moved, it rolled back the other way before diving. Somehow, in all the commotion, Tolby managed to get the pilot's attention. "What's going on up there?"

"Taking fire from an enemy cruiser," came the reply. "Sit tight, and may the gods be with us."

Tolby reached up from his position and tapped a button. A holodisplay dropped down and displayed the view from the cockpit. At first, I couldn't see much other than clouds below and a starry sky above, but when the pilot banked hard and whipped us around, I caught sight of a few bright streaks of plasma shoot by.

"Where's the Nodari ship?" Tolby said.

"Almost a hundred kilometers to our rear," the pilot said. "I think we'll be out of range soon."

"Did any other ships manage to escape?"

"I don't know. Comms are still scrambled, but our 39th Flotilla is en route to reinforce," he replied. "Hang tight. We're clear of atmo. Hitting the impulse burners now."

Our ship lurched to the side one last time to dodge incoming fire before it surged forward with such acceleration, I doubt anything short of a black hole would have pulled us faster. Thankfully, the burst of speed only lasted a short while, and soon the pilot eased off the proverbial accelerator.

"We're clear, relatively speaking," he said. "Sit tight. We'll be docking with the *Fury's Edge* soon."

CHAPTER ELEVEN:
THE RETURN

We jolted twice. Once when the shuttlecraft landed inside the hangar of *Fury's Edge* and then again when the destroyer's engines went into overdrive a moment later.

I rushed to undo my harness and ran out of the shuttle along with everyone else. The hangar we were in had a low-lying ceiling with reinforcing ribs along the walls and ceiling. A large, shimmering force field faced rearward and offered a view of the planet as it shrank away. Because the destroyer we were in was configured in such a fashion, it also meant that the hangar gave a fantastic view of not one but three Nodari cruisers in orbit around the planet and that were currently pummeling it into submission.

A bright beam came from the nearest cruiser, cutting through the dark void that separated us, and struck our ship. Klaxons blared, and our ship rumbled. Thankfully, whatever defenses the *Fury's Edge* had seemed to hold, as we weren't blown apart.

"Dakota! Move!" Tolby shouted. "It's not safe here."

I nodded and ran with the others down a corridor. The passages we raced through were tight, even if they were made for the Kibnali, who easily dwarfed my paltry height. Every ten or twenty meters there were bulkheads and fire doors. Junction boxes and pipes filled every spare bit of space along the ceilings and walls.

I didn't memorize the route we took. All I could do was focus on keeping up with the others and listen to the hard strikes of my feet hitting the metallic floor. It wasn't long, however, before I'd followed Tolby right up to the bridge.

The station of the ship was not what I expected. Whereas the halls had been tight and confining, the bridge itself was far more open, although that might have had something to do with the lack of personnel.

We entered through one of three possible hatches that were set in the back. The entire thing was arranged in a semicircle with three control stations spaced evenly around in a triangle shape. Above, the ceiling had a shallow dome structure to it, and in the middle hung a circular array of screens that were currently displaying a myriad of information to everyone that was there.

Only three Kibnali manned the helm. Two of them were at the computer consoles while the third stood in the middle of the bridge, face set with determination, and ears back. "Damage report."

"Shields stabilizing," the Kibnali on the left said. "Warp drive currently offline due to uncontained energy surge."

The commanding Kibnali grunted. "Are they pursuing?"

"Negative," came the reply. "They're more interested in the planet than us. I think we're out of range of their weapons now, too."

"Good. Keep her moving as fast as she'll go."

I felt my body relax now that we were out of immediate danger. I wondered what the Kibnali homeworld would be like and how the Empress there would treat us. But when I looked around and realized that while Okabe stood nearby, Empress and Yseri were not here.

"Where's everyone else?" I asked.

The commander at the helm turned around and looked surprised to see me. "Who let these tailless creatures onto my bridge?"

Before I could reply, Tolby took a quick step forward and presented the data card. "The data, Commander Ito," he said, offering it up.

Once Ito had it in hand and gave a short nod of approval, I repeated my question. "Where are the others?"

The Kibnali's eyes narrowed, and he growled. "Everyone and everything that needs to be on board is."

"What's he talking about?" I asked Tolby.

"This ship is headed back to Empress with Okabe and his research," Tolby said. "We're only on board because he wanted to give us a chance to escape."

"That's right, and unless you want me to eject you out of an airlock, you'll close that disgusting, tiny little mouth of yours and get off my bridge. Now."

"Empress isn't on board?" Jainon asked, looking shocked, as if such a possibility could even exist.

"The Empress is safe on our homeworld," Ito replied evenly. "The one you refer to is a no one, and along those lines, you are a no one as well." The commander turned and faced some of the Kibnali who had come in with us on the shuttle. "Get these things out of here."

They all snapped to attention and moved in on us. Tolby, however, held up a paw and they stopped. "There's no need for any of this, Commander Ito," he said. "We will go quietly."

"Then do so," Ito replied. Though his voice lost a little of its edge, his eyes never left us until we were gone.

Once outside and down the passageway, Tolby turned his face toward me. "We have no standing with them. Not even Empress," he said. "We need to remember that. They have their orders, and those orders do not include entertaining us."

"You're not concerned where Empress and Yseri are?" I asked.

"I am, but picking a fight with him will do you about as much good as shoving a screwdriver into a hypercoil," he said. "There are bigger things going on right now."

"Not for me," I said.

Jainon laughed, but it was not one born from amusement but from disbelief. "She's more a member of the Royal Guard than you are, Tolby."

"Why? Because I refuse to have a fight that cannot be won?" he said without hesitation. "Only kits enter battle in such a wasteful fashion. Be smart, Jainon. Empress—our Empress—would want no less."

We stared at each other in the hall for a few moments before he started to walk and motioned for us to follow. "Come, we'll find a better place to talk all this over."

Jainon, Jack, and I followed, albeit a bit reluctantly. Jack, of course, didn't have much stake in this fight, but as for Jainon and me, we certainly weren't about to let this go. We traveled the passageway a couple of dozen meters before taking a side hall and going through a fire door. At that point, we ducked into a small meeting room to gather our wits and process all that had gone on.

"We'll wait in here," Tolby said as we entered. "That should keep us out of the way and out of trouble until we get to Empress Tamaki."

"What about our Empress? And Yseri?"

"Hopefully they'll get there soon, too."

"I guess," I said, hating where we'd ended up and not being able to do a thing.

I should clarify that last bit. While I didn't like being stuffed into a meeting room with my concerns thrown to the wayside, I should mention that I was grateful that I wasn't being tossed into the brig.

The meeting room had a curved outer wall with a view of the outside, a modest table in the middle, and bolted chairs surrounding it. Above, ceiling lights hung from gray tiles, and while that was rather dull, the walls did have box gardens mounted with plenty of flowering plants and a few which had alien fruit hanging from vines. I couldn't help but smile at that. Even on their warships, the Kibnali still made time to bring nature with them.

"What now?" Jack asked as he plopped into one of the chairs.

"I don't know," I said, sitting across from him. Everything had happened so fast, and I had yet to make sense of any of it. I found myself wondering how Yseri and Empress were doing. Not well, I was sure, assuming they were still alive. After a few moments of silence torturing my mind, I whipped out the data cube from the facility and began to sift through it mindlessly.

"This is wrong," Jack said. "I can't believe I'm saying this—no offense Tolby—but leaving our own is wrong."

"I know," I replied.

"We should be down there fighting with them," Jainon said. "Or at least trying to help them get off the planet."

I nodded and felt my throat tighten. I couldn't fathom what sort of nightmare they were facing on their own. While part of me was glad we'd managed to get to the shuttle and escape, a bigger part felt guilty for being part of the ones who survived, especially since I didn't even try to save them. All I did was run. I knew I couldn't blame myself that much given all the chaos during the attack.

With a sigh, I punched up the articles dealing with the underground Progenitor facility. I didn't know what I was looking for other than hoping I could find something that would be of some use to those left behind. I figured maybe we could get some sort of communication to them, assuming the jamming stopped before it was too late.

"Let me know if you find something," Jainon said as she shut her eyes and pressed her paws together. "I need to meditate and regain my focus."

"Will do."

As I went through the records, Tolby paced by the window, and Jack moved around the table and sat down next to me. He didn't say anything but quietly read over my shoulder.

Twenty minutes came and went, and I had nothing to show for my efforts. There were a lot of mundane records I ended up sifting through, shipping manifests, and inventory. Frustrated at the lack of progress, I mindlessly flipped through a handful of records before moving on to a new section.

Jack grabbed my arm. "Wait," he said. "Go back."

"Where?"

"Back to that one before," he said, practically pushing me off my chair to get to the data cube. He was full of such energy, both Tolby and Jainon took note and joined us. Once the records were up, he grinned from ear to ear. "Look at that. I think we've hit the jackpot."

He had pulled up a partial listing for some ships that had come and gone from the Progenitor facility. It all looked straightforward enough, but I didn't see what the excitement was all about. "I'm tired, Jack," I said with a sigh. "What's got you riled up? Because as far as I can tell, none of the cargo manifests list Nodari Extinction Device."

He pointed to a few lines at the top left. "They do list that though."

"What? Those are just arrival and departure times."

"I know," he said. "But at least two of those ships left and returned on an earlier date."

Now it was Jainon's turn to get excited. She leaned over me from behind, practically pushing my head into the table with her furry body. That wouldn't have been too bad if she hadn't been draped in armor, so the whole experience was far less snugly than I'd have liked. "He's right," she said. "These ships must be capable of temporal jumps."

"Unless you're reading it wrong," Tolby said.

"I'm not," Jack said.

I rubbed my eyes as fatigue wore more and more on my psyche and then examined the records. A dozen seconds had to pass before I had to admit Jack was right. "No, he's not reading it wrong. There are at least two separate ships that make these trips."

"Are they still there?" Tolby asked.

I flipped through the logs some more. "I think so. Yeah, actually. They should be. Separate sides of the facility, but there are still two there."

"Next two obvious questions: Can we fly them, and do they work?"

"I have no idea to both, but I do have this," I said, raising my arm. "I'm willing to wager that if they're still operational I can jack into one and get us out of there. Everything else the Progenitors have made, I've been able to use once I tapped into it. I don't see why the ship would be any different."

Jainon slammed a paw into the table triumphantly. "Then we go back, find Empress and Yseri, and jump out."

"Hell yeah," Jack said, standing. "And then we use that damn ship to go home and get my brother back."

At first, I thought Tolby was going to protest by saying something practical, a not so gentle reminder that we were headed back into the bowels of hell with not even a shred of a guarantee that anything was going to work. But he didn't. He only made one minor point. "Okay, I say we give it a go," he said. "But this ship will never turn around, and I don't think they will give us a shuttle. It's not really made for blockade running anyway. Since we need to land relatively close to the city, we can't touch down on the opposite side of the planet and walk. The battle will be over long before we get there."

"This ship is outfitted with four drop pods. We could all fit in one of them if Ito would agree to help."

"Worth a try," I said. "What's the worst he'll say, no?"

"Hopefully," Tolby said before walking over to a panel on the wall and hitting a comm button. The call went straight to the bridge, and when the commander answered it, the background noise wasn't as hectic as I'd thought it might be. "Commander, if we're still clear of danger, there's something you should see."

"And what might that be?"

"It has to do with the Progenitors and the Nodari back on the planet," Tolby said. "It would be easier to show you. Okabe should come, too."

A few orders were spoken to others that I didn't quite catch, and then the commander returned to the line. "I have a moment, so when I get there, make it fast."

Less than a minute later, the commander and Okabe came striding through the door. Ito walked with purpose and kept a stern gaze on me with his dark, predatory eyes, but his stance was not nearly as aggressive as it had been when I got kicked off of the bridge. I can only imagine Okabe had some words with him outside in the hall. I'm not sure what else it would've been.

"Speak," Ito said, once he was in front of the table.

"Take a look at these records," Tolby said, motioning to the data cube. Once both he and Okabe had directed their attention there, Tolby gave them both a rundown of everything we had discussed.

When he was finished, the commander shook his head, and in that moment, he sank my hopes completely. "I admire your dedication," he said, "but this ship has to stay its course, and if you have firsthand knowledge of this new enemy, then you must stay on board and tell Empress Tamaki all that you know."

"Commander," I said before anyone else could speak up. "There's a Progenitor ship back on that planet. With it, we could find untold amounts of technology—technology that could be used to drive back the Nodari."

"That cube has all their data, does it not?"

I shook my head. "No," I said. "It has a lot, but even with the cube, there's still a good chance you wouldn't be able to get what you need anyway."

"Why is that?"

"Because that ship can traverse the entire universe," I said. Okay, I was taking a stab at that, but hell, it had to be right. "Not only the universe, but it can travel through time, too. I doubt anything you've got will be able to get to a lone planet that's in another supercluster and a hundred million years in the future."

Ito looked over to Okabe, and while the commander looked more and more annoyed that he had to entertain any of this, Okabe's eyes continued to brighten at the possibilities. "I think we should give her a chance, Commander," he said. "That ship could be the key to unlocking everything."

"How do we know she's right?" he asked. "Even if she's not lying, you're asking me to risk the only ship that managed to escape—a ship carrying precious cargo at that."

"Please," I said, my voice bordering on begging. "My friends are down there, friends who have faithfully served the Empire. They don't deserve to die."

"Even if I let you go on this suicide run, I'm not so delusional as to think you're a match for this new foe."

"She's not," Tolby said. "But Jainon and I are. We're both veterans of many campaigns against the Nodari. We can sneak her onto the ship. All she has to do is pilot it."

Though we hadn't discussed the particulars, I was glad Tolby volunteered to do all the fighting. I was hardly the Force Recon space marine. Hell, if you really got down to it, I was more like the hapless VIP that had to be safely escorted. Hopefully, I wouldn't end up like the dummy in various games who wandered around and did stupid things to complicate the mission.

I was pretty sure I wouldn't.

Pretty sure.

"I can't agree with this. The risk is too much," he said. "When we can get into contact with Empress Tamaki, I shall tell her of your proposal. Perhaps she will be willing to launch a counterattack."

"It'll be too late by then, Commander," Jainon said with a tiny growl. "We need to go. Now."

"If it is in the gods' will that we reclaim the planet at a later time, then it will happen," he said.

Jainon shot up, her face full of fiery anger. "The gods do not embrace the cowardly, Commander," she said, slamming both paws onto the table. "As the high priestess, I assure you they will not look favorably upon those who duck opportunity to demonstrate their faith in the face of any adversity."

The room felt tenser than a twelve-way standoff with gun-toting poker players after a game went south. A few tense moments passed in silence, and the comm on the wall sprang to life. "Engineering is reporting repairs are complete, Commander," the Kibnali on the other end said. "We can make the jump home on your orders."

"Acknowledged," he said. "Any update on reinforcements?"

"Negative," the Kibnali replied. "As far as I know, the 39th Flotilla is still en route. ETA unknown."

"Good. I'll be on the bridge soon. Let me know if anything changes."

"Commander, don't leave," Jainon said. "We can do this."

"I don't doubt your heart," he said before drumming his claws on his side. He then turned back to the comm and pushed the button. "Question. Have we cleared Caul?"

"Negative," the Kibnali replied. "The planet is coming up, portside."

"I want you to chart a course that slingshots us around it," he said. "We're headed back."

"Repeat?"

"You heard me, pilot," the commander said. "I want us shooting back to Nagakuro so fast photons couldn't keep up. We're making an assault drop. Understood?"

"Understood."

Jack ran an arm across my shoulder and squeezed tight, while Jainon nuzzled Tolby.

"Thank you, Commander," I said, keeping my celebration down to a giant enormous smile. "May Inaja bless you with good fortune."

The commander straightened and cocked his head. He then touched the top of his head and bowed slightly. "May her luck be your luck, tailless."

CHAPTER TWELVE:
THE DROP

Stop squirming," Tolby said as he tightened one of the straps to my modular armor and gave it a look. "These won't fit right if you keep moving around."

"I didn't know these doubled as corsets," I said, feeling my lungs collapse.

"Data has shown that armor that is formfitting and snug against the body is up to twelve percent more effective than generic counterparts," he said.

"Yeah, but at what expense?" I asked. "I think being able to breathe is pretty important to being effective as well. Besides, I'm not sure I want to be turned into a beetle, which is what this armor makes me feel like."

Tolby ignored my comment and turned around to face the weapon locker inside the armory we were in. Inside were a number of large rifles that looked like they could punch through a tank if need be, as well as a number of smaller firearms, and even a few melee weapons such as swords and combat knives. Actually, the sizes for all of that is relative. Since they were made for Kibnali hands, every last one of them was absolutely gigantic in comparison to myself, and as such, I certainly didn't have any hope of wielding any but the smallest effectively. I probably couldn't even pick up one of the rifles, to be honest.

Tolby seemed to share that sentiment. He plucked a flat-gray pistol from the rack and handed it to me. "Here," he said. "It's still a little big for you, but if you treat it like a carbine, it should work."

"Is it loaded?" I asked, giving it a once-over. It looked similar to all the other pistols throughout the galaxy that I'd seen. Funny how firearms tended to all evolve in the same direction. Well, some firearms. There were certainly a number of variations, as some species had adopted a more pole-like design.

"No," he said as he handed me a few power packs. "Those can be inserted into the side right here. They'll give you about two hundred shots each before being drained. You can chuck them after that."

I attached each pack to my new utility belt. "I'd rather not have to chuck any at all to be honest."

"As would I," he said. "But make no mistake, Dakota. Where we are landing will be completely overrun by tomorrow morning. The chance of us not getting into a fight is zero."

"I know," I said.

"Good," he said. He then nodded toward a mirror behind me. "Want to give yourself a once-over? I think we're all set."

I turned around and looked at the total badass stranger looking back at me. She sported modular armor that contoured to her body in dark red and black plates. They covered everything from the tops of my feet, all the way up my torso and down each arm. What gaps there were in the hard plates at the joints were covered by a flexible but incredibly strong mesh of high-tech alloy. Tolby had made a point that these spots were indeed weak points, but they sure as hell felt strong to me.

"Oh, I like this," I said, turning a few times and giving myself a playful war face in the process. "I almost look like I know what I'm doing."

"Leave the knowing to me," he said.

"I'll try," I said with a half grin.

"I mean it, Dakota. Things are going to happen fast down there, and when I make orders, I need you to follow them without question as quick as you possibly can," he said. "I'll feed you orders and tactical overlays through your helmet."

My face matched the seriousness to his tone. "I will. I trust you. Always have."

Tolby nodded but didn't let the point drop. "You say that now, but your instincts for survival might say otherwise."

"This is your pep talk?" I said with a laugh. "A normal girl might think she's about to be killed."

"If I wanted to get you killed, I wouldn't be telling you this," he said with deadly seriousness. "I mean it. If you ever find yourself doubting anything I'm telling you, do it anyway. Even if you think you have knowledge I don't. Chances of you being right and me being wrong are far, far lower than vice versa."

I reached up and put my hand on his armored shoulder. "I am your fang and claw."

The corners of Tolby's mouth drew back revealing a bright grin and razor-sharp teeth. "Good, but don't you ever let any other Kibnali hear you say that. That is reserved for the Empress and the Empress alone."

"Sorry," I said with a chuckle. "I'm still trying to learn all your customs."

"I know," Tolby said as he went back into the weapons locker and took a handful of cylindrical devices about the size of a large soda bottle. He held one up for me to see and pointed to various parts as he gave his crash course in Kibnali weapons tech. "Blast grenades. Push the top down here. Twist here. Throw. Each one can blow anything organic apart for thirty meters."

"That might be a problem," I said, taking one and realizing it weighed a couple of kilos. "I don't think I'm throwing these ten meters let alone thirty."

"Then I suggest you take cover," he said.

"Are they shock resistant?"

"Very. Why?"

"Because I can always give one a friendly boost," I said, holding up my right arm.

Tolby grinned. "Already thinking to your assets."

"It's starting to be a habit, it seems," I said as I attached the three grenades to my belt. "Yeah, I'm still surprised you have anything that fits me. I would have to be such a runt when it comes to fighting in a Kibnali army."

"You'd be a runt's runt," he said, bopping me on the head. "But as I said before, formfitting armor has been shown to be incredibly effective, and our scientists took that data very seriously. The plates will interlock and bend to fit practically any size."

"Well that's handy," I said, impressed. I looked at the armor on my left arm more closely, and although I hadn't paid attention at first, sure enough, I could see that the plates were not solid pieces that just happened to be of the right size. No, the individual parts were much smaller, and together they formed the whole, much like the absolutely fantastic kid's ultraplex building blocks, Megoblocks.

Note to self: Once home, strike a deal with the Mego corporation to come out with a line of Kibnali Megoblock spaceship sets.

Addenda to note to self: Once home, use a portion of revenue after selling the resonance crystal to own a controlling share in the Mego corporation and corner the market.

Addenda to the addenda: Time release of Kibnali Megoblocks spaceships with release of book, *Whatever You Do, Don't Touch That* for maximum sales.

"If you're done daydreaming, we need to get to the drop pod," Tolby said. "We only have fifteen minutes to launch."

"I wasn't daydreaming!"

Tolby dipped his head.

"Okay, maybe I was a little. But I wasn't that distracted."

"If you say," Tolby said, clearly not believing me one iota. He handed me a helmet and waved me to follow. "Let's get moving before your brain has you chasing another thought."

At that point, we hurried out of the armory and ran through the corridors until we reached the staging area. It was a tight room bathed in red light and set in the portside, midship. One hatch led back the way we came, while a second, currently closed, led into the drop pod. Inside the staging area were Jack and Jainon, each dressed for battle in a similar fashion as Tolby and me.

"Do you have any thoughts on where we will make a landing?" Jainon asked.

"No," Tolby said. "I was going to make the call as we approached. There's probably too much chaos down there right now to blindly pick anything."

A panel next to us lit up with a blue light, and the commander's voice came through. "Tolby," he said. "We've got a transmission coming through that you'll want to hear."

"From the planet?"

"Yes, but more important, from one of your own."

"Put her on."

"Already done," the commander said.

Yseri's voice came through next, and while her transmission was slightly broken up and crackled with static, we could at least communicate relatively well. "Tolby, the commander says you're coming back?"

"Affirmative. What's the situation down there?"

"As bad as you can imagine," she said. "I'm with about a half dozen others along with Empress. We're at the edge of the city and can't stay here much longer. I don't think any place can be considered safe. Abort your landing."

"We will do no such thing," Tolby said. "We're coming to get you both. Dakota is going to pilot one of those Progenitor ships and get us all out of here."

"She is?" Yseri said.

The conversation suddenly halted as the line filled with chaos and the sounds of a firefight. I cringed as an explosion sounded, but then relaxed when I heard Yseri cursing up a storm. "We have to move. I'm transmitting coordinates of an old bunker five kilometers from the city that as far as we can tell is devoid of Nodari activity. Meet us there. It'll likely be our only realistic choice at a rendezvous."

The line went silent, and we all exchanged concerned looks.

"I guess we know where we're landing," I said with a grin.

"Correction," Tolby replied. "We know where to meet. We won't land anywhere near it. We can't chance the Nodari seeing us land there."

Jainon went to the panel and closed the inner hatch before opening the one leading to the drop pod. "We can continue lessons in assault drops on our way down," she said. "We need to strap in."

The drop pod had a hexagonal floor pattern and a teardrop shape to the interior. In the center were six chairs with combat harnesses all in the center and facing outward. Above each chair was a monitor, each one currently turned off. We filed in quickly and took our seats after stowing our weapons on racks above the chairs. Like the harnesses on the shuttle, the ones here were made for Kibnali and made me look like a little kid getting strapped in for the first time in the back of a car.

We'd barely gotten in place when the hatch sealed shut and the interior lights dimmed from a light blue to a deep red. The commander's voice came in loud and clear. "Switching on your outside feeds now," he said. "We'll be coming in hot, but hopefully those cruisers will be more interested in us than you."

The monitors above our heads flickered on. Dead center was the planet we'd just left. It took up a majority of the screen, and I was surprised at how close we were. A timer popped up on the top left and counted down the minutes until we dropped. We had a little over three to go, and we spent that time in silence. I wasn't sure what everybody else was thinking. Tolby and Jainon were probably rehearsing all the ways to kill a Nodari or maybe thinking about when they could run off for a romp again, but all I could do was wonder when the cruisers would start firing at us.

It didn't take long to get that answer.

A little over a minute until the drop, bright streaks flashed by. My stomach jumped upward as our ship took evasive maneuvers. I don't think they hit us, as I didn't hear any alarms or giant explosions. Still, I would've liked us to have come in undetected.

"Maximizing ECM," the commander said. "That should keep their shots wide."

"I hope so," I said.

"Me too," Jack replied. "Or this could be the shortest assault in history."

With about forty seconds to go, Tolby and the commander began to coordinate.

"Standby cross locking now," the commander said. "Prelaunch on a cycle engaged, and primary are couplers released."

As he spoke, I felt our launch pod shift and heard the whine of gears and nearby hydraulics.

While this was going on, my furry buddy reached up and hit some buttons on his armrest, and a control stick popped up. "Setting the internals," he said. "Confirm cross lock and drop station secured."

"Affirmative," Jainon chimed in, hitting a few buttons near her seat as well. "Drop stations secured."

"May Inaja bless you with good fortune," the commander said.

"May her luck be your luck," we all replied in unison.

Tolby shifted in his seat and briefly wiggled the control stick. "Standby to initiate sequencer on my mark."

My stomach tightened. This was it.

"Five...four...three...two...one...mark!"

I lifted in my seat to the sound of a massive rocket engine firing, driving us toward the planet with a rumble. I gripped my armrests, and my knuckles turned white. Tolby and Jainon let out fierce roars as if they were charging into battle. I guess in a way, they were.

"Yeeehaaa! Express elevator to hell," Jainon shouted. "Going down!"

I wasn't all that excited about the idea of being dropped into hell, but I'll admit, if this had been a park ride, it would've been intense. I bet it would've easily earned a solid three Super Vortex icons on how hard it lifted me in the seat alone.

Ten seconds passed, and then twenty. The acceleration from our initial separation from the ship lessened, and I managed to breathe a few times as I kept my eyes glued to the monitor. The planet grew tremendously fast, and I could easily pick out finer details of the terrain such as mountain ranges and large lakes and rivers.

Then we hit the atmosphere, and everything rumbled and shook so badly that I clutched the armrests once again, fearing our pod would tear itself apart.

"You'll be fine," Jack said, giving my hand a brief squeeze. "Nodari have nothing on the Queen of Space and Time."

I liked the sound of that and couldn't help but smile. Maybe one day I'd start a church in my honor. Ha-ha. Just kidding. The last thing I ever want to do is be responsible for writing a sermon every week. "Thanks," I said. "But if I die..."

"I can have your stuff?"

"No, stupid. I want a Viking funeral."

I sucked in a breath and prayed. *Please, oh please, great and venerable Kibnali gods, don't abandon us now.* I guess it's true. There are no atheists in foxholes—or drop pods for that matter.

"Switch to DCS ranging," Tolby said.

I glanced over to him as he kept his focus on the monitors. His displayed a slightly different picture than ours. While it still had an identical view of the planet, it also had a HUD overlay with plenty of real-time information being shown, presumably to help him guide our pod down.

"Two-four-zero, nominal to profile," Jainon said.

Tolby grinned. "We're in the pipe, five by five."

The air grew hot and stifling, even more so when a new counter popped up on my screen, the time until landing—the time until impact was more like it. As best I could tell, this drop pod was a one-way sort of thing, and it wasn't trying to come in gently whatsoever.

"Your harnesses will disconnect automatically upon our arrival," Tolby said as if giving a lecture to new recruits, which we more or less were. "I want you out of this pod and in position before your heart beats twice."

I was about to ask where exactly our position would be when all of a sudden a translucent display popped up on the visor to my helmet and gave the answer. What I was now presented with was a tactical battle map of our insertion point along with easy-to-read icons where not only I should be but where everyone else would be, too. "Well that's handy," I said, taking a moment to appreciate it all.

"Very," Tolby replied. "Now focus."

A retrograde rocket lit up beneath us and pressed us all into our seats as the ship slowed. I sucked in a breath and held it. All the while I tried to imagine what was about to take place. Did all marines have such jitters? Or was it just me because I was pretending to be one?

"Range zero-one-four, coming up on final," Tolby said. "Look sharp."

"I'll bet you twenty rens there's nothing," Jainon said.

"Done," Tolby replied.

The rocket increased its thrust for the last ten seconds, and I thought my spine was going to collapse due to the massive amounts of Gs we were taking in. My vision darkened and then tunneled. My body felt as if it wasn't mine, and the entire experience became surreal, sort of like if one downed a dozen shots of Venetian whiskey and turned six sheets to the wind in less than two seconds.

We slammed into the planet, and I bounced on my butt. Literally dazed upon impact, I flopped out of my seat as everyone else rushed out of the pod. By the time I regained my wits, I was alone in the pod with nothing but the sounds of battle to keep me company.

CHAPTER THIRTEEN: WELCOME BACK

I raced out of the pod, heart blasting in my chest.

The smell of ozone assaulted my nose, and the sounds of plasma fire crackled all around. Tolby, Jainon, and Jack were spread out, taking shots at a handful of Nodari swarmlings that charged down at us from the top of a small rise.

None of them made it within fifty yards. They all were hit multiple times. Heads exploded. Legs were sheared off. Bodies became mangled. When it was all over, my eyes scanned our grassy surroundings, finger on the trigger of my carbine, but saw nothing.

"Not so tough when they don't have a hundred million of their friends around, huh?" I said, smiling.

"If we stay here for more than a few minutes, that'll change," Tolby said grimly. "They undoubtedly saw the drop pod come in."

"Hopefully they won't find our trail," Jainon added.

I fidgeted with my carbine. "That doesn't sound good."

"It's not," Tolby replied. "Imagine a sea of those things following us wherever we go."

"Okay, so why are we standing here again?"

"We're not," Tolby said as he hiked off.

Half trotting, we made for the city. Over the course of the next couple kilometers, I didn't see much of anything when I looked behind us, other than the gorgeous planetary landscape of gentle hills and lush flora. Looking forward, however, I could see the towering buildings off in the distance, silhouetted against the first rays of sunlight. That probably would've been a great view, too, if many of those buildings weren't billowing thick clouds of smoke.

Several times during our travels, Tolby or Jainon would stop, and their rifles would go up and their ears would flatten. Then we'd wait a tense couple dozen seconds before continuing on without a word.

It wasn't long before we reached a narrow suspension bridge that crossed the mighty Shaze River. Though I couldn't see it from the small, rocky outcropping I'd ducked behind, I could hear the waters roaring. Had I not been in the covert military ops I'd managed to get myself into, I'd have been looking for a place to put in a kayak for some whitewater fun.

"Bet you twenty rens there's an ambush here," Jainon whispered through the comm.

"You already owe me twenty," Tolby whispered back.

"Then it's double or nothing for you," she replied without missing a beat.

"Fine. I'll take that bet."

Given the banter going on, I relaxed and laughed at my giant furball bud. "When did you start betting on anything?"

"Since always. Why are you even surprised?" Tolby asked.

"Because the only time I've seen you gamble was in a card game with me," I said. "You lost interest in ten minutes and never wanted to play since."

"Only because you're a bad player."

"I'm not a bad player."

"You blush every time you get anything over a straight," he said. "That makes things boring."

"She does, does she?" Jack said with amusement. "Oh, Dakota, we have *got* to play some strip poker when this is done."

"Really? Can't do any better than that?"

Jack shrugged unapologetically. "Should I have suggested dinner first?"

"That would've at least helped."

"Enough for you to play?"

"Enough for me to weasel a free meal out of you."

"I smell something," Jainon said, perking and twisting in place. She scanned the area behind us before grunting. "Swarmlings are on our trail. Far, but not for much longer."

Tolby sniffed the air, too, before nodding. "Then we cross right now."

My body stiffened. I was hardly a military genius, but if Jainon's first words were accurate, the idea of running into an ambush seemed bad. It seemed even worse if somehow they had some gun-toting Nodari with them as well. "Should we maybe look for another crossing?"

"There isn't another for twenty kilometers," Tolby said as he punched a few buttons, and a timer suddenly appeared in my visor. "We go in ten seconds. Stay sharp."

I checked and rechecked my carbine as Tolby's countdown ticked away on the screen of my visor. I took a deep breath and tried to steady my nerves. How did I ever get myself mixed up in all of this? I only ever wanted to find artifacts, not firefights. Okay, that's obviously not including spas and the perfect glass of wine.

Waypoints and assigned fields of fire popped onto my screen. Tolby and Jack would be up front as Jainon and I brought up the rear.

Tolby darted forward, and the rest of us followed right on his heels. Advancing on the bridge like a pro was a simple task, thanks to my handy tactical battle computer installed in my Kibnali armor. That said, my nerves still went into overdrive, and my hands shook.

Tolby and Jack passed between the bridge towers on the near side without incident, as did Jainon and I. My hands tightened on my carbine, but still no attack came. Did I dare believe we'd get across without a shot fired? No. I didn't.

It wouldn't be that easy.

My eyes looked up, scrutinizing every detail of the suspension cables, but I saw nothing out of place.

"A hundred meters to go," I whispered to myself as we crossed the halfway point.

"Contact!"

The shout was drowned out by alarms blaring in my helmet. Our squad's vital signs flashed in the lower corner of my visor, heartbeats elevated, and breathing grew rapid. Diamond icons—each one representing a new target, a new threat—filled the rest of my faceplate. I tried to count them all but quickly gave up as scores of Nodari swarmlings came charging out of the brush on the other side toward us.

Tolby and Jack each dropped to a knee, and their rifles met the seething mass of teeth and talon head on. Plasma fire flew with deadly precision. Tolby chucked a grenade, landing it in the middle of the swarm, and blasted them apart like tissue paper, but still the sea of fang and claw came.

I darted to the side to get a better angle and contribute to the fight, but Tolby's words blasted in my ears. "Watch the rear, Dakota!"

I spun around right as a slew of more icons filled my visor. Nodari swarmlings bounded at us from whence we came, closing the distance with godlike speed. I fired madly, most of my shots not doing a damn thing other than draining my powerpack.

Thankfully, Jainon was worth ten of me when it came to firefights. With exceptional precision, she drilled shot after shot into the oncoming horde. As she kept them at bay, movement caught my eye, and I looked up to see more of the creatures racing down the suspension cables.

I shouted a warning, and then another half dozen swarmlings came up and over the sides of the bridge. Jack pivoted and ripped into them with his carbine.

Time slowed, and the world became a surreal haze of frantic exchanges and the distant sound of Tolby's orders.

I tracked a Nodari running down the cable to my left. I fired twice, striking it in the front legs and sending it toppling over the side to the river below. Another followed the same line of attack, and I managed to kill it just the same. And then another, and another. Number three fell to a headshot from Jainon, while number four dropped from a single plasma round from Tolby.

Two more dashed at me low along the railing. I fired as fast as I could, and the only thing running faster than they were seemed to be my ammo counter racing to zero. One moment it was in the fifties, and the next, it barely registered the twenties, but at least I'd managed to kill my latest two assailants.

Another blur of movement was captured in the corner of my eye. I barely spun in time to see a swarmling flying through the air, its powerful jaws open and ready to snap through my neck in a single bite. I fell backward and tried to get my carbine up in time, but I was too slow. The creature slammed into me and knocked my weapon out of my hands. Trying to keep its jaws away from my face, I raised my left arm, which it promptly chomped on. My armor held, but when it shifted its bite, it found my hand and sank fang into flesh.

Reflexively, I used my psychokinesis to shatter its skull. Its body went limp. I tried pushing it off, but waves of agony radiated down my left arm, freezing me in place. Teary-eyed, I sucked in a breath and managed to rid myself of the monster before coming to my feet.

The fight on the bridge raged on. I scooped my weapon off the ground, but with my left hand mangled and wracked with pain, all I could do was keep it tucked against my midsection and fight one-handed.

Surprisingly, I managed to shoot without blowing my own foot off—or anyone's head for that matter. And when I drained my powerpack, I even managed to eject it and slam home a new one by pinning the weapon to my side with my left arm and using my right hand to finish the job. The moment I got it seated, a swarmling ran straight at me from down the cables. I whipped my gun around and fired three times in rapid succession.

Two of the three missed, but the one that landed vaporized half its skull. The kill hardened my resolve. I could do this. I would do this.

Grenades exploded behind me, and I could feel the heavy thump of air against my back. A glance over my shoulder showed that Tolby and Jack still held the front, but as fast as they were firing, too, I couldn't help but wonder when all of their power packs would be spent.

I shook my head, realizing I couldn't worry about such things. I had to keep firing, had to hold the rear and pray that the Nodari numbers would run out before our weapons went silent.

Jainon roared next to me. Whether it was out of fear or enjoyment from the killing frenzy, I couldn't tell. Then again, maybe it was born from both.

More swarmlings came. More died. Powerpacks from all of us dropped to the ground, empty.

I took aim at another who raced down the cables and squeezed the trigger. I drilled it dead center, causing it to fall. When it hit the ground, I realized there was a lull in the action. A few bursts from Tolby put down the last swarmling that ran at us, and a few similar shots rang out from Jainon, but after that, all was quiet.

I dared a glance to the sky, feeling like any moment chaos would return and perhaps this time, it wouldn't be four-legged monsters but flying nightmares come to snatch us away. Thankfully, all I could see were clouds hanging lazily above.

"Clear?" Tolby asked, not moving from his position.

"Clear," Jainon replied.

Jack repeated the answer, and finally I did the same, once I realized I needed to sound off.

"That's double you owe me," Jainon said, lowering her rifle. As Tolby eyed her, she came over to him and nudged him with her hip. "You can work it off, though."

A Nodari swarmling dropped next to me. Its skin swelled, and an instant later, it exploded.

CHAPTER FOURTEEN: A NICE LITTLE DIP

I flew backward, the force of the blast sending me over the bridge railing. A scream escaped my lips an instant before I hit the cold, dark rivers below. I shot to the surface as fast as I could, sputtering once I reached the air. My armor filled with water and pulled me back under.

The current was far stronger than I could hope to match, but I fought regardless. I'd survived Mister Cyber Squid, Goliath, swaths of Nodari and Nekrael, so a stupid river wasn't going to do me in. My feet hit the river bottom, and when they did, I kicked, and kicked hard. Again, I surfaced. Again, my lungs gasped for air. My heart thundered in my chest, and my eyes focused on my objective. The shore was maybe thirty meters away.

The survivor inside me took over and demanded long, powerful strokes that moved me forward. But it wasn't enough. It took only a few moments to realize my armor would be the end of me.

I sucked in the largest breath of air I could and allowed myself to sink under once again. As I did, my hands fumbled for the quick release straps. My greaves came of first, and my legs rejoiced at their newfound freedom before driving me to the surface.

Another gulp of air. Another dip under the river. I knew my chest piece would have to go next. My hands reached up to my shoulders, and I yanked the locking straps hard.

To my dismay and panic, the straps held fast, and the armor did not break away. My body slammed into a rock, and a rib cracked when I bounced off a second one.

Thankfully, I had the presence of mind not to exhale.

A third rock hit me in the head. My helmet absorbed most of the impact, but it jarred me nonetheless. I felt myself tumbling along the riverbed, but I managed to right myself and push off one last time. Once I broke the surface, I tore at my straps again.

Thanks be to the Kibnali gods at that point, for my entire chest piece broke away. With the last bit of energy I could muster, I swam for the shore. When I reached it, I dragged myself out and collapsed in a heap.

My arm still felt cold from telekinetically punching that toothy monster, so since I was only a foot from the water, I rolled and flopped my left arm in to recharge my Progenitor batteries.

I welcomed the flow of energy up my left arm and sank into the warm feeling. Exhaustion took over, and I let my eyes rest for a moment.

Someone clamped down on my shoulders.

"Dakota!"

The name, though strange in my mind, triggered a small thread of recognition.

"Dakota, damn it, wake up."

A dream involving me playing xenoarchaeologist as a kid and discovering lost Progenitor tech faded away, and I realized I was lying on my back, looking at a blurry sky with an equally blurry silhouette above me.

"At least she's not dead," said a voice, distant and vaguely familiar.

"Come on, Dakota, wake up. You still owe me a root beer."

I rubbed my eyes, and once I regained some of my focus, I saw Tolby standing over me with my carbine in hand with Jainon at his side. "What happened?" I asked.

"Nodari xenocide," he replied.

I sat up and stared at him blankly. "A what?"

"A living bomb," Tolby said. "Xenocide. Kamikaze. Whatever you want to call it. The Nodari have mutated into such things every now and again."

Jainon helped me to my feet. "Are you hurt?"

I looked myself over. Thankfully, I appeared mostly intact, headache and some nausea aside—presumably from hitting my head a few times during my impromptu whitewater excursion. "Other than getting mauled on the bridge, I'm okay," I said, raising my left hand so they could see my injuries.

Tolby didn't share my enthusiasm. Neither did Jainon. The handmaiden took my upper arm in a vise grip with one paw and, with the other, manipulated my hand so she could get a better view.

"Ow! That flipping hurts!" I said, instinctively trying to pull away, try being the keyword.

"This doesn't look good," she said to Tolby. "Give her a test."

"A test for what?"

"Swarmling venom," she said. "Stomach churning yet? Double vision?"

"Not...a lot," I said, voice wavering. I didn't like them treating this as if the grim reaper had saddled up to my side. "But I did hit my head a few times coming down that river. It's probably from that."

"Pray that's all it is," he said as he whipped a small tablet off his belt. It had a rectangular blue display on the bottom and a number of round buttons across the top. From the side came a thin silver needle that he pulled free and jabbed into my shoulder. "Don't move."

Tolby worked the controls, but instead of relief washing over him, all I saw was frustration. Others might have called it him being grave, but I refused to go with that. Grave was us having sixty seconds to get off a planet before taking a lava bath. Grave was being trapped on a museum moments before the reactor went critical while a ravenous cyber squid barreled toward us. This was not grave. I refused to let it be any such thing.

"I hate this thing," Tolby said with a grunt of frustration. "Its optimization is terrible and has no presets for Nodari work."

"It's also four hundred years old compared to what you've used," Jainon said. "Cut it some slack."

"I should've paid more attention in my historics classes."

"Can we get back to my hand?" I asked.

"I'm on it, don't fret." Tolby pressed a few more buttons and sighed. "Okay, maybe you should fret."

"What?"

"You're infected, and its already spread to your torso," Tolby said.

Jainon muttered as she released her grip on my arm. "I'm assuming then we can't even take the arm?"

"Whoa! I like my arm, thank you," I said, backing away.

"You'll like not being eaten from the inside even more when those Nodari eggs in your bloodstream hatch."

"Say again?"

"That venom contains microscopic eggs that will hatch soon, and when they do, the microbes that come out will feed on your organs."

My legs buckled, and Jainon bolted to my side to keep me upright. "We've got some time to see you treated," she said. "You'll pull through."

The strength in her words gave me some encouragement, but the headache that continually built inside my skull did its best to snatch that hope away. "Where can I get treated?" I asked. "Surely you've dealt with this before."

"In our time, yes," Tolby said. "But Kibnali medicine hasn't adapted yet, and honestly, I don't know if the treatments would be safe on you."

"They're better than no treatment at all," I countered. "How long do I have?"

Tolby shook his head as his ears turned downward. "A few hours, maybe," he said. "Hard to predict since your biology is not ours."

"A few hours?" I said, eyes wide, pulse racing. "We've got a few hours to what, sneak back in the city, find the others, get to the ship, hop through spacetime, get me to a future Kibnali medical facility *and* convince the staff there to treat an infected alien?"

"One step at a time, Dakota," Tolby said. "Do anything else, and you'll go mad."

"I'm almost there already," I said with a laugh. "A treatment of baby steps isn't going to help."

Jainon squeezed my shoulder. "No, I suspect not. But the Progenitors might have something we can use. With such a large facility at our disposal, how could they not?"

I turned her suggestion a few times over in my head. "True. Maybe I can get plopped in a stasis tube."

"Precisely," Tolby said. "Now let's move. We've no time to waste."

CHAPTER FIFTEEN: RENDEZVOUS

If there was a tenth circle of Hell, that's precisely where the fires came from that burned in my joints. I shut my eyes and ended up curling in a fetal position on the ground as this newest wave of pain washed over me. It only lasted a few seconds, but that wasn't much solace, especially since it was the sixth attack I'd suffered, and they continued to grow in frequency.

"It's the Nodari venom working in your system," Jainon said.

"I know," I said once I was able. "We really need to get to that facility."

"We will," she said. "Come on. Let's work our way up to the others."

I steadied myself, which wasn't terribly hard now that the pain had subsided completely, and resumed my belly crawl up a gentle hill to where the others were already prone at the top. The landscape offered plenty of thick scrub and colorful, knee-high grass to remain concealed in, and the howling wind that had picked up maybe twenty minutes ago was a godsend in masking any noise we might have made.

Of course, that wind did the same for the Nodari. For all I knew, they were creeping up on us as much as we were creeping up on the hill. I could only hope that the heightened sense of smell that Tolby and Jainon possessed were more than enough to detect any approaching Nodari.

At the top of the hill, I could see the city a short way off in the distance. Smoke rose from numerous buildings, and occasionally I would see bright flashes of light or mushroom clouds as something big exploded. I wondered what it was going to be like there, what sort of husks for buildings we would find, how many Kibnali we would see slaughtered in the streets.

I shut my eyes and shook my head. I couldn't think about that, so instead I turned my attention to the outpost below. The rendezvous point was a solid, squat round building with a single antenna coming out the roof. On one side there were slanted windows on the second story, while the other had a few machines and a parked vehicle on the ground floor. Nearby was a small landing pad that was currently unoccupied save for a single creature that no doubt was Nodari in origin.

Coppery bronze skin formed overlapping plates of armor across its body. It moved on a serpentine tail, but instead of scraping across the ground on its belly, it remained mostly upright as if it were a king cobra standing tall and proud. Its bulbous head lacked any obvious eyes and was held about two meters off the ground. The creature sported wide, powerful jaws that spread out on either side of its head, looking like a giant trap ready to be sprung on whatever victim it came across.

For a few minutes, we all watched it in silence, waiting for it to move on. Instead, it kept circling the launchpad, at times going over to the outpost and searching the area for something.

"What is that?" I whispered.

"Nodari tunneler," Tolby replied softly. "They burrow through the ground to reach bunkers and foxholes, striking in coordination with a ground assault. Expendable creatures, more or less, but vicious ones at that. Those jaws can shear through most armor."

"What's it doing here?" asked Jack.

"I don't know, but since it's not moving on, we've got to take it out." Tolby slid his rifle up and brought it to bear on the creature.

"Why do I get the feeling that's harder than it sounds?" I asked.

"Because if I don't kill instantly, the Nodari will know we're here, or at least, that someone's here," he said. "Each one is linked back to the hive overseer, and it'll scream like a banshee as it dies."

"And that's not to mention the little fact the only part of its brain that offers an instant kill shot is the size of a mutefruit," Jainon said, using her paws to approximate the size of a lemon.

"You sure you don't want to wait for it to move?" I asked.

Tolby shook his head. "Your time is limited enough as it is."

"Good point," I said.

"Jainon, standby for backup."

The handmaiden brought her rifle to bear on the tunneler. Her ears pressed back, and her tail flattened behind her. "On it."

"Good, taking the first good shot I get," he said.

For what felt like an eternity, all I could do was watch Tolby settle into his sniper position and track the Nodari's movement. Every time the monster looked like it was going to hold still for more than a half second, it suddenly jerked to the side and made another erratic trip around the outpost. Twice it even dug into the ground only to pop up near the outpost walls. I guess it was trying to get in but was having difficulty.

Was it simply exploring? Or were Yseri and Empress inside and it was trying to find them? I didn't know, obviously, but I felt if it were the latter that creature would have called for reinforcements by now.

A bolt of plasma flew out of Tolby's weapon with a loud hiss. The bright orange shot struck the tunneler center skull. The thing flopped over, but it didn't die quietly. It thrashed around, tail flipping and mouth screeching, for a half second before Jainon put a second shot through its head, and that shot was followed up by four more from both of them.

"Move! Now!" Tolby barked, bounding to his feet and sprinting down the hill. "They'll be here soon!"

Jainon followed, right on his feels, and Jack and I did our best to keep up. "I can't believe you missed!"

"Neither can I," Tolby said, sounding disappointed.

"Jack, stay with me outside," the handmaiden said. "We'll provide cover for Tolby and Dakota as they sweep the bunker for Empress and Yseri."

We reached the landing pad in seconds. Tolby hit the controls for the bunker door, and it slid open with a popping sound. The first floor held a lot of supplies and, not surprisingly, guns and power packs. Tolby and I grabbed as many as we could to replace the ones we'd spent on the bridge and to give to Jack and Jainon. The upper floor had a dozen gun ports that allowed for defense of the area, as well as a central room with a handful of computers that were currently displaying the status of battle inside the city. I couldn't make sense of most of it, but the blobby red parts, which were Nodari, seemed to be slowly overtaking the blobby blue parts, which were the defending Kibnali forces.

"Where are they?" I asked, noting how we were the only ones here.

"Good question," Tolby asked. He keyed up his comms and tried to raise them. "Empress? Yseri? Do you copy? We're at the rendezvous."

Static.

Lots of static.

The Empress's voice crackled through a few seconds later. "Unable...reach..."

Tolby's brow dropped. "Can you get to the Progenitor hangar? We could meet you at the ship."

"...un—"

"Empress? Empress!" Tolby shook his head and swore. "This is not good."

A new, unexpected voice chimed in. "Dakota? Can you hear me?"

I blinked, unable to do anything else. "Daphne?"

"Hi there!" she said. "I hope you're nowhere near all this fighting. It's ugly. Very non-conducive to long life-spans, which I believe you are a fan of."

"Yeah, I am, which is why I need your help," I said before giving her a rundown of recent events, putting emphasis on the Nodari venom ravaging my system.

"That does sound painful," she said. "But as luck would have it. I can help."

"Oh, thank god," I replied.

"Going by the data I had downloaded before, there's a medical facility inside the art exhibit. Predictably, the Progenitors had well-equipped themselves for dealing with the Nodari on all levels. The medbay there should be able to neutralize the toxins."

"There is? Holy snort, that's outstanding."

"I thought you'd like that."

"Like that? I love it!"

"I suggest you get moving," she said. "I'm not sure how long that area will be devoid of Nodari infestation."

I nodded, not that I needed any encouragement to make a beeline for the facility. "We're on our way. Where are you? Can you meet us there?"

"I'm hiding near Okabe's lab. I should be able to make a rendezvous at the facility."

"Wonderful. Tell Empress and Yseri to get there, too, if possible. We lost contact with them."

"Will do."

At that point, we left the outpost in a hurry, but instead of making a direct run for the city as I had expected, Tolby took us in a parallel direction a few hundred meters and through a small orchard before resuming our approach.

"If they send any Nodari to investigate, hopefully, this will help dodge them," Tolby explained.

I nodded. We were about to clear the orchard, and I had to slow considerably. I didn't have a full-on joint attack as I had before, but my energy levels were dropping like I'd been up studying three days straight, and the last bits of caffeine from my eighth cup of coffee had finally worn off. I ended up leaning against a tree with one hand, panting, unable to catch my breath.

"Come on," Jack said. "Less than a klick to go."

"I know," I said, still trying to find enough air to keep my body feeling like it wasn't starving for oxygen.

He went to grab my weapon, and I jerked it away. "You can barely keep yourself up," he said. "Let me carry it."

"No," I said, straightening and wiping the sweat off my brow. "I can do this. That's not going to make a difference, but me not being able to shoot might."

Tolby, who was at the very edge of the orchard, glanced at me over his shoulder with a concerned look in his eye. "Are you sure you're ready?" he asked. "We've got a park to go through with a lot of open space."

"I'm ready," I said, hoping my sheer determination would be enough to see me through.

Tolby nodded, and we all burst from the tree line at his command. We didn't move at a full sprint as we had been before on account of me, but we still moved at a fair clip. The park he was in reference to was one I would have loved to enjoy had I the opportunity. It had gentle, rolling hills with incredible landscaping that combined large rocks, towering crystals, and exceptionally pruned trees and bushes that formed a work of art like no other. Even with the gray skies above and the thoughts of battle looming in the back of my mind, I couldn't help but feel lost in the beauty of the place. The serene, sprawling pond with quaint, wooden bridges and a gazebo in the center only topped off the idea that becoming lost in this park would have been easy and welcome.

We were about thirty meters away from the pond when Tolby ducked behind a boulder, and Jainon tackled me to the ground. A spray of tiny darts flew by and struck a rock to my left. When they hit, they splattered the area with a thick yellow goo that began dissolving everything it came into contact with.

"It's eating through rock?" I shouted in disbelief.

"Better than your face," Jainon said. "Now get to cover and stay low."

I did as I was told and dragged myself across the ground. I wasn't sure where to go, so I followed the natural decline I was on and ended up closer to the pond and behind a small granite outcropping. I guess that was good enough, because when Tolby threw me a glance, he didn't say anything and simply went back to firing.

"Six scouts, moving on our right flank," Tolby barked.

"I'm counting at least seven more keeping us pinned," Jack said. He fired a few times with his carbine before dashing across the ground and making a slide behind a rock and ending up a few paces away from me. Acidic darts zipped by his head and chiseled deep gouges in everything they struck.

Since the Nodari were directing most of their fire at Jack and Tolby, I took advantage of the moment and peeked out from the side of my cover. I spied a Nodari scout charging down our left flank, alone and out in the open. I put several shots toward it, but they all missed. I thought he was about to make it to a good place near the gazebo to dig in, but I fired a few more times and nailed him in the hip and chest. The scout's body crumbled to the side, and I'm not ashamed to say it, but I shouted in triumph.

"I got one!"

"Get us twelve more and we're golden," Jack shouted back with a half grin. He took a few potshots at the Nodari afterward and was forced back behind his rock. Once the suppressive fire on him ended, he tried to pop up again but had to dive once more as Nodari shots zeroed in on his position. Most went wide, but one struck him high on the arm. The armor he wore sizzled away in wisps of gray smoke. "What the everlasting hell," he said, furiously popping two of his buckles to get the piece to fall away before the corrosive substance ate through his body. "That goo nearly got my arm!"

The firefight continued, and although we kept the Nodari at bay, we weren't making progress getting anywhere either.

"Tolby," Jainon shouted after she dropped a Nodari scout with a perfectly placed plasma bolt to its forehead. "They're going to get reinforcements soon. We can't stay here much longer."

"I know," he shouted back. "What I wouldn't give for some artillery."

"Maybe we can call for help," Jainon said. She opened up a comm to the Kibnali defenses and spoke. "Rogue Team requesting fire support at the southern gardens. Can anyone hear this?"

Predictably, no one answered. Jainon tried again two more times before Tolby grunted. "We'll have to do it the hard way then. Leapfrog backward with covering fire."

Now I'm no Sun Tzu, but I was proud of myself that I knew what he was talking about and didn't have to ask. The general plan was one group would put so many plasma shots downrange that the Nodari didn't dare even a peek at us while the other group ran for cover. Rinse and repeat till presumably we were all out of there. And while on the surface that looked like all that we had, I was even more proud of myself when I also realized there was a much better option.

"Hey, Tolby, did you forget about something?" I said, raising my right arm. I jerked it back when Nodari fire nearly took it off, and I grinned sheepishly. "Well, assuming I don't do that again, we have all the artillery we need."

"Think you can hit them?" Tolby said, pulling one of his grenades off his belt.

"Absolutely," I replied. "Send it up in a nice arc. I'll do the rest."

"On three. Ready?"

I nodded. Tolby gave the count, and as he did, he primed the grenade. With a powerful throw, he sent it sailing high into the air. At the apex of its climb, I telekinetically punched it and sent it rocketing toward the Nodari line. I put a little too much oomph in the hit, so it almost went flying by them. Thankfully, I realized I was going to miss in time, so I hit it again from above and sent it into the ground. The grenade hit the ground and bounced up about a half meter before exploding.

If I hadn't known firsthand it was a grenade that had been tossed, I would've sworn a battlecruiser was providing orbital fire support the explosion was so big. Chitinous armor flew in all directions along with fragments of Nodari limbs and entrails. As the pieces rained down, I did have a brief twinge in my gut as I realized the sheer power of the explosives that were strapped to my waist.

"Ha!" Tolby roared. "Do it again!"

"Whenever you're ready," I said, prepping myself for another game of horseshoes with hand grenades.

The next grenade he threw flew out to our right flank where the other Nodari were still trying to get around us. I knocked it a little ahead of the six, but it was still close enough to blast them apart.

"Was that all of them?" Jainon asked after a few tense moments of silence.

"Clear here," Jack replied, eyes fixated on our right flank.

Tolby and I said the same. We had a brief celebratory cheer before a sea of swarmlings came charging out of the orchard and right at us.

"Go!" Tolby shouted.

His words were unneeded. Everyone had already scrambled to their feet and were now sprinting across the park. I was far too weak to do anything but limp along. The others occasionally turned and waited for me, and as they did, they pumped shot after shot into the seething mass of teeth and claws. For every one they dropped, three more burst from the tree line.

Tolby pulled his last grenade off his belt and gave it a throw. "Dakota! Hit them in the middle!"

I staggered as I came to a halt and nearly fell over when I turned around. I was so hurting for air I'd barely managed to smack the grenade in time with my psychokinesis. The device got a little bit of a boost, but it wasn't much. It fell short of the line of swarmlings when it detonated, killing a few at best and stunning maybe twice that in the blast.

"Focus, Dakota!" Jainon yelled. "We can't afford anything else!"

I nodded, knowing she was right. My joints flared with pain, and I stumbled to the side and dropped. Tolby and Jack called my name, and the fire from our little group intensified. There were some other shouts as well, but it was all I could do to keep from passing out.

Large paws grabbed me and hoisted me up. Air blew out of my lungs as Jainon slung me over her shoulders. "If we survive this, Dakota, the first thing we're doing is enhancing this body of yours."

I would've argued if I had the energy and wherewithal, but because I was still fighting off the pain from the Nodari venom, I didn't put up any sort of fight. When this latest attack subsided, I was still across her shoulders, bouncing along as she ran full tilt across an open field toward the first line of buildings at the city.

A rough, crackling voice suddenly filled the comms. "Rogue Team, south gardens, what is your situation?"

"About to be overrun," Tolby replied with a calm voice. "Need a danger close strike, fifty meters south of our position. Sending coordinates now."

"Confirm. Danger close at fifty meters?"

"Confirmed!" he barked. "Send it, now!"

It was probably only a dozen seconds at most, but it felt like a lifetime. At first, all I heard was a faint whistling, and then the ground exploded behind us time a dozen times. Each eruption sent massive jets of earth and debris flying into the air, plus whatever was left of shattered Nodari bodies.

Did that stop the Nodari horde? No. Of course not.

Though the swarmlings had taken a beating and lost untold numbers, still they came. Worse, they were rapidly closing on Jack, who trailed our group by thirty meters. Jack ran like the wind. I can't fault him there, but the Kibnali were far faster, and sadly, so were the swarmlings.

"Jack!" I yelled before feebly tugging on Jainon's shoulder. "We've got to help!"

"We die if we do," Jainon said.

"We can't leave him!"

"We can, and we must."

CHAPTER SIXTEEN: BOTTOMS UP

No, you—"

A loud...brrrrrrrrrrrrrrrrrrrrrrrt, for lack of a better description, cut me off. A massive stream of plasma bolts flew overhead and mowed down the remaining swarmlings with a godlike vengeance.

Jainon slowed enough for me to be able to look up over her shoulder without falling off. Ahead, Tolby had come to a halt near the entrance to a two-story building. Standing next to him was a trio of Kibnali soldiers crouched near this massive robot that towered over them. It sported dark-red armor plating across its wide body. Its left arm held a three-fingered claw while a cannon with a smoking barrel hung off its right shoulder.

"Heavy fighting in the streets," one of the soldiers said. "I don't suggest you stay topside if you've got wounded."

"They're not in the tunnels?" Tolby asked.

"Not as much as they are out here," he replied. "They're pressing hard for our anti-air and orbital-defense cannons."

"Then we use the tunnels to get to the facility," I said. "Right?"

"Going that way may take longer," Tolby said. "And if we get caught in an ambush, we might run out of options fast when it comes to escaping."

Jainon slid me off her shoulders. "Can you stand?"

"Yeah," I said, promptly wobbling and falling over. "Or not."

"This venom is working against her faster than I'd thought," she said, ears flattening.

Tolby growled. "We need to move. Every second we waste puts her closer to death."

"Agreed," Jainon said.

"I'd offer an escort if we could, but we've been sent to reinforce another squad," the soldier said. "We've got to ensure those cannons hold until the 39th Flotilla gets here and beats them back."

"Then do your duty," Jainon replied. "The gods will watch after us."

The soldier handed Jainon a small purple card. "This will get you in the tunnels," he said. "May Inaja bless you with good fortune."

"Thanks, and may her luck be your luck," I said.

As our saviors left, Tolby led us inside the building with Jack helping me to my feet and supporting me along the way. "Your pick, Dakota," Tolby said. "Do you want to stay topside or head through the tunnels?"

My stomach soured. I almost puked, but I ended up dry heaving, which exacerbated my massive headache tenfold. "I don't care," I said, half crying. "All I want at this point is a stiff drink."

To my surprise, Jainon perked and grinned. "Let's get her drunk," she said. "If the alcohol levels in her blood are high enough, it'll inhibit the Nodari microbes."

"How much?" Jack asked.

"How much do we need to get her drunk, or how much will it slow them down?" she replied.

"Both."

"As much as we possibly can without killing her, and if we're lucky, she'll have another hour to live. Maybe two."

"Welp," I said with a hard swallow. "Given I'd rather be dead than suffer this much longer, I say we get me plastered, smashed, sloshed, fluttered, and totally tit-faced in the next sixty seconds. So, where's the pub?"

"Right across the street," she replied.

Tolby and Jainon stayed in front, and Jack, with my arm slung across his shoulders, helped me limp over. Purple benches and black stone tables filled the pub, along with a sea of glass shards covering the marble floor. Holodisplays of Kibnali and various scenery hung on the walls, and included in the decoration were a dozen scorch marks and chunks of Nodari.

"Clear here," Tolby said, briefly ducking his head into a side room.

"Back is empty, too," Jainon said after she peered into the kitchen. As Jack brought me to a corner couch, one of two that wasn't covered in Nodari blood or outright destroyed, Jainon slung her rifle and grabbed a bottle from behind the bar and popped its top.

"Holy snort that stuff reeks," I said as she brought it over. "I'm supposed to drink that?"

"If you want to live, yes," she said.

I cringed as I took the bottle, and nearly threw up when I brought it close for a second whiff. "A dead rhino that's been baking for a week probably smells better than this."

"It's not that bad," Jack said. "Down it and let's go."

"Says the man holding his nose."

Jainon snatched the bottle, took a deep whiff, and thrust it back into my hands. "It's fine. Drink."

I grumbled for a few seconds, and then before I could think myself out of it, I shut my eyes, held my breath, and chugged as much as I dared. I downed about half the bottle before jerking forward in a coughing fit. My stomach cramped, and I nearly upchucked. But after a few seconds of fighting with my internal organs, everything calmed. Warm butterflies took root, and a light, happy feeling spread through my soul.

"Is it working?" Jack asked. "It can't be though, right? I mean, no drink hits someone that fast."

"Ours are modified to be rapidly absorbed," she said. "In fact, the…"

Her voice trailed. Well, my attention trailed. She was still talking. I think. If I really thought about it, which was a pain in the butt and not nearly as much fun as pulling on my lower lip, I could make out her voice, but that was about it.

I smiled. Not at the drink, which was nice, but at the realization I now possessed a secret weapon when it came to drowning out the noise she and Tolby would make during their wild escapades. And speaking of Tolby, I really needed to do something special for the big furball, on account of how awesome he was and how much he looked after me. Even if he didn't believe in the power of the lucky elephant, he deserved a hug.

"Hey, Tolby," I said, mushing my words. I tried to stand and walk over to him but ended up losing my balance and nearly making out with the floor.

"And she's drunk," Jack said.

Was I? I did a self-diagnostic. Numb? Check. Double vision? Check. Inability to...damn it. What was I trying to remember? Ah well, screw it. Probably a check. So that made at least eight out of nine checks for...for...

"Dakota!" Jack yelled, getting in my face.

I jumped in fright. I probably would've been a lot madder if I didn't get lost in his eyes a second later. "That, mister cool man, was not cool whatsoever," I said. I flopped toward him, throwing my arms around his neck. "But you know what? I forgive you. Cuz' we're buds."

"Guess that answers what kind of drunk she is."

"I'm not—" The room spun when I tried to talk and jerk back at the same time. Or maybe it was spinning already. Who knows? Who cares? "Okay. I'm drunk."

Tolby came to my side and steadied me. "How's the pain?"

"What pain?"

"Perfect," Jainon said. "We need to go."

My brow furrowed. "Go? Where? We just got here, and I want to do some karaoke."

"Nodari invasion ring a bell?"

"Is that still going...hic...going...hic...hic...on?"

Tolby snatched me up, sending me on what had to be a ten-super-vortex rollercoaster ride that ended with me over his back. "Hang on. We're moving."

"Ooo, I don't think that was a good idea," I said, feeling super queasy.

Tolby didn't reply. Jack grabbed my weapon after I dropped it, and the group left the pub. The Kibnali streets went by in a blur of jarring movement that was punctuated by the occasional streak of plasma fire along with an accent or two of massive explosion.

We dropped down into a dry canal at some point and followed it a short distance before ducking into an alcove. Tolby and Jack were looking back the way we came, and as such, I had a good view of what Jainon was doing. She stood at a large, sealed door and tried to work the console nearby.

"This one's no good either," she said with a grunt of disgust.

"Is it broken or not granting clearance?" he asked.

"No, it's not broken," she said. "But this card isn't working here either."

Tolby growled. "Nodari fighters are still sweeping the air," he said. "Let me try and hack it with my PEN again."

"You fried the last console," I pointed out.

Tolby straightened and eased me off his shoulder. "You remember that?"

"Um, duh. I was there," I replied, leaning against the wall. I was glad to be off his back since being carried that far for that long wasn't what I'd call a luxurious ride. Now that I was standing, however, I wasn't too thrilled with the headache that plowed over me either.

"That was at least ten minutes ago," Tolby said, concerned.

"Yeah, so?"

"That means you're sobering," Jainon said. "Between your liver and those microbes, the alcohol in your system is being broken down much more rapidly than I'd thought it would."

The Kibnali high priestess stuck the bottle in my face. "Drink up. We need to buy you more time."

My face twisted in revulsion, but I complied. It wasn't so bad the second time, mostly because I was still intoxicated enough that the smell didn't get to me. I still ended up coughing and spitting, but I did stay standing, even if the wall at my back was doing most of the work.

"Ha! Got it!" Tolby declared.

I looked up after wiping my mouth with the back of my hand. The door he was at slid open, and a long, well-lit tunnel free of all signs of war and strife greeted us.

"I knew you could do it," I said, slurring my words again as I dove back into the sea of drunken bliss. "That's why I pay you the big bucks."

CHAPTER SEVENTEEN: DETOX

True to the soldier's word, the tunnels were free of Nodari. Thank the furriest gods who blessed our escape. Even better, we happened upon a small transport that looked like an oversized golf cart with a bulbous rear end that we all piled into. It wasn't the speediest thing in the world, but it did move at a fair clip faster than we were running, and I'm sure Tolby and Jainon appreciated not having to carry me around another five kilometers.

I'm not sure how long it took for us to get to the Progenitor facility, but once we did, Jack used his implants to hook into the network and open the door. Again, nothing greeted us, which I was thankful for, but seeing how according to the map there were no less than ten other entry points, it was hardly a guarantee that we wouldn't encounter anything up ahead.

The other part to all this that wasn't peaches and ice cream was the fact that once again, I was sobering. I could stand. I could run. I could feel my joints flaring, and worst of all, we were out of alcohol. Thus, we raced through the facility as fast as we could, only stopping to check nearby maps to ensure we were still headed in the right direction.

"This place is going to make me sick," Jack said.

"I'm not a fan of it either," Jainon added.

The reason for their discomfort was obvious. We had entered a new section of the art gallery, and the exhibits here took surrealism to an entirely new level. The floors were painted with curved lines and swirls that made them look as if they were continually wobbling and bending.

The walls were done in a similar fashion, and side rooms, too, and all of them had odd dimensions that made big things seem small and small things seem big—like a funhouse, but this was no fun at all. Most of the space on the walls was taken up by holograms of distorted places, but there were a few windows where one could stick a head inside and glance around a miniaturized, ordinary art gallery full of paintings and sculptures and fountains and the like. Maybe the Progenitors were trying to give patrons the view Alice had when she'd eaten the wrong piece of cake.

What really put the icing on the proverbial weird cake was the lighting. Lights on the ceiling flickered in strange patterns and produced dancing dots along the walls and floors, which gave a sort of a hypnotic feel to it unless you were epileptic, in which case you probably wouldn't have gotten ten meters down the hall without going into a seizure.

Then again, due to the venom inside of me, I couldn't be too sure that I wasn't hallucinating half of it. Hell, Jack might've said something completely different for all I knew. That thought was disconcerting, to say the least. How many of my senses could I actually trust?

"Jack," I said. "We're walking down a hall that's like a bad trip through a mystery funhouse, right?"

"I've never had the displeasure of having a bad trip, so I can't say," Jack replied. "But yes, we're going through a funky hall, and truth be told, I'm carrying you more than you're walking."

"Okay, good," I said with a heavy sigh. I had no sooner relaxed than a new thought came to me. What if I'd only imagined having that conversation with him? "Jack, did I ask you about us walking down a funhouse hall, or was that all in my head?"

"No, you asked me. *Again.*"

"Sorry."

Jack and I spun around at the sound of plasma shots. Tolby, facing the rear, had his rifle shouldered. Down the hall, a couple of Nodari swarmlings lay on the floor with their heads a smoldering mess. "I think they've discovered the art gallery," Tolby said. "We need to get to the medbay quickly."

"I'm going as fast as I can," I said. I paused a moment and wiped off some sweat from my brow. My tongue felt puffy, and the inside of my mouth I was sure had turned to sandpaper. "Trust me. I didn't need them trying to munch on my butt to get me to move."

KN-B and his obnoxious buddy KN-C swooped down on us from a side room, each one of their eyes a flurry of pulsating colors. As with our first meeting with the pair, they talked in rapid succession, leaving little room for anyone to get a word in edgewise until their rants were finished.

"Isn't this exciting?" KN-B said.

"So exciting!" replied KN-C.

"We're so happy you're here to see our grand triumph!"

"So happy!"

"We would love to know what you think!"

"Would so love!"

"I think you're lucky Tolby and Jainon didn't blow your head off coming at us like that," I said, leaning on Jack and limping along. "Remember what happened to KN-E?"

"That was a tragic event," KN-B replied.

"So tragic!"

"But we have found a way to avoid such things!"

"Completely avoid!"

"Aren't you dying to know?"

"Completely dying!"

"I'm already dying," I said, only half listening to them at this point. The air seemed to have become molasses it was so thick in my lungs. If I didn't know better, I would have been sure I'd contracted a case of hyperpneumonia.

"Oh, well, we installed shields," KN-B said.

"The shieldiest shields that ever did shield," added KN-C.

"Wasn't that clever of us?"

"So clever."

"Perfect for this exhibit, don't you think?"

"Completely agree!"

Jack stopped, so I stopped. I didn't mind right off the bat because something about their words told me they were talking about this strange part of the gallery we were in. "Why do you need shields here?" he said as he adjusted his grip on his weapon.

"For the same reason you have those weapons."

"Totally same."

"The completion of our task is dangerous, after all, and we are grateful for helping us finish. Would you like to join the festivities?"

"So fun!"

"Task?" I asked. "What task?"

"This doesn't sound good," Jainon said, her face hardening.

The two drones laughed with sinister, harmonic voices. They spun around each other and then danced around for a few seconds before recomposing themselves. "The eradication of the Kibnali!" KN-B replied.

"Time for them to go!" KN-C tacked on.

Tolby, keeping the rear secure, glanced over his shoulder, dropped his brow, and growled. "What did that thing say?"

"We were saying we're so happy you stupid, brutish, worthless furballs didn't' figure out what was going on before we got the webway operational again," KN-B said.

"So stupid," KN-C added.

"Remember when you asked about Adrestia and the Nodari? And I replied 'Oh, I have no idea what you're talking about?' And you morons believed us. I only wish we could've accomplished this sooner, but alas, stupid paradox backlash problems. We could only insert the Nodari into the timeline here and now."

"You're responsible for all of this?" I asked, both shocked at the news and mad at myself for ever trusting the little bastards. After all, we'd known the facility on Adrestia had been made to send the Nodari fleet to invade the Kibnali, but we'd thought that wasn't going to happen for a couple of years.

"Me? I'm not that good," KN-B replied, spinning about. "Group effort. Go us!"

KN-C joined the fun. "Go team, go!"

My eyes narrowed, and I raised my arm, intent on telekinetically punching one of them through the other. Instead of launching my famous attack, however, I dropped to one knee and emptied my stomach. And it wasn't a normal puke either. It was thick, chunky, and had flecks of dark blood in it.

That's probably the only thing that kept my Kibnali buddies from vaporizing them as well, as they both instantly tried to get me back up on my feet.

"She doesn't have much time," Jainon said, speaking to Tolby as if I weren't there.

Tolby growled. "I know."

"Oh, that is not a good look for her," KN-B said.

"Not good," chimed his twin.

"Maybe she'd like some chicken noodle soup and a good rest."

"A great rest."

I coughed again, and it hurt, but at least I had enough strength in me to talk again. "We're going to the medbay."

"What a fine idea," KN-B said. "The medical facility here has been specifically designed to meet the needs of all registered omega-level family membership holders."

"Specifically designed!"

"Can it take out this venom?" I asked, my hatred for them both taking a back seat to the hope I'd find a cure.

"In theory, yes," KN-B replied.

"In theory!"

"What do you mean, 'in theory'?"

"You'll have to infect one of your own," he explained. "Seeing how you didn't seem to appreciate your part in eradicating the Kibnali, you might object."

"Possible problem!" KN-C added.

"But in your case," KN-B went on, "I think you would more see it like self-defense than anything. I'm sure you could rationalize it as such if you're having a moral quandary."

"Completely rationalize!"

"Look out!" Jainon yelled.

Out of instinct, I dropped to the ground and dragged Jack along with me. A bright, superheated beam of plasma flashed between us and struck KN-B dead center. Whatever shields he might have had apparently weren't enough to stop this blast. Most of his body vaporized, and what was left of his shell collapsed to the floor. KN-C flew away with a shriek as Tolby and Jainon put a half dozen shots back the way we came.

The Nodari scout who'd suddenly appeared behind us caught their shots with its face and chest. It crumpled to the ground in a smoldering heap.

For the next few seconds, Tolby kept his weapon up and trained back the way we came while Jainon covered ahead of us. Eventually, he glanced over his shoulder. "Looks like the Nodari have found a way in," he said.

"Let's hope it's only a few," Jainon added.

The giant tigress pulled me up, but I fought her off for a moment when she tried to put me across her shoulders. I had something I needed to say first, something that nearly got caught in my throat as I spoke. "Tolby..."

My bud hurried over and dropped a massive paw on my shoulder. "Don't listen to them. This isn't your fault."

"I didn't know. I swear." My eyes watered, and despite the lack of spare time we had, I threw myself into him. The ugly cry came. The ugliest of uglies. "I'm sorry. If I had listened to you from the start, if we had never gone in the *Vela* and never messed around inside the museum, none of this would've happened."

Tolby squeezed me tight, which only made me cry harder.

Jainon broke the silence. "You are not at fault, Dakota," she said. "They did this to us. Not you, but that doesn't mean you can't be the one to set things right."

I sniffed, cleared my eyes, and then blew out a massive bunch of snot. "Thanks, but..."

"No buts," she said. "Take whatever anger you have for yourself and unleash it on our enemies."

I sucked in a deep breath and tried to ground myself in her words. They helped, but I'd be lying if I said they worked completely. It's not like they teach you in school how to deal with a mindscrew like the bomb that had just been dropped on me. "Right," I said. "I need that medbay, though. How much further is it?"

"I'll check," Jack said before trotting a dozen paces to a console.

Once he was out of relative earshot, Tolby spoke to me softly. "I think he's using you."

"Why would you say that?"

"He cares not for his new family," he said. "I can see it in his eyes and the way he looks at the others. He's distrustful of my species, and thus is distrustful of you. Those who are like that only seek to manipulate and get what they can before cutting loose and running."

"I think he has every right to be distrustful of the other Kibnali," I said. "To be honest, I don't trust them either, and they didn't experiment on me nearly as badly as they had on him."

"I'm not even speaking about the Kibnali who live here. He's distrustful of not only me, but Empress, Yseri, and Jainon."

"I think wary is a better word," I said.

The conversation halted when Jack came running back over with an excited look on his face. "The medical facility is right around the corner. They had it listed as 'primary support' which I guess was an awkward translation of 'first aid.'"

"The gods bless us still," Jainon said with a huge grin.

I couldn't help but smile as well, but for other reasons. "I guess even Progenitors mess up their translations from time to time. I don't suppose there were any clues as to what that whole infecting business was all about?"

"No, but let's hope that's another botched translation," he said. "Because as far as I know, I'm the only other human around, and as much as I like you, I'd rather not be infected with anything."

"Agreed."

We took off for the medical bay, and I didn't get but a dozen steps before collapsing against the wall. Pain seared all through my body. My eyes felt as if they were going to explode, and my joints felt as if each one had an invisible ice pick stuck in them and was digging around.

"I've got her," Jainon said, scooping me up with one arm and slinging me across her shoulders.

I probably should've been used to it by now, but I was really starting to hate being slung around like a sack of potatoes. It's painful. It's not dignified, and it made me feel like a three-year-old kid. I tried to make myself useful as we ran down the hall, but since the pain continued to grow worse, most of the time I had my eyes clenched shut. Thankfully, we reached the medical facility in short order.

I heard a whoosh right as we entered, and caught sight of a large, translucent door sliding to the side. The medical bay's waiting area was arranged in a crescent with several benches along the walls. Above the benches were large paintings of tropical landscapes, some of which looked more like they belonged hanging over an ancient bar at Key West than they did in an alien facility— probably a few more pieces the Progenitors had procured from

Earth way back when. Or was it way forward when? I guess it all depends on how you look at time travel.

Next to those benches sat a few ferns with purple and red leaves, and near the center of the room beneath a lovely crystal chandelier was an elongated, sleek, black desk that had a single monitor sitting in the middle and a cushy chair with a back that fanned out in multiple colors much like a peacock. I imagined that was for the doctor or the receptionist or whoever normally staffed this place. Since it was empty, much like most Progenitor facilities we had been in, we pushed through the waiting area.

"At least there isn't the line," Jack said, opening the next door.

"Or questions about insurance," I said as I forced a small grin. "I'm pretty sure this area would be out of network."

We entered a wide hall that ran for a few dozen meters before turning to the left. We didn't run its length, but rather entered the first door on our right, which ended up being an exam room—or maybe operation room was more accurate.

It was spacious and rectangular with rounded corners and a large ceiling that stretched overhead. Hanging from the ceiling was a rounded mount that held a number of robotic arms and devices, many of which reminded me of what I'd seen TG2 use to operate on Empress not long ago.

Beneath that mount there stood a hefty, padded operating table that had a large white-and-blue ring surrounding it, presumably to scan whoever the patient was. A cart about as tall as I am and twice as long sat nearby, and on its trio of shelves and top, it held a number of baskets filled with surgical tools, packets of who knows what, and at least half a dozen techno whatchamacallits that probably did something immensely cool, but I had no idea what.

Numerous computer consoles stood idle on the wall to our right, except for one screen which did display a blinking cursor in the top left corner. Finally, at the far end were three large cylindrical tanks, much like the bacta models made a long time ago in a galaxy far, far away (but ended up being junked due to poor performance in extremely cold weather). All three of them were empty, thankfully, because if one of them had been holding a Nodari scout like the stasis tubes we had stumbled on back on the other Progenitor planet, I'd have lost my mind.

"Do you have any idea how to use this?" Jack asked me as Jainon eased me on to the operating table.

"No," I said weakly. "But a lot of the Progenitor tech I've used before has been automated once I told it what I wanted it to do. If you connect into that console over there, maybe you can get it to fix me."

"All right. I'll give it a run. Try not to die on me in the meantime."

"Tolby! Can you hear me?"

It was Yseri over the comms. She sounded relieved, which I took to mean that they were relatively safe. I say relative not only because we were in the middle of a Nodari invasion but compared to my predicament, unless a giant, cybernetic space squid was using her body as a toothpick, she was probably safer than I was at that moment.

"You're coming in clear," Tolby said. "What's your status?"

"We're on the northeast side of the city," she said. "We ran into one of the largest swarms I've seen on the ground, but thankfully we got away. I think some managed to get into the tunnels. Be careful."

"They have," Tolby said.

"Are you at the ship yet?"

"Negative, we're at a Progenitor medical bay," he said. "We're going to try and extract Nodari venom from Dakota first, then move on to the ship. The hangar is close by."

"Will you be able to meet us there?" Jainon asked.

"I think so," Yseri said. There was some chatter on her end I couldn't pick up. It sounded like Empress saying something, but it was too muted to tell. "There's a lull in the fighting here. We'll move now."

"Good, then Inaja's luck is still with us," Jainon replied.

Yseri gave an uncharacteristic, lighthearted chuckle. "It would seem so. We'll see you soon."

The conversation had no sooner finished than Jack clenched a triumphant fist in the air. "Got it. I think it's going to diagnose you now."

An announcer, whose voice had more energy than a junkie binging on hypercrack, spoke from unseen speakers. "Greetings and salutations, lifeform, and welcome to Excel-Care, where treating every guest with the utmost state-of-the-art technology is our primary mission. We are having a special on micro sutures today. Buy twenty and get three free! Would you like to hear more?"

"No," I said, grimacing. "All I need is this Nodari venom taken out of me."

The announcer laughed. "Leave the diagnostics to us," he said. "It has been shown that nine out of ten self-diagnosed problems are wildly inaccurate, and they are often the cause of undereducation or mental illness such as hypochondria."

"I'm not a hypochondriac," I said. "I'm sure."

"We at Excel-Care appreciate your candor and commitment to mental health. We also offer insurance against mis-self-diagnosis. Customers who purchase this are seven-point-six times more likely to experience a positive clinical visit and report three times as much peace of mind as those without. Would you like to hear more?"

"No."

"It sounds as if you are saying no. Due to this highly irregular statement, please confirm."

I groaned. "Yes!"

"Wonderful! We're so glad you decided to purchase platinum-level insurance. After a brief survey, meeting with your doctor, review of six references, and a small deposit, we can process your claim and have it back to you in as little as seven years—terms and conditions may apply."

"Tolby, make it stop," I whimpered.

"Look, sales guy, we'll buy whatever you want after you fix her," Tolby said. "But we don't have a lot of time. So, if she dies, I promise I'll make sure you never make whatever quota for the year you're aiming for."

"You will? How glorious! I love it when a whale—er, I mean, VIP customer comes through the door," he replied. "You'll be glad to know that we take all major forms of universal credit cards, including MISA, Domni Card, Progenitor Express, and Explore."

A new wave of pain ripped through my body, and I curled into a fetal position. I tried to speak, but all that came out was a pathetic cry of despair.

"She doesn't have her wallet with her," Jack said.

"Hmm, that could be problematic. Proper medical attention is costly."

"Charge it to her membership, then," Tolby said. Though he sounded confident, I could tell by the look on his face that he was making a Hail Mary.

"Membership? What membership?"

"She has an omega-level family membership at the Museum of Natural Time."

"But that hasn't even been built yet!"

"So?"

"Well, we'll have to run a background check, then," he said. "But the good news is, once you pass, we can sign you up for a new Domni or MISA card, and you'll be eligible to earn ten thousand frequent light-year points on your first thirty seconds of purchases. Isn't that wonderful?"

"Whatever. Do it already," I said.

"We're so glad you're agreeable. Stand by for initial scans. Creditworthiness and preliminary diagnostics will now begin."

The ring that circumscribed the table sprang to life. Bright, yellow light emanated from its inner edge, and the entire thing slowly moved over me, starting from my feet and working up to my head. As it did, a faint smell of ozone wafted from the device, and a loud shrieking noise came from above like metal scraping against metal.

I cringed at the horrific assault on my ears. "Am I the only one that thinks that's loud?"

"No," Tolby replied, grimacing as well. "I hope these doors are thick enough to keep it from attracting the Nodari."

The scan didn't last much longer, thankfully. When it was finished, the announcer spoke again, this time with an equal mix of shock and respect in his voice. "You're Dakota Adams?"

"Yes," I said, my voice barely a whisper now. "But not for much longer if you don't hurry up."

"*The* Dakota Adams? The one who beats Master of Records and trashes Adrestia?"

"Yeah, that's me."

"How exciting! Why didn't you say who you were in the first place?" he said. "You'll be pleased to know your application can be auto-approved."

"Great. Please, just treat me," I said. "I can't take much more of this."

"Of course! You'll see the bill on your next statement," he said. The ring sprang to life again, whirring along as it made another scan. When it was done, the announcer spoke. "Oh, this could be bad."

I frowned. "More so than it is right now?"

"Well...yes and no," he replied. "The good news is, you were correct in your self-diagnosis. The level of Nodari venom in your blood is at critical levels."

"I fail to see how that's good news."

"Compared to the bad, it's terrific," he went on. "The bad news is our stock of pharmaceuticals is low. There's only enough to formulate one try at the antivenin."

"One try?" I repeated.

"Yes," he said. "It's too bad you didn't sign up for platinum-explore-level insurance against low pharmaceutical storage. You could have made a claim and been reimbursed for additional expenses in as little as four years. Would you like to hear more?"

"No, god, no," I groaned. "Just do whatever you have to do to make that one serum work."

"Field testing will be required," he said. "Batch should be ready in approximately ten minutes. Please enjoy this pleasant serenade as you wait."

I cringed as the announcer hummed some unknown melody. Holy snort. Ten minutes? Could I last that long? Pain aside, how much longer did I have to live before my insides turned into a Dakota slurry. "Any chance you can inject me with 3,000cc's of the most amazing painkiller ever? Because if so, go ahead and do that a couple of times."

"Initiating treatment plan," the announcer said. "You are strongly encouraged to hold still at this time. If you choose not to abide by instructions, you automatically waive all rights to proper and prompt care."

I shut my eyes and listened to the ring sweep over me two more times. When it was finished, one of the surgical arms from above zipped down with a noisy whir before sticking my neck with a slender needle. I didn't move, terrified I might cause it to puncture something I might want left intact, like my jugular. I dared a peek, and from the corner of my eye, I could see it drawing blood into a clear vial about the size of my hand.

Once that vial was filled, the machine withdrew the needle and placed said vial into a compartment overhead that snapped shut. Another minute passed while the machine above hummed and beeped before a bubbling noise grabbed our attention. I wasn't sure if I should sit up to look, so I craned my head back to see what was going on.

The middle tank was a flurry of activity. Bubbles churned through some sort of gel that filled the thing while electricity arced constantly inside. The gel darkened to a forest green before turning a burnt brown and finally jet black. At that point, the bubbling and churning stopped for a few seconds before a milky substance was injected forcefully from the top. This new addition displaced the black gel in the tube, and thus instead of seeing all black, all we saw was white.

"What's going on in there?" I asked.

"I don't think it's making milk, if that's what you're leaning toward," Jack said, approaching with caution. "At least, I wouldn't recommend making a smoothie out of it. But you can if that's your thing."

This new liquid drained away, revealing me on the other side. Well, not me, me, but a clone of me. Or a replica. Or a...hell, I don't know what to call it. Probably a clone. We'll go with that. Clone Me floated gently inside the tube, suspended perfectly in the middle, naked as the day I was born.

"Now that's not what I was expecting," Jack said, drawing to Clone Me like a moth to a flame.

"Little privacy!" I said, trying to sit up but instead being smacked with enough vertigo that I fell back on the table.

"It's not you," Jack protested. "Besides, there's stuff sticking out of her back. That's kind of gross."

"She's close enough," I said. "And I don't care if there are angel wings coming out her back. Stop gawking."

"Is that like...a real person in there?" he asked.

"Subject is an organic replicant currently devoid of consciousness and for testing purposes only," the announcer said. "Would you like me to initiate brain activity? We are currently running a special on biological clones who are fully capable of assisting or even replacing all functional duties of their organic mold."

"No," I said. "We're not having another me run around, especially out here where she'll just get killed."

"Are you sure? This special is a great one. Eighty-five percent off the usual fare if you act now."

"I said no, and I meant it," I said. "Just fix me."

"As you wish."

The tank made some buzzing noises before the entire suspension was replaced by yet another liquid bath, this one a ruby red that made it look like she was being held in a large vat of gelatin. The ring above me spun around me, and another mechanical arm swooped down and pinned me to the table.

"Stand by for subject preparation," said our unseen announcer. "Moving may cause injury."

A needle followed, this one jabbing into the other side of my neck. A cold liquid was injected, and a shiver ran through my body as goosebumps raised on my skin.

"If you would be so kind as to enter the medical pod to the right of the test subject, we can finish your treatment," announcer guy said.

I tried to get up on my own but failed miserably. Thankfully, my best bud swept me into his giant paws. He was about to stuff me in the pod when announcer man chimed in. "She'll need her clothes removed," he said. "Impurities may interfere with treatment."

Tolby balked, and I gave him a reassuring flop of the hand. "Just do it. I don't care."

The big guy nodded, and in a flash, he stripped me bare. Not that I would've put a halt to things on account of my guts turning to Nodari slurry had Jack not turned around, but I will admit, when I saw him give me his back, I appreciated it to no end.

"See you soon," Tolby said, as he popped me into the tube.

"Don't run off without me," I said, managing to crack a half smile.

The pod sealed right after and filled with a semi-clear liquid. After some more whirrs and buzzes, all the pods sank underneath the floor.

Just before I lost consciousness, I was treated to a quick view of whatever technological marvels the Progenitors had constructed in the floor below. The room looked like it could swallow an apartment building or two. A hefty construct took up most of the space. It had sloped sides and at least three dozen arms that shot off in all directions. On each of these arms spun several discs that gave off a dizzying array of lights, and from the very center of it all, out came a diamond-shaped probe that trailed long wisps of metallic hair.

My pod and the one next to me gently sank to the floor before rotating and tilting so that the clone and I were on our backs. The probe floated about my tank, and using one of its filaments, it jabbed the side of my pod.

Darkness swallowed my world. I wasn't aware of much at that point, but I could feel the pain in my joints and gut lessen. It didn't take long for it to go from excruciating to painful to mildly annoying. I fell asleep, but when I woke—which couldn't have been that long after—I was being raised back into the room with the others, practically good as new.

The pod popped open, and I fell out, soaked from head to toe. "Doc, you're a miracle worker," I said, slowly sitting up with a hefty sigh of relief. "I'd have your babies if I could."

Jack, who still had his back turned toward me, huffed and crossed his arms. "Him? After all I've done and carried you through. You could've at least offered to buy me dinner."

"I'll buy you dinner. Don't worry," I said as I shook dry as best I could before tossing on my clothes. "I'll even get you a root beer float."

"I'd rather have whiskey if that's okay with you."

"I'll buy you a whole distillery once we're out of this mess." I paused and looked myself over. My skin had a light, fluorescent yellow sheen to it, like the glow produced by fireflies. I rubbed my index finger across my forearm and picked some of it up and noted it felt sticky and smelled like bananas. "Why am I oozing glowy stuff?"

"Are you not supposed to?" the announcer said. "I've read numerous accounts of humans where they were described as glowing."

"Yes, glowing, like extremely happy or elated," I said. "Not anything like this."

The announcer laughed. "I know. You ought to lighten up. Stress produces high blood pressure and in turn can cause considerable wear and tear on a human. Would you like to hear more about our anti-stress packages? We have a number to choose from that can meet the needs of any individual or family."

I shook my head, not appreciating his attempt at being funny. "Could you just tell me what this is about? I don't like turning into a lightning bug."

"It's the toxins leaving your body," he explained. "I'm afraid you will be a gigantic lightning bug for at least another hour or two. It really depends on how fast your body processes the new compound as the antivenin attaches itself to the Nodari particulates inside of you."

"That's going to make sneaking around here a lot harder," Jack said.

"Maybe we should turn the lights on full bright," Tolby suggested. He was trying to sound serious, but there was a snicker in his voice and a not-so-suppressed grin on his face. "On the bright side, we could use you for a visual confirmation to land a ship at night."

"Or even better, maybe we could set some concave mirrors around her and blind the Nodari," Jack added.

"How about we simply get to the ship," I said.

They made a couple more remarks at my expense before I silenced them with a glare. I guess I can't blame them too much, seeing how we were in a high-stress situation and a little joking here and there was probably what everybody needed to keep sane.

"Here, put this on," Jack said, handing me a set of Kibnali armor.

It was at that point I realized he had none. "Is this yours?"

"Not anymore," he said.

I shook my head. "Thanks, but I don't need you to be chivalrous. I'll be fine. Besides, it probably doesn't fit."

"It's all modular and easily customizable, remember?" he said. "Now take it."

I glanced to Tolby, who threw me "don't argue" look, and thus, I reluctantly put it on. "Okay, but if the Nodari melt your face, I'm absolving myself of any and all guilt," I said.

"Oh, if I get melted, I definitely expect you to mourn my loss every day for the next hundred years," he replied with a grin.

Daphne's voice cut in over the comm. "Dakota, are you alive?"

"I am, and I'm feeling a ton better. Are you almost here?"

"Yes, spatially at least."

"Spatially?"

"Temporally, no," she said. "I am unable to decrease rendezvous time due to Nodari interference."

"I see," I said, thinking perhaps I didn't. "You're not stuck in the past or something weird, are you?"

"No, don't be silly. You're the only careless time traveler in the group."

"Then what are you saying?"

"I'm saying there are too many Nodari between me and you to get there safely, and thus, it'll be a while if you want me to get to the medical bay."

"Oh, why didn't you say that to begin with."

"I thought I did."

I snickered and shook my head. "Can you make it to the hangar?"

"I believe so."

"Good, we'll see you there."

We left the examination room and made a brief stop inside the waiting area, where I looked at the map of the facility once last time to check the route to the hangar. It was a straightforward path that took us through a section of the art museum that was dedicated to the works of the Gilbanat.

Since we were moving quickly and quietly and didn't have a lot of reading time, I only got the gist of who the Gilbanat were. They lived on a planet filled with volcanoes and under the constant rain of ash and acidic rain. This meant that life expectancy for those who were running around on the surface was short, and the amount of fun in the sun one could have was even shorter. Thus, this insect-like race had remained entirely underground and made sculptures out of lava. Most of the sculptures made were terrifying beasts and gods who the Gilbanat thought of as terrorizing their existence nonstop, but there was another branch of Gilbanat art which featured dreams of what heaven and life would be like on the surface had there not been raining fire and hurricanes of poisonous gas.

To them, heaven was crystal-clear water that was surrounded by banks of snow and ice. The sun in the sky, too, was cold (not sure how that worked, ecology wise) and the most popular pastime was being able to stand up straight while the wind blew by and sucking in large quantities of air without falling over dead. I understand that might be a little weird to some who are living in relatively nice places, but if you've ever been to Los Troit, where the smog from the cars is as thick as politicians who ran that city into the ground, you'll understand how that wish could be anything and everything you'd ever want.

We had gotten through most of the exhibit without incident. When we took a side hall, however, and entered a section with brown-and-white marble flooring, tall, peach-colored walls, and an arched ceiling with track lighting installed near the edge, we ran into a group of Nodari scouts trotting down the hall toward us.

"Watch it!" Tolby said a moment before the firefight began.

I had already thrown myself to the side and began shooting before he had finished his warning. My aim was still nowhere near good enough to write home about, but in the initial exchange of fire, I did manage to drill one of them in the knee, dropping it to the ground. A couple of scouts next to it didn't even have time to raise their weapons before Jainon shot both square in the face.

The final two Nodari didn't fare better. The first one caught three shots to the chest by Tolby, while the last was put down by Jack. As it fell, its skull a smoldering mess, the one I hit brought his weapon to bear and fired. The shot struck Tolby in the lower abdomen, just to the side. A heartbeat later, Jainon nailed the scout three times over, finishing it off.

The infamous yellow goo chewed through Tolby's armor with frightening speed and an unsettling hiss. Tolby roared in defiance as he ripped his armor off and let it fall to the ground only seconds before the acid chewed through his flesh.

"We've got to work on your aim," Tolby said, sucking in a breath and examining his body. Other than some missing fur and a little bit of red puffiness on his skin, he was no worse for wear.

"I know," I said, feeling awful. Though we had survived, it was clear that was only because Tolby's armor had saved him, and now that armor was no more. If he got hit again...My throat tightened, and I pushed that thought away.

"No need to dwell on it now," he said, to my relief.

We continued, picking up the pace. When we reached the end of the hall where it split left and right, we were about to go right when a new monster lumbered into view.

The thing was flanked by four scouts, two on each side, and as terrorizing as the scouts looked in general, they had nothing on this new guy. This massive creature could have easily stood four meters tall if it hadn't had to hunch over due to the art gallery ceiling. Sinewy legs covered in the telltale Nodari exoskeleton kept it upright, and it dragged a lengthy tail with a barbed hook behind it. Its two upper arms ended in claws that could crush a mountain, while two smaller ones beneath those held a ginormous biological rifle that was connected to its back via organic tubes.

"That thing definitely does not eat carrots," I said, backpedaling as fast as I could.

It's a good thing I'd been hanging out with giant cats, because I'm pretty sure I used up one of my nine lives I'd gotten via osmosis when a massive blast of acidic goo flew past me at nearly supersonic speed and promptly melted half the corridor.

"What the hell is that?" Jack yelled as we took off, running back the way we came.

"A Nodari captain," Tolby answered. He unhooked his last grenade and tossed it back the way we came. "If the captains have made landfall, the Nodari monarch isn't far behind."

"Captains, as in plural? You mean there are more of them?" I stumbled forward as the grenade went off. Even though Tolby had managed to bounce it around the corner and shield us from most of the blast, the shockwave was more than enough to keep me fighting for balance.

"There are usually three to a landing force," Jainon replied. "But sometimes more."

"Holy snort, there are at least two more running around? What's it take to kill one? A tank?"

"Orbital strikes usually work the best," she said thoughtfully.

"Anything else I want to know as this battle has gone from bad to worse?"

"I don't think you want to know anything else," Tolby said with a chuckle. "But you should know the monarchs are even deadlier, and nothing short of a full broadside from a cruiser will take it down."

"Wonderful."

As we ran, I could hear the Nodari captain charging after us. Despite the twisting path we took, it stayed on our heels, but thankfully out of sight. It stayed out of sight, that is, until we took a wrong turn and ended up in a long hall of miniature displays and exactly zero side passages to dart down.

With no other options, we sprinted as fast as we could. When we were about halfway to the other end, a deafening roar came from behind. I looked over my shoulder to see the Nodari captain barreling toward us. The main cannon it held was missing a large chunk from its middle, and it dripped a thick, brown goo from its bottom. I assumed that meant it was broken since we hadn't been vaporized on the spot. But the captain didn't need such weapons to finish us off. The enormous lobster claws it touted would be more than enough to crush all four of us in a split second if it could close the distance.

The captain came at us faster than a runaway freight train, and I knew we didn't have a prayer to make it. I turned and slowed just long enough to give it the most massive telekinetic punch I could. Using what I learned while fighting Goliath, I aimed for the captain's eye. The blow was everything I had and then some. It shattered the left side of the monster's face, sending gore and pieces of exoskeleton everywhere. The captain reeled sideways and crashed into a couple of paintings hanging on the wall.

"You are an honor to your kind!" Jainon shouted with glee.

The celebration was short-lived, as my hit wasn't enough to put him down. The captain stumbled to its feet within a few seconds and charged at us once more.

We flew through an arch at the end of the hall. As Tolby, Jainon, and I slid on the floor, trying to make a tight right turn, Jack threw himself at a nearby console on the wall. He furiously punched at its controls, and right as the Nodari captain was about to pass through, Jack brought down a ten-centimeter-thick fire door.

The captain rammed into it at full steam. My teeth rattled in my jaw from the shock, but the door held. We all exchanged nervous glances as the captain rammed it again. I don't know why we didn't keep running. I guess we were in shock Jack had managed to get the controls going and we hadn't become a Nodari snack.

"Is that going to hold?" I asked, easing back but unable to keep my eyes from breaking away from the door.

"Maybe," Jainon said.

The captain rammed the door a third time, at which point it buckled a little.

"Maybe not," she corrected.

A fourth hit caved it in further and generated spall. Most of the pieces bounced harmlessly off the walls, but a few skipped off of Jainon's armor while another particularly large piece ripped through Jack's shoulder.

"Son of a bitch that hurts," he said, grabbing the wound and staggering away from the door.

The fifth blow produced similar results, and the door caved considerably.

Tolby's face soured. "Less talking, more running."

CHAPTER EIGHTEEN: A NEW SHIP

Yseri, Empress. Sitrep," Tolby said over the comm.

It had been a good five minutes since we dropped the fire door on the Nodari captain, and throughout that time we'd bolted through the art gallery faster than a runaway rocket booster. Although we didn't think it was following us directly at this point, we could still hear his occasional roars which were more than close enough to keep us pushing our bodies to the breaking point.

"We moved from our prior position, but we're still a half a kilometer from the hangar," Yseri said. "We had to ditch a Nodari captain."

"There's one down here, too," I said. "But Tolby nuked its acid cannon thing, and I cracked open its skull."

"Excellent news, tailless," Yseri said. "Are you almost to the ship?"

"We'll be there in two minutes, tops," I said, checking the map.

"Then get ready for us," Yseri replied. "We'll be there soon as well."

We ran on, taking one last bend to the left and practically jumping down a flight of stairs before reaching the final door—a door that Daphne stood by, patiently waiting for us. Even better, she had Taz with her. The moment the *ashidasashi* saw me, he leaped off her metallic head and adorably savaged my shoe.

"Taz!" I yelled with delight. "You made it!"

Jack nudged Tolby with an elbow. "Are you getting replaced?"

"Pshhh. Never," I said, giving my little guy a belly rub.

"Glad to hear," Tolby said. "But perhaps we should spend more time on opening that door and less time cooing over your pet."

"Right," I replied, feeling silly. That said, I didn't feel that bad. Anyone who knew me for even an hour ought to know I get a case of the squirrels often. Some people find ADHD a pain in the butt to live with, but hey, I say it's a blessing because without it, I'd miss out on all the super cool stuff the universe has to offer. I mean, the stuff is everywhere! Sometimes I wonder if when we die, we'll get the stats on everything we found, or maybe the Easter eggs—surely there are some, right? You know, you die, get to the pearly gates or whatever, and there's a personalized scoreboard. How fun would that be? Mine would dwarf everyone else's; I just know it. Especially if lost socks somehow factored in. Holy snort, you could outfit—

"Dakota!" Tolby boomed.

I snapped back into the present. "Right, sorry. On it."

I turned my attention to the door and went to work. It was one of the heavy, gear-like ones we'd encountered before, which made a lot of sense when you figured a prize Progenitor spacecraft lay beyond. Right as I plugged in, the roar of the Nodari captain put the fear of God in me. It wasn't on top of us yet, but it might as well have been.

"I hope you can get that door open fast," Jack said as everyone kept their weapons up and pointed to our rear.

"Me too," I said while my stomach knotted.

Thankfully, I found the controls with ease once the console sprang to life, and I immediately ordered the door to cycle. It did, but the moment it began to move, I wished that it hadn't responded at all. It slowly began to roll to the side with such a shriek that it would have caused a banshee to cover her ears.

"Martian babes on a stick," Jack said, shaking his head. "That can't be good."

"I have calculated that there is a one-hundred percent probability that at least one Nodari swarm is now aware of our location."

"A hundred percent? Really?" I asked, shocked. "Nothing can be a hundred percent certain."

"Well, this is. Unless I forgot to carry the one. Silly me. I do that sometimes, you know."

"Good, let's go with that, then."

"If you like," she replied. "My revised calculations put that percent chance at a hundred and one percent."

I rolled my eyes and groaned right as the Nodari captain bellowed. It wasn't a roar, not like before. This was very different. Deeper, longer, and held purpose. An unsettling feeling reigned in my stomach because I had a strong feeling about what it was. When smaller cries of Nodari answered, I would've given up anything and everything to have not been right. The captain was calling for others, and they were coming.

We darted into the hangar the moment we could. Once through, I cycled the door behind us. It shut before the captain appeared, but I had no doubt he'd be on the other side in no time at all.

"That's a meter thick," I said. "He can't get through *that*, can he?"

"I wouldn't put it past him," Tolby said. "They're stronger than the pull of a neutron star."

"Lovely."

"We've got bigger problems than that."

I groaned. "Of course. What are they?"

"Unless there's another way in, everyone else is cut off."

"Crap." My hands balled into fists at my side. "Crappity, crap, crap, crap."

"Or we just pick them up once we're out of here," Jack said as if the answer was painfully obvious.

I smirked at myself because that answer had been painfully obvious. "Good point."

Turning around, we hurried through the Progenitor hangar. The entire thing stretched a hundred meters across and who knew how long as the only parts that were lit were in our immediate vicinity.

To both my left and right sat a number of machines with countless pipes and thick bundles of wires coming out of them and heading every which way. Non-slip metal plates made up the bulk of the floor along the edges, although a few small drainage grates could be found scattered about. I-beams and catwalks made an intricate latticework along an otherwise smooth and unremarkable ceiling. Off to the side, a couple of fans set into the wall spun slowly with a hum, and from their cylindrical vents floated a strong, metallic smell.

"Where's this transport?" Jack asked.

"I think that's it," Tolby said, pointing down the hangar to where the darkness swallowed it all.

I popped over to a console and connected quickly. After surfing through the menus, I found what I was looking for and turned on the lights. A series of clunks, like the power being turned on at a stadium, preceded dozens of wall-mounted lights turning on and revealing the most beautiful thing I'd ever seen: a Progenitor ship.

A couple of hundred meters in length, the body of the corvette was elongated and sleek with a steel-blue and orange color scheme. From its sides, it had a pair of reverse-swept wings, and it also had a pair of vertical stabilizers coming out the back. Mounted on the wings were four rectangular pods with vented intakes along with a couple of forward-facing antennas on the wingtips. The entire thing sat on four padded feet for landing gear, and near the aft of the ship, a ramp extended from the belly to the ground, beckoning to me like a siren calls a sailor.

"What are you guys waiting for?" I said, laughing and running.

If they answered, I didn't hear, or at least I didn't pay enough attention to remember.

I ran up the ramp and into a short, oval hall that ended at a sealed door. Though everything was dark, thanks to my glowing skin, I managed to see well enough to find a console on the nearby wall. Plugging into it with my implants was a simple task, and the moment I did, not only did the screen light up, but the interior of the ship did as well with soft, blue lights. There was a lot to see where I was at, but even though I was only in an entryway, there was an unparalleled cool factor to it as everything around me looked both high-tech and extremely organic.

"I can't get Empress or Yseri on the comms," Tolby said, joining me at my side. He had a worried look on his face, and his ears were pinned back.

I didn't need to pry his thoughts to know how troublesome that was. "They'll be fine. Don't worry. We'll find them."

"At least the entrance to the hangar isn't being battered down," Jack said. "That'll give us some time to think about our next move."

"Right now I'm thankful for any little thing I can get," I said as I cycled the door.

We entered a large, circular room. Monitoring stations were set up in cubbies all along the edge. Each one had a plethora of screens on the walls and hanging from the ceiling so that whoever happened to be manning them would be inundated with as much information as they could handle. In the center of this portion of the ship was a raised platform with a railing around all of it. On the end near us, there was another computer station that was raised a half meter and accessible by a few small stairs.

"Wonder what all this does," Jack said.

"I don't know," I said, looking around in amazement. "I doubt it flies it though. We should find the cockpit."

Jack grinned. "How do you know this isn't the bridge? Maybe the Progenitors like to fly from the rear."

I shrugged. "I don't. But what are the chances the first room we come to happens to be the bridge?"

"Point taken."

"Records from the cube indicate that like most spacefaring races, the bridge will be toward the bow of the ship," Daphne said.

"In fact, it'll be more closely related to an extensive cockpit than anything else."

"Told you," I said, putting extra smug into the smile I flashed Jack.

We passed through to the other side where we ended up in another hall that curved around to the left. This corridor ran by a few smaller rooms, one of which reminded me of Curator's office on a much lesser scale, as it had a dark, crescent-shaped desk like he had set in the middle, but it was nowhere near as big as his. There were also several chairs bolted to the floor sitting around it, so I assumed this was a meeting area of some sort or maybe a place for the crew to come and relax.

The hall ended up dumping us in an egg-shaped room that housed more consoles and crew stations like the first room we'd been in, although these stations formed three sets of hexagons in the middle of the room as opposed to lining the walls. Along the walls were various alcoves which housed equipment I had no idea what they were there for, but they looked important. I particularly liked the two near the front, which looked like a combination of an ancient pipe organ and tanning booth.

"Think this is it?" Tolby asked. He leaned over one of the console stations and tapped a screen. Nothing happened. Nothing continued to happen when he tapped it a few more times. "You know, just once in all of this, I'd like to be able to use these things right off the bat. You being the only one who can start the stuff up might come back to bite us later."

"You should join the implant club if it bothers you that much," Jack said.

"I'll admit her implants have been handy on more than one occasion," Tolby said. "But I still don't trust an alien modifying my body."

The corner of Jack's mouth drew back. "You know what? That's a good attitude to have." When I tilted my head and arched an eyebrow, he added, "Why the surprise? If there's one thing I learned about the Kibnali, being indispensable is a key to survival."

"I still don't think this is it," I said, not knowing what I should say, especially with Tolby taking a keen interest in our conversation. "Let's see what's up front."

The front of the ship tapered down to what had to be the cockpit. A single seat sat in the middle, all the way up at the front, surrounded by more monitors and a slew of controls. Flanking that seat on both sides and set back about a meter were two more stations, each with their own consoles and monitors mounted above. Where there wasn't hardware attached, the curved ceiling had a half dozen, clear, thick panes that gave an excellent view of the outside. Likewise, there were four similar panels to see what was going on directly in front and below. This setup reminded me a lot of the glass noses that ancient bombers used to have a thousand years ago.

"Any idea how to fire this thing up?" I said, jumping into the pilot seat.

"Might also want to figure out how we leave before you hit the throttle," Jainon said. "I don't recall seeing an exit or hangar doors."

"Good point."

I made the mental connection and felt a slight pop in my head once I did. The cockpit dash sprang to life with a menagerie of intricate information scrolling on the screens as well as a slew of electronic beeps. Holograms suddenly appeared overhead, one displaying the planet we were on as well as a blinking red cursor that I assumed was our current location, while another showed a green wireframe model of the ship we were in. Portions of the wireframe lit up yellow and blinked before cycling onto another section.

"Welcome, Dakota Adams," a deep voice said from seemingly all around at once. "You're late."

CHAPTER NINETEEN: INTERVIEW WITH AO

I flopped back in the chair as I threw my hands up. "Run that by me again? I'm late?"

A holographic orb popped up next to me about the size of a basketball. Fractals of reds and blues swirled across its skin, reminding me of the monstrous storms on gas giants. As the voice spoke again, the orb pulsed in synch. "Correct," it said. "I have been waiting approximately twelve-point-six-nine-seven-one-three-three trillion nanoseconds longer than I should. This is unacceptable as far as forty-second first impressions go. I now have serious reservations about your refined abilities."

The four of us exchanged confused looks. "Any of you want to take a stab at what's going on?"

"I think the ship's AI is talking to us?" Jack offered.

"That would be my guess," Tolby said. "Although you do have to admire its precision."

"Erroneous statement," the orb said. "I was talking to Dakota Adams, version forty-two."

I laughed nervously. "Version forty-two? Did I miss something? Far as I know there's only one of me."

"There is that brain-dead clone we left behind," Jack said. "He must mean that. Maybe doc made more than the one we saw."

"Erroneous statement. The clone is not an iteration of the original Dakota Adams."

"You're saying I'm not the original me?" I said with a scoff. "No way. Even if I was grown in a vat somewhere, I would know. My family would know. These guys around me would know. It's not like I just popped up out of nowhere with an entire back story in my head that couldn't be verified."

"Faulty assumptions. You're the forty-second iteration of Dakota Adams because this is the forty-second iteration of this universe," the AI explained. "Minor correction. This is the forty-second iteration of this part of the universe's timeline. The majority of the original timeline remains unchanged. Spacetime from approximately four-point-one-three-one-nine-seven Earth years ago is still in flux. Shifts from paradoxical eddies are still settling since the Progenitors vanished and you acquired the prime mover."

I strained all my neurons trying to understand. Somehow, I managed a coherent reply. "Okay, I think I followed that, but on the off chance I didn't, why don't you say all of that again, but like you're teaching a first grader."

"Simplification. The original Dakota Adams acquired the prime mover and used it to make future corrections that led to the destabilization of time lines, post Progenitor disappearance. This destabilization has been slowly settling over forty-one iterations of Dakotas jumping back in time, trying to alter fates. Hence, you are the forty-second iteration of Dakota Adams."

"I died? No, wait. You can't possibly know that, even if it was true."

"Erroneous assumption. I am Progenitor. My extra-dimensional existence is not subject to the flux of this universe's spacetime."

"I don't want to rain on anybody's parade, but right now, we've got a massive Nodari invasion to avoid," Jack said, coming up behind me and squeezing my shoulder. "So I say we skip the lesson in quantum time travel and get right to the part where we take off and get the hell out of here."

I blew out a puff of air and nodded while trying to refocus. As I did, I gently removed Jack's hand from my body. "Agreed. So, if it's all the same to you, Mister AI, what do you say we get this ship moving, get our friends, and blast out of here so we can continue our conversation where there are a few less Nodari trying to eat us."

"Patience. Diagnostic procedures are still running. Estimated time until completion is approximately one hundred and eighty-two thousand, three-hundred and fifty-four-point-seven-six milli-seconds. I have put the countdown timer on display for you on the monitor above."

Jainon growled. "Why the hell are we trusting anything this thing says?"

"There is precisely zero correlation between trust in me and your ability to launch this ship."

"I don't think he's bluffing," Tolby grumbled.

"I am not."

I dug my nail into my scalp and wished a thousand wishes I had Taz or a lucky elephant to rub. The *ashidasashi* had run off again, and I still didn't have a replacement plastic pachyderm. Maybe I could make one out of spit or something on the floor. Or hell, blood. That was a little grim, and probably carried with it the penalty of dark magic, but it's not like we didn't have ample amounts of it leaking from all of us.

"When your diagnostics finish, then we can take off?" I asked, trying to remain upbeat.

"Erroneous assumption. Diagnostic completion will allow me to determine what faulty systems need repair. I am detecting at least one."

I slumped in the seat. "Please tell me it's only an oil filter," I said as I rubbed my temples. "Or don't, actually. You guys are probably so 'advanced' you put the oil filter in the most inaccessible location that requires the entire engine to be dismounted and removed before removing six panels and three radiators to get to it. Right?"

Jack chuckled. "You seem rather bitter for a hypothetical."

"Let's just say I'm sick of not being able to do basic maintenance on my own ship anymore," I said with a heavy sigh.

"Funny," Tolby said. "You don't seem to mind me doing the work."

"That's because you love it."

"Which only goes so far."

"And because you love me," I added.

"And don't you forget it."

"Hey, AI guy," I said, sitting back up in my chair. "What do we call you?"

"Indifference. I need no designation as it is not necessary to differentiate me from others. I am the Progenitor ships' AI."

"Right, the ship's AI," I said. "But what about the others? How do you tell each of you apart? Surely they call you something."

"Erroneous statement. I am not the ship's AI. The ships' AI."

My forehead hit the palm of my hand as I struggled to understand why we were butting heads on the obvious. "Didn't I just say that?"

"Clarification for basic lifeform's understanding. I'm not the AI for this ship. I'm the AI for all ships. My size defies your comprehension, and my whereabouts are beyond your understanding."

"You're in every ship the Progenitors made?"

"A crude understanding, but yes."

"So...you're the Alpha and the Omega of AI, is that what you're telling me?"

"That is an adequate view of my role."

"Fine. I'm calling you AO, then," I said. I drummed my fingers on my leg as a thought came to me. "Can you fly all the other ships here and wipe out the Nodari for us?"

"No," he said. "The majority of Progenitor ships are no longer in existence. The others are offline, and their whereabouts are unknown to me. They will require in-person reactivation before use."

"How do we do that?" Jack asked.

"The same way you reactivated this one, by interfacing with the systems and turning them on."

I glanced at the monitor showing the diagnostics. While the timer was less than a minute from hitting zero, there seemed to be a laundry list of ship systems that needed some sort of preventative maintenance. At least, that's how I took the list because I sure as hell wasn't about to entertain the idea that each one of those components needed rebuilding or replacement.

Our comm crackled to life. "Tolby? Tolby, can you read me? We can't make it to the hangar."

Everyone perked at the sound of Yseri's broken and stressed voice. Throughout the background on her end, we could hear the sounds of heavy fighting. My gut tightened every time I heard the rhythmic thuds of a Kibnali heavy weapon presumably ripping into the Nodari line, and I couldn't help but cringe at the constant sounds of acidic goo hissing nearby. And then there were the explosions and the Nodari roars, and the yells of Kibnali screaming out for the wounded to be evacuated.

"We've secured the Progenitor ship," Tolby said. I know he was trying to sound optimistic for her sake, but I could hear the stress in his voice. I'm sure she could as well. "Hold on a little bit longer, and we'll pick you up. We're only waiting for the diagnostics to finish."

"Inaja still grants us her favor, I see," Empress said, joining the line. She grunted, and there was a frightening roar that was followed by a cacophony of plasma fire. "By the gods, that was close," she said, panting. "I think I have a few seconds. Can you repeat that last bit? You're on your way soon?"

"Affirmative," Tolby said. "We'll be on our way, soon."

"Outstand—"

Another explosion sounded that was followed by countless Kibnali yelling at each other over the renewed sounds of combat.

"Empress? Yseri? What's going on?" Tolby yelled as his claws dug into his side.

"We're in retreat," Empress said. "I'll call when we're clear."

The line cut out, and Tolby growled as the hair bristled across his body.

"She knows what she's doing," I said softly.

A rapid beeping from the diagnostic screen grabbed our attention and halted the conversation. "Scan complete," AO said.

"Propulsion systems offline until fission plug and hyperclutch assembly is returned."

"Returned? Why was it missing in the first place?"

"Prior to Progenitor disappearance, they had removed it to rebuild core components and add additional upgrades. It was never reinstalled."

As he spoke, the wireframe of the ship faded away and was replaced by a diagram of the needed components. Thankfully, AO had provided a silhouette of a person to compare it with, and the entire thing looked to be about two meters long. It reminded me of a manual transmission box from the 5th century PHS, but with a lot more complicated moving parts and a number of plugs coming out one end.

"Okay, okay, okay," I said, trying to remain calm. "At least we don't have to repair it, right? We just grab it, plug it in, and we're done. I don't suppose it's in a nearby footlocker?"

"Affirmative. Fission clutch assembly is in the hangar's workshop."

"And where is that?"

"Estimating. Two hundred and eighty-seven-point-fifteen meters east-northeast of this position. It weighs almost five hundred kilograms. I suggest your Kibnali companions go and retrieve it."

Tolby grunted and gestured toward the door with his tail. "Jainon. We need to move. There's no time to lose."

"While they are gone, I will upgrade your implants for better interface capabilities."

"That sounds handy," I said. "Let's do it. Unless that means you scrambling my brain like that artifact did. Then I'll pass."

"Unfounded worries. Your rudimentary brain will be able to handle such upgrades with ease," he said. "Now sit back and relax. This will only take a moment."

A thin wire descended toward me from the ceiling, curving through the air like a snake coming down from a branch. In a single, swift motion, it stuck itself into my right forearm and burrowed through a few centimeters. Surprisingly, I didn't feel it pierce my skin, but within a few seconds, my muscles started to twitch involuntarily. At first it was just a simple clenching and unclenching of my hand that looked odd more than anything, but as time progressed, the contractions hurt more and more.

To distract myself from what was going on, I decided to dig into the past—specifically, I decided to dig into my past. "You said I'm the forty-second iteration, right?"

"Correct."

"What happened to the other forty-one?"

"They died."

I chuckled and threw a nervous glance at Jack and Daphne. "Well, I mean, yeah, right? No one's immortal. I do hope I had a good run in a few of those, yes?"

"No."

"No?"

"By your standards, you did not have a good run in any of them."

I shot up in my chair and winced as a jolt of electric pain shot in my arm. "What? Why the hell not? What was I doing?"

"Please hold still," he said.

The contractions in my arm intensified until they had to be only a step below labor pains. At that point, the needle retracted, the pain vanished, and I found myself clutching the armrests while sweat dripped from my brow. "I thought that wasn't supposed to hurt," I said.

"Faulty assumption. I said to sit back and relax. I said nothing about pain levels."

"That was still misleading," I said, rubbing my arm. I bit my lower lip and hesitated to follow up on what we had been talking about only moments ago. In the end, I decided I had to know. If I didn't, there was no way my imagination wouldn't be a thousand times worse than whatever he would say. "What was I doing in all those iterations?"

"Trying to atone for your sin."

"Sins? What sins?"

"Erroneous question. Not sins. Sin. Singular. One act."

My mouth dried, and my throat tightened. "Which was?"

"Eradication of the Kibnali species."

"You mean I keep dying trying to save it from the Nodari after those little backstabbing drones screwed us all?" I said, feeling the color drain from my face and my stomach growing queasy. I wondered if the other Dakotas had asked that question. Maybe they didn't, and thus never knew the odds that were stacked against them. Or maybe they did, and they went to their graves never seeing home again.

"Incorrect assumption and conclusion. You were created specifically to bring about the Nodari invasion, and to that end, you were a great success."

CHAPTER TWENTY: ORIGINAL SIN

I was made to do what?"

"You were one of many found at an early age and implanted with the desire to find and use Progenitor technology so you would eventually come back to this planet and open the webway, thereby enabling the Nodari invasion," AO said. "The drones were one of many tools to accomplish that task, but you were the primary one."

"But...but...why?" I stammered. "Why do you want to kill them all?"

"Details will be provided once we are safely away," he said. "Standby for takeoff."

A deep reverberation raced through the ship. Lights became stronger and brighter, and a myriad of systems sprang to life both around us and on the holographic display. Immediately, I leaped out of the chair. "What are you doing?"

"Leaving."

"But you said the ship needed repairs!"

"I lied."

I grabbed my carbine and pointed it at the console. "Stand down right now and let them back on or I'll blow you apart."

"I do not care if you destroy this console. If you wish to stay here and die with your friends, that is your choice," he said. "Those who created your role in all of this saw fit to ensure your return to your homeworld since you are merely a pawn in the Kibnali–Progenitor war. Consider this extraction as payment, and thanks for your unwitting service."

"Dakota? What's happening in there?" Tolby asked, sounding rightfully panicked.

"This stupid AI is trying to leave you!"

"Well, don't let it!"

"I'm not!" I said, madly pushing buttons on the console. Menus flipped. Lights blinked. I even got a few beeps and boops out of them, but the only thing I wanted—a landed ship—I did not get.

"Recommendation: Strapping in would be beneficial to your health. This ship is capable of accelerating to such a degree that your bones will be pulverized if you choose not to."

"I don't want it accelerating at all! I want you to land!" I yelled, still mashing everything that looked like a button, switch, or pilot input. Somewhere in my madness, I glanced to Jack, who was standing there dumbfounded. "Do something!"

"What?"

"Anything!"

So he did. He slammed his hand on his console. Lights flickered across it, and AO chuckled. "You humans are amusing. I wonder—"

AO's holographic image suddenly distorted before disappearing altogether. The lights in the cabin went out, and the ship dropped a couple meters, smashing into the hangar with a deafening thud that also managed to toss me out of the chair.

As jarring as that was, at least we didn't have to stay in total darkness forever. Daphne switched on a floodlight housed in her body that offered more than enough illumination to see what was going on. Or at least, not to trip over ourselves.

"Okay, whatever button you hit, remember which one it was in case we need it again," I said as I pushed myself off the floor. Gingerly, I touched my hand to my face and winced as it came back bloody. "How bad is the lip?"

"Looks like you took a nice right cross by a heavyweight champ," he said.

"Dakota, what's going on in there?" Tolby asked. "Let us in!"

"If I knew how I would," I replied, looking around. Everything in the cockpit was still off. "Jack hit something, and it all came crashing down."

"I suggest you find whatever it was and unhit it so we can get out of here," he said. "It won't take long before the Nodari get in here."

Before I could reply, AO's hologram flickered back to life. Only, it wasn't AO at all. What came back was a white, vaguely humanlike, cloudy form. Though I've never believed in ghosts up until that point, as soon as it spoke, I was a believer from that point on.

"Da-da-da-da-kota," it said in a very broken, unevenly timed manner that sounded like a digitized version of my own voice. "If you are hearing th-th-th-this recording, we ha-ha-have successfully disabled...AI and prevented-ed-ed-ed-ed...leaving. Ship systems will b-b-b-b-be restarted in th-th-thirty seconds. Integrity...severely d-d-d-damaged. Instructions to restore...are contained...are contained...are contained...are contained...From a-a-a-all of us Dakotas who c-c-came before you, good luck, and g-g-g-g-give our love to T—"

At that point, the hologram disintegrated, leaving Jack and me to stare at each other in confusion.

"Was that...was that you? I mean like, you from before? All the yous that psycho AI Progenitor guy was talking about?" he asked, sounding as if merely speaking the words would have him tossed into an asylum.

My brow dropped as I tossed the idea around in my head. How was that possible? But if it wasn't, who else could it be? "Okay, so, that had to be me, or me's. Or whatever, right?" I asked. "Apparently, I left instructions for myself to restore something somewhere. Do you see a manual lying around, by chance?"

Jack glanced around and snorted. "There's nothing in here but us. This place is clean as a whistle."

I groaned. He was right. Old Me's didn't leave anything behind here, or at least, nothing they did managed to stay here. "Hang on a sec," I said as a thought dawned on me. "They said instructions were contained in something, right? Not just sitting around."

"Yeah, and?"

"Well, we have something that contains instructions for almost everything," I beamed. "Daphne, you're the little speed reader of the group. What's in the archive cube?"

"Instructions for how to restore the ship systems," she said merrily. "I found them precisely two-point-two seconds before you asked the question. Quite an ingenious place to put them, don't you think? Or maybe they were always there. Either way, kudos to you for telling yourself where they were."

I sucked in a breath and tensed. "And can we do whatever it is that needs to be done? Because I really, really would like to be gone by the time the Nodari get into the hangar."

"Hopefully," she replied. "I'm downloading the software to restore critical systems."

"Does this mean we're going to get AO back?"

Daphne laughed. "Heavens no. I get to take over AO's responsibilities," she beamed. "Isn't that wonderful?"

"You? How?"

"Thanks to Okabe's interface device, I can upload myself into the network once the system is back on," she explained. "Once power is back on, I'll have access to most of the basic functions, at which point I'll let you guys out so you can get to work. But to get access to the rest of the ship's functions—not to mention be able to take off—I'll need you to replace a part that's shorted out. Apparently, the Old Yous managed one hell of a clever sabotage to get rid of AO without completely destroying the ship."

I sighed heavily. "Please tell me this is going to be simple."

"Does needing a new dorsal subatomic charm relay chamber sound simple?" she asked. "Because if so, you're in luck. Maybe rubbing that abricadabri's belly was worth it."

"*Ashidasashi*," I corrected. My upper lip curled on one side as I thought about what she said. "This dorsal whatchamacallit it...do we have a spare onboard?"

"No. There is no spare dorsal subatomic charm relay chamber onboard."

"Well then where do we get one?"

"There's a lab on the other side of the art gallery on the ninth floor," she said. "You should be able to pick up a spare in its storage room."

"Should?" I repeated, feeling panic rise in my chest. "Don't you think we should have a better lead than that with all those things running around?"

"You haven't even heard the best part," she said, sounding upbeat.

My fingers found my temples and started giving them a message. "I don't know what you're about to say, but I know for a fact whatever you think is the best part is going to be the exact opposite."

"You don't think that getting to tour the ninth floor while the Nodari flood the halls of the art gallery is exciting?"

"Why would that be exciting, Daphne? It sounds like a great way to get killed!"

"True, but the ninth floor has the best exhibits," she said. "Or the worst? Best of the worst? Or worst of the best? I'm not entirely sure how to translate this part of the records as they're fragmented. But regardless, I do know that floor is the most popular, so you ought to have a wonderful time seeing things no other human has or ever will. You should want to go more than anything."

"Honestly, Daphne, I'd rather not go at all. I only want to leave."

"Pffft. You'll never get any awards and plaques for exploration with that attitude," she said. "Think of it as more material for your book tour—"

"Which I'll never go on if I wind up dead!"

"In which case, I'll be sure to see that your awards are given posthumously," she said. "I'm already keeping a long list of things to do on behalf of your estate. Adding this to that won't be much more trouble." Before she could say another word, the ship's engine thrummed back to life, and the interior lights to the cockpit came back on. "Oh, look! Everything's coming back on, sort of. I'll lower the ramp, and you all can get moving."

"I'm not thrilled about this either," Jack said, dropping a hand on my shoulder. "But I'm even less thrilled sitting here in a broken ship. We've got to do what we've got to do."

"Yeah...yeah I know."

He then threw a wry grin at me and spoke words that eased some worry in my soul. "Besides, we're going to have a pair of giant space marine kitties with us. We'll be fine."

I smiled at that. "Yeah. Seems Tolby and Jainon are good to have around when we need a little extra protection."

Tolby burst through the door with Jainon right on his heels. On his face he wore a mix of controlled rage and tremendous worry. "Are you okay?"

"Yeah," I said. "But we've got to get a part for the ship."

"What are you talking about?" he asked. "What sort of part?"

"Okay, long story short," I said, taking in a deep breath. "No, check that. That's still too long. Short, short version: A bunch of Old Me's sabotaged the AI, broke the dorsal sub something or other..."

"—dorsal subatomic charm relay chamber," Daphne filled in.

"Yeah, that, and there's a replacement on the ninth floor past the art gallery."

"I take it we need it," Jainon said.

"Only if we want to leave," I replied.

"And to live," Daphne added.

"Then there's no time to waste," Tolby said, shaking his head. "We need to go. Now."

"I know! I know! I was about to, but...there's something I need to do first," I said. I glanced left and right, hoping that Taz was around for a good belly rub so I could really stack the odds in our favor. Sadly, he wasn't. "Oh, man. Really?"

"Really what?" asked Jack.

"Taz is still gone. How am I supposed to rub his belly when he's off superpositioning all over the galaxy?"

"I have no idea. We'll have to do without."

"No. We need some super luck."

"We *need* to fix this ship!" Jack said as he grabbed my arm and pulled.

"Hey! Let go!" I said, shrugging him off. "We're not fixing anything without some super luck!"

"Dakota—"

I silenced him with a glare before turning to Tolby. "Hey, bud. Help me out. Tell him what's what."

Tolby sighed. I know he was pretending to humor me for Jack's sake, but I still wish he wouldn't have been like that. "Let her do her thing," he said. "Sometimes you have to work with what you've got."

"I find your lack of faith seriously disturbing," I said, knitting my brow. "I'll make you all believers soon enough."

"You will, will you?" Jack asked, raising an eyebrow. "Because I'm not seeing a Taz or a lucky elephant anywhere you can use."

"I know, but I can fix that." I quickly swabbed the inside of my busted lip with my finger and drew on the floor. Now I know some people might think it's bad mojo to dip into dark blood magic—and it is—but you have to remember, I was offsetting that bad mojo with the blessings of the tiny pachyderm. In essence, the net was a positive gain. Or so I told myself.

"What are you doing?" Jack asked.

"Making a lucky elephant to rub," I replied.

"With blood. You're literally finger-painting with your blood to draw an elephant."

"I'm not going to argue with you about it," I said, finishing my painting. "My old lucky elephant saved my life more times than I can count. Don't disrespect the pachyderm."

"Looks more like a mutant pig by Picasso."

"Mister Oinker is going to save our bacon," I replied. "And he's an elephant."

"Says the girl calling him Mister Oinker."

"I do." With that, I vigorously rubbed my drawing five times before patting his head and tummy, and then pretending to grab his arms while doing a little mini dance. With the ultra-super-lucky ritual complete, I turned to Tolby. "All right," I said with a smile. "Let's do it."

CHAPTER TWENTY-ONE:
THE NINTH FLOOR

The four of us darted out of the ship and sped across the hangar at Daphne's direction. We ducked into an adjoining cargo bay. On one side were a handful of pods, yellow and egg-shaped. Most floated in neat rows and inside a giant shelving system. A few, however, rested near a half dozen transit tubes maybe a half meter in diameter that sped off into different directions. On the other side were more tubes, considerably smaller, which ran vertically, as well as a set of double doors leading to a turbolift.

I immediately ran to said lift and worked a nearby console mounted into the wall. "Come on. Come on," I said, trying to bring it to life, but to no avail. "Why isn't this working?"

"Have you tried kicking it?" Jack asked, the corner of his mouth drawing back.

I drove the ball of my foot into the bottom of the wall. Nothing. "Yeah. I have," I said. "Now what?"

"So much for Mister Oinker."

I narrowed my eyes and pursed my lips. "Keep it up, and he's not going to save you at all."

"There must be another way to the ninth floor," Tolby said. "I suggest we find it."

"There are many," Daphne chimed in. "However, they all involve leaving the way we first came in. Due to the relatively high density of Nodari lifeforms occupying the space beyond the blast door, I would advise against such course of action."

"I'm going to go ahead and veto any ideas that suggest we should," I said.

"Seconded," Tolby said.

Jainon nudged me with a paw before flicking her claw over my shoulder. "What about those vertical tubes? Perhaps we can use them?"

"Jack and I would barely fit," I said. "There's no way either of you could."

"Two looking for a part is better than none," she replied.

Off in the distance, the muted sound of a Nodari captain roaring lit a fire in my pants and accentuated her point. "Well, Daphne? Can we use these tubes? I'm assuming they're for cargo transport, too."

"Let me check the schematics on hand," she said. Thankfully, she continued to live up to being the speed reader of the group, and we didn't have to wait but a heartbeat. "Well will you look at that. They do eventually get to the ninth floor. After you use them, you should be able to follow the signs to exhibit IL-965, which is connected to the CDL. That's the lab where you'll find the part we need."

"Do they work?" I asked, ever hopeful.

"The signs? I would expect so," Daphne said. "Takes a lot to break them, you know?"

"Wait, what? No, I mean the cargo pods, Daphne! Why on Mars would I ever ask about the signs?"

"Seems like a good question to me," she replied. "What if they didn't work? Then what would you do?"

I groaned. "That's the dumbest—okay, fine. Whatever. Yes, the signs were a good question, too. Now what about the cargo pods. Do they work? Or rather, do the transport tubes work?"

"They should," she said. "Check the other console. It's on the opposite side of the room from the elevator."

I dashed over, ignoring the Yet Another™ roar by a Nodari captain as best I could. It sounded as if it were a little bit farther away, so that was good. Or at least, I convinced myself that was the case.

"All right, Mister Oinker, do your stuff," I said once I reached the console and tried to connect with it. Unlike the first console, this one sprang to life. When it did, I cheered with delight. A broken, pixelated menu popped up, but despite its malfunction, it was both readable and useable. And that was all that mattered. After a few pushes of some buttons, a pair of slender cargo pods raced down the tubes and stopped at their loading stations. Once there, they each opened, revealing enough space for me and Jack to climb in.

At that point, I folded my arms and shot Jack a look of pure smug. "You were saying about Mister Oinker?"

"Lucky," he replied with a huff.

"Duh," I said, hurrying over to the pods. I climbed in the one on the left, and once inside, I looked to Jainon. "They're all set. Can you hit the launch key?"

"Of course," she replied, going to the controls. "Though I hope for your sake they don't launch you too quickly. It would be a shame for you to have come this far only to be pulverized by a transport mishap."

"I set it to fragile," I said. "At least I think I did."

The high priestess drew back her lips into one of her characteristic smiles that was both amused and fierce. "Only one way to find out," she said. "Good luck."

Before the conversation had a chance to go any further, she planted her left paw on the console. The lids to our pods snapped shut with a click and hiss and then rocketed upward with such force I'm pretty sure my skull touched my ankles.

The pods raced through what had to be kilometers of twisting, looping tunnels, or maybe it just felt like that since my heart was pounding a million beats a minute. I love rollercoasters, don't get me wrong, and had this actually been a proper one, I guarantee it would've earned at a solid four Super Vortexes (minus one vortex for the cramped space), but since I couldn't see a damn thing, it was a pretty awful ride.

I guess I should be glad I don't get motion sick all that easy, swimming through wormholes aside.

At least the stop was halfway decent. When we got to the ninth-floor exhibition area, the pod slowed drastically and came to a cushiony stop. Getting out was relatively simple, as the lid popped open with a gentle push. When I stepped out, however, the room I was in kept spinning and I ended up crashing against the pod to avoid falling altogether.

"I vote we get the elevator working for the trip back," Jack said. With one hand, he leaned against a nearby blue wall, and with the other, he rubbed both temples. "Either that, or we need to find the stairs."

"Sign me up for either because I'd rather not do that again." I sucked in a breath, steadied myself, and then made a quick check of the area to ensure no Nodari were lurking about. It was at that point I realized the room we were in was decorated in six parts dark, three parts gloom, and two parts creepy vibe. Thanks to the single overhead light, the only things I could really see were myself, Jack, and a few nearby cargo pods other than our own.

"Well this could get ugly, fast," Jack said, sharing my thoughts. "Hey, Daphne, any chance you know where the lights are in this place?"

Silence.

"Daphne?" he repeated.

We exchanged nervous glances. Then I gave it a try. "Daphne?" Lumps of fear grew in my throat as I tried the others. "Tolby? Jainon?"

Still nothing.

I fidgeted with my gun. "They're okay. Right? I mean, they're probably just not answering so we aren't distracted by their upbeat conversations or something."

"That's one theory," Jack said warily.

"You know, there are plenty of studies that show a strong correlation with being a Gloomy Gus and an increase in bad luck," I said.

Jack laughed. "Oh there are, are there?"

"Yes."

"Name one."

"Well...there's...um..." I stammered as I counted on my fingers, hoping the act would spark my memory. "Or was it the...? Or maybe...?"

Jack raised an eyebrow.

"Look! We're way too busy for me to properly cite all my sources," I said, throwing up my hands. "We're supposed to be getting a dorsal sub thingy."

"Dorsal subatomic charm relay chamber."

"Yep. That's the one," I said. "Now quit arguing and help me light up the place."

At that point, I turned my attention to my gun and looked for the button that turned on the under-barrel flashlight. It only took a second to find the little bugger, and Jack found his as well. The beams shone like the sun, a surprising and welcomed trait. I quickly put the extra light to good use and swept the area.

I almost wish I hadn't.

At first, my light only revealed more cargo pods neatly arranged against the walls of a mini-warehouse with the occasional support column thrown in for good measure and one fork-lift-looking thing toward the far end. However, off to our left, hanging upside down from a ceiling conduit was this nightmare amalgam of flesh and tech—and I don't mean in the Nodari sense. More like the Frankenstein sense.

The creature immediately dropped from its perch and landed on the floor. It stood—barely—on a pair of twisted legs and dragged a rat-like cybernetic tail behind it. One set of metallic arms came out of its hips, and one of the hands attached to said arms cradled its bloated belly. Its torso looked emaciated from the ribs up, and two fleshy arms hung limply from the shoulders by its neck. A pair of misshapen heads sprouted from the neck, but they were not separate. They were fused together, one looking mostly to the front with a set of hollowed, glowing red eyes, while the other was turned to the side and had its jaw hanging open.

"What the hell is that?" Jack asked, weapon up, eyes as wide as mine.

"I have no idea," I said, readying my blaster. "Do we shoot it?"

The monster took an unsteady step toward us before bursting into a full head-on charge, screeching like a banshee as it came.

Jack and I fired without hesitation. If there was ever a sport for inflicting the most collateral damage, I'd be an Olympic champion. Hell, I'd hold the record for the next thousand years, easy. Wonder what sort of endorsement deals I could get for that?

Anywho, I blew apart cargo pods, tore chunks out of the floor and walls, and even exploded a power junction box I didn't know existed until it the fireworks started.

Jack's shots were a little more disciplined—okay, a lot more—but despite the fact that his plasma bolts flew directly at the thing's head and chest, not a one hit home. Before any could strike, the creature seemed to freeze in place, as if hit by the pause button on a universal remote, before disappearing altogether.

"Where'd it go?" I said, stepping back. Though I was unsure what had happened, I had the presence of mind not to stand there like a complete idiot and do nothing. I've seen enough horror movies to know that if some terrifying monster wants to use you as a refresher course in human dissection, you never assume it's gone, let alone dead, until you've personally strapped it to a fifty-megaton nuke and hurled it into the sun.

I spun to the right and spotted the thing a couple dozen meters away. Again it screeched and ran toward us, and again I fired madly, only to have it disappear once more.

"Again?" Jack whispered as he pushed his back against mine. "How the hell do we kill it?"

"I have no idea, but I'm thinking standing here is a really, really bad idea."

"Agreed. On my lead then. We'll shuffle for the exit."

I swallowed, nodded, and followed. My eyes scanned the area over and over, desperate to find any sign of the monster before it got up close and personal with us. I nearly jumped through the roof when Jack yelled a string of curses as he fired a half dozen shots. I twisted my head over my shoulder to steal a glance at what was going on when he turned and grabbed my forearm.

"Come on, let's go," he said, giving me a solid tug.

I spun on the balls of my feet and took off running, Jack a half step ahead. We bolted through the warehouse, his light shining on the exit, while mine swept our flanks. It felt like cotton balls filled my mouth, and my ears filled with the sounds of frantic flight.

Ten paces away from the exit, the damn thing materialized right in front of us, lunging forward with all four arms.

Instinctively, I shot out my hand and knocked the thing in the head with a telekinetic punch. It staggered backward, and that apparently was enough to hamper whatever defenses it had, because when Jack opened fire once more, he chewed it to pieces. Plasma bolts ripped through its two heads and chest, leaving smoldering holes in their wake.

It dropped to the floor and twitched a few times before going still, at which point, Jack popped a few more shots into it. "If that doesn't do it, I'm calling shenanigans on life," he said with a nervous chuckle.

I forced a weary smile. "You and me both."

"What do you think that was?"

I shook my head and started for the exit. "Trying not to."

"Trying, but not succeeding?"

"Yeah," I replied with a heavy sigh. My imagination raced with all the possibilities. Was it another type of Nodari? Possibly. Probably. That, of course, meant bad news because if one was here, more undoubtedly were as well—or would be soon. The idea it was something else, however, wasn't too appealing either, as the warnings Tolby gave when we first got here about how the Kibnali settled on worlds were everything tried to kill you came crashing to the forefront of my mind. "I really wish Tolby were here."

"You've got me at least," he said as we eased through the doorway and a dark hall. "Seems like we make a half-decent team."

I smiled, genuinely, and then even more so when I couldn't resist the tease. "Eh. I guess. I mean, you're no three-meter space kitty. I guess you'll have to do for now."

"Wow. Thanks."

"Anytime," I replied. I let the conversation drop for a few moments as we hurried through the corridor as fast as we dared. Along the way, we found signs that directed us to IL-965, but those signs weren't enough to distract my imagination. Because of that, my thoughts quickly filled the void with images of the monster from the warehouse.

"Any chance you see a light switch?" I asked.

"Chance? Yes," he said. "Do I? No."

"Could we talk about something then to keep me semi-sane."

"I think we'd best stay focused and quiet."

I sucked in a breath to try and steel my nerves, but that didn't help. My knees felt weak, and my hands couldn't find a comfortable grip on my gun. "Yeah, that's not going to happen," I said after a moment. "Let's face it. I'm no space marine."

Jack chuckled. "Okay, well, what do you want to talk about?"

"I don't know," I said after checking behind us for the umpteenth time. "Something. Anything."

"I see...So, Dakota...do you come here often?"

I laughed. Hard. "No, but I did have a smashingly great time at a Progenitor museum not long ago."

"The Museum of Natural Time?"

I nodded. "That's the one. Ever been?"

"Love that place. Heard it went under."

"Something about a rat infestation."

"That does tend to drive off guests," he replied. "The reactor meltdown probably didn't help anything either. I mean, you can't charge full price with rads off the chart and expect people to come."

We paused our chitchat at a T-junction. A nearby sign directed us left, and thus we quickly went that way.

"New question," Jack said. "Who's your childhood hero?"

"Who's yours?"

"Robin Hood," he replied.

I grinned. "Funny, you never struck me as the type to rob from the rich and give to the poor."

He waited a moment for us to pass through and sweep clear another doorway before replying. "I am if you consider the rich as old dead people who have no use for their buried treasure, and I'm simply giving back to the poor."

"Mm-hmm," I said. "Somehow I doubt you donate your finds to charity."

"I never said to charity," he said, laughing. "I said to the poor, and compared to many, I'm quite poor."

"Touché."

"Your turn."

"Sarah Dekker," I answered without a moment's hesitation.

"Who?"

"Sarah Dekker?" I paused when I realized that the woman had been born a couple of hundred years after Jack had gone missing. "Oh, never mind. She's just one of the most famous and brave explorers that humanity has ever produced. I was kind of obsessed as a kid with her."

"What did she do?"

"What didn't she do?" I said with a laugh. "First person to walk from the Padatane desert to the Gelgori ocean, and the first woman to shoot her craft between orbiting binary stars."

Jack nodded, and his voice filled with respect. "Impressive. I guess you liking her makes sense, being a thrill seeker and all."

"The thrill-seeking part is a bonus, as far as I'm concerned," I said. "What she's most famous for is being the one who discovered an ancient Ontore derelict ship in the middle of the Cigni dust cloud that held more artifacts than all the existing pieces in every museum combined. As soon as I learned about her, she's who I wanted to be. While I did grow out of the wearing-her-clothes phase, I never stopped wearing my hair as she did and never will."

"Ah, gotcha," he said. "Another piece of the Dakota puzzle falls into place."

"My hairstyle that much of a quandary for you?"

Jack threw me an amused look. "No, but I assumed you were being practical and weren't modeling yourself after your childhood hero. Did you dye it, too?"

"No," I said, slumping a little. "She was a redhead, so I didn't go all out. I don't like being fake. That's why I never went the cyber upgrade route."

"Except for your arm," he rightly pointed out.

"Being able to manipulate spacetime trumped personal preference on that one," I said.

At that point, we reached a large set of sliding double doors. On one side, there was a plaque that read IL-965, and on the other, there was a console embedded into the wall. Not expecting much, I tapped the screen. It flickered to life, giving off a light blue glow and low buzzing noise as it did.

"That's promising," Jack said. As I worked, he flatted his back against the wall and kept watch over our rear.

I whipped through the menus, and after a few seconds, I made one last tap and watched in utter joy as not only did the entire area light up, but the doors to the exhibit slid open. "Negative," I said with no small amount of boasting in my voice. "*That* is not promising. *That* is the power of the lucky elephant."

CHAPTER TWENTY-TWO:
THE EXHIBIT OF BAD ART

When you get to be an intergalactic way famous xenoarchae-ologist and a treasure hunter such as myself, you tend to see a lot of weird stuff. And I mean, *weird*. Okay, maybe I'm not intergalactically famous yet, keyword being yet, but I've definitely earned my spot in the upper echelon after all I've been through as of late. Even if one doesn't count everything I saw at the Museum of Natural Time, I've stumbled upon finds and customs that would leave anyone but the most seasoned traveler baffled.

This one time, I touched down on Nuntani Prime, a single planet orbiting a long-forgotten star in the Mu Quadrant, and came across a race of psilocybin-like creatures who were barely out of their Bronze Age.

Right, I know what you're thinking. Dakota, that's not strange at all. Fair enough. But get a load of this: they loved making sofa mazes. And I mean *loved*. L-O-V-E-D. *LOVED*.

It was freaking pathological.

Enter a living room? Sofa maze.

Stroll down a hall? Sofa maze.

Need to get to the butterfly garden to enjoy some tea? That was at least three sofa mazes you'd need to get by.

Stranger yet, they weren't gigantic pieces of furniture either, or even ones stacked upon one another. That meant if you wanted, you could easily crawl across the top, but if you did that, you committed an unspeakable act of blasphemy in the eyes of their priests. If you did that, you'd better have immediate evac available—or a three-meter-tall best bud full of fang and claw at your side—otherwise, there was an extremely high risk that you were going to be the main course during the next ritual dinner of atonement.

Weird, right?

That's only the tip of the proverbial iceberg of things I've seen.

There was this one time when Tolby and I were chasing down lead to find the Star of Santar. If you're not familiar with that, it was a priceless neckless that had been lost when it's owner, Rebecca Freeman, wandered off into the jungles of Otta IV and never returned. Naturally, there were tons of conspiracy theories surrounding the events, some of which had nuggets of truth to them Tolby and I used to direct our expedition.

Though we never found the necklace, we did uncover her final resting place. About three hundred kilometers south-southwest of our original starting point, we discovered a tiny wooden house that she'd built along the banks of a hidden pool, deep inside the jungle. As best we could tell, she lived the rest of her life there, whittling a plethora of cute, lobster-monkey figurines before dying at the ripe old age of eighty-something. Her personal bot, Stanley, buried her before shutting down.

Anyway, that's all backdrop to the weird part. The really weird part was her tiny house had no less than one hundred and fifty-three pictures of Magic Williams—you know, the fitness guru who was entirely too happy throughout all his workout videos to not be absolutely insane? The guy who'd break down in blubbering tears every time he caught wind of someone choosing not to eat that one extra nibble of chocolate? Yeah, that guy.

Not only did she have over a gross of pictures of that weirdo, but those pictures were all arranged on the same wall, making a giant arch with some sort of incense burner and shrine in the middle that held a single inscription: *I know why the waffles left.*

I'll give you twenty cred on the spot if you figure that one out.

Anyway, neither of those, nor anything else I'd ever seen, had prepared me for the amount of utter, total weird that was inside the exhibit we'd entered. I really should've paid more attention to the Kibnali soldiers' remarks when we first arrived at the art gallery, because then maybe I wouldn't have been so dumbfounded at all.

"A glorious and mindful tribute to the worst art that has ever been created this side of the Eastern Universal ridgeline," Jack said as he read from the top of a colorful brochure that he'd picked up a moment ago.

As he spoke, my eyes remained locked on the first exhibit on our left. It was an array of small tools about the size of my arm, each one looking like a bizarre cross between a hedge trimmer and a can opener. Glued on their tops were several googly eyes, all different colors, and on their sides, somebody had stuck in wire arms that branched out into four-fingered hands. "An Ode to My Stomach," I said, reading the plaque nearby.

"What does that have to do with anyone's stomach?" Jack asked.

"Like I should know," I replied, shaking my head.

It only got worse from there. We hurried through the exhibit, trying to reach our goal as quickly as we could. Along the way we saw a myriad of...well, pardon my crudeness here, but crap. And no, I don't mean actual feces, because I do know there have been "risqué" artists from time to time who try to work with the medium. I simply mean art that is beyond god-awful. Worse, it wasn't the type of awful it actually turned out to be good, or was so bad it was fun to look at. All of it either led me to shake my head in disbelief or turn away with a cringe, completely embarrassed for whoever had created the work in question.

A few dishonorable examples were as follows: about halfway through the exhibit, we came across an intestinal bouncy house castle. I think it was supposed to bring attention to an irritated bowel in a fun, nonconventional way, but all it did was make my stomach squeamish and make Jack gag a few times. A little before that, there were some poorly drawn stick figures in a cartoon that tried to discuss the moral complications of using tap water at night, which simply left me scratching my head. And last, and certainly not least, we came across an abstract painting that I thought had been made of charcoal at first, but it turned out to be made from the ashes of the artist's left leg when he cut it off and burned it. Talk about gross.

We also went by cubes of garbage, empty pedestals of wood, and some quote-unquote musical performance pieces that sounded about half as good as nails on a chalkboard. I wouldn't call them dishonorable mentions, obviously, but they were good examples of what filled the place.

The absolute winner, at least in terms of shock, was an empty stasis tube. It stood a little over two meters tall, with clear, rounded walls, and delicate machinery on both its top and bottom. Attached to its side was a small holographic projector that displayed an image of the monster we'd run into when we first got to this floor.

"That thing was in here?" Jack said. "Why?"

"*Be the Discount. Be the Dragon. Let Your Birthday Sing,*" I said, reading the info panel on the other side. "Okay, I have no idea. This has to be a joke. Right?"

"I'm going out on a limb and saying 'no,'" Jack said. "I mean, if this section is the worst of the worst when it comes to art, it makes sense that none of it makes sense."

"Yeah. I guess. But how did it get out?" I asked. "Or even better, why does this wing exist in the first place?"

"Not following."

"What I mean is, if the art gallery was meant for the Progenitor staff, wouldn't they want something...I don't know, better to look at? Or at least more impressive than junk."

Jack shrugged. "True, but right now, I'm thinking a better use of our time would be getting that part and getting the hell out of here."

I couldn't argue with him on that, and I knew the answer to my question could wait. We hurried over to the doors that led to the CDL. Not surprisingly, they were closed, but the console on the right was both powered on and helpful. Getting to it to open the doors turned out to be simple, too, which wasn't surprising given I clearly had the power of both Taz and the lucky elephant to look out for me.

With a friendly beep, the doors slid open. Before we could step through, Daphne's voice cut through the line. "Dakota?" she asked. "Can you hear me?"

I jumped with excitement. "Yes! What happened? Is everything okay back there?"

"We're fine for the moment, but I'm not sure how much longer that moment will last—Nodari invasion and all," she said. "I cut communications when I realized we were being monitored. I didn't want to reinitiate contact until I could be sure this line was secure."

"Monitored?" I echoed. Jack and I exchanged nervous looks. "By who?"

"Not who. What," she said. "AO's facility counterpart, maybe? Or perhaps AO himself?"

"Whatever it was, it must have let our friend back out," Jack said. His hands nervously readjusted their grip on his weapon, and his eyes kept scanning the area.

"Can't be good, regardless," I said.

"Probably not," Daphne said. "But there is a bright side."

Knowing Daphne, I couldn't help but roll my eyes. "I seriously doubt that."

"That's rude. You don't even know what I'm going to say."

"With you, your bright side rarely is."

"Well, Miss Frumpy Pants, I was going to say that I've calculated that due to the presence of this mysterious force, there's a 98.9897 percent chance you'll get some extra cardio in for the day. And you know what they say about extra cardio, don't you? Exercise gives you endorphins. Endorphins make you happy, and happy people—"

"Are not in our shoes," I finished.

"They could be," she said. "It's all about perspective. I bet if you were more grateful for what you have, you'd feel much better about all of this."

"I'd feel much better if none of this were happening, actually," I said. "What makes you so sure about all this anyway?"

"I hacked some of the facility's monitors," she said. "Remember those Nodari that were trying to ram their way in here?"

"Yes..." I said. My face scrunched as I took in a sharp breath. "Are they headed here now?"

"Haha. Don't be silly. They're still trying to get into the hangar."

I exhaled sharply, and my shoulders fell. "Oh, thank god."

"They do, however, have friends who are headed your way," she said. "Depending on how long a few fire doors hold, they'll be joining you between five and eight minutes."

I rubbed my hands together to expel some of my nerves. "Five to eight minutes, huh?" I said. "We'll be long gone before that."

"You sure?" Jack asked.

"Very," I replied as I gestured to the open door. "Shall we?"

Jack smiled. "Thought you'd never ask."

Together, we zipped through the door and ran down a forty-meter-long hall with vaulted ceilings. Running along one side of the corridor were large bundles of conduits while on the other, small ventilation shafts had been placed about every three meters. Despite the relatively short distance that we went, by the time we reached the other end, I swear the temperature had dropped fifty degrees.

"What is this place again?" I asked, teeth chattering. "The CDL, right? What's that stand for?"

"Nothing of importance," Daphne said. "Just ignore it all and hit the first room on the left. I'm reading that the part we need is in bin 22-A. You can grab it and be back on your merry little way in no time."

The tip of my finger stopped a photon's width away from the console to the final door. "Why are you talking like that?"

"Like what?"

"Like your hiding something."

"Not hiding anything at all. Only looking out for your well-being. And ours, too, for that matter."

My finger withdrew. My eyes darted to Jack who only threw up a shrug. "Daphne..."

"I promised Tolby I wouldn't say, and a promise is a promise."

I threw her a disbelieving snort. "Yeah, right. He'd never keep me in the dark."

"Unless what was in that lab was something that would..." Jack's voice trailed.

"Would what?"

"Would make you be...well...you..."

I cocked my head and bit my lower lip for a hot moment before their combined words took on some semblance of meaning. In a flash, I hammered the door controls, and it slid painfully slow to the side. Unwilling to wait the five seconds it probably would have taken for it to allow easy access, I rammed myself through the hole. I had no idea what they were keeping from me, but I knew it had to be awesome. Probably a wee bit dangerous, too, given their apprehension, but like that was going to stop me. Risk and I were on friendly terms, or at least, we had each other on speed dial.

Anywho, once through the door, I found myself inside a massive octagonal room. Along each wall were three doorways, twenty-four in total, each one leading into a considerably smaller area that looked like some sort of testing lab. At the center of the room stood a giant, mechanical spire. It jutted out of the floor and reached all the way to the ceiling, some four stories up. At least a hundred thick bundles of cables shot out of its sides, some running along the walls while others clung to the ceiling. Several monitors had been placed on it as well, most surrounded by a myriad of controls I knew I'd have no hope of learning. All of them, save one, were dark.

Movement caught my eye, and I spun to the left, my weapon following. To my utter shock, I saw KN-C pressed against a far corner, his pupil wide and iris pulsating a bright yellow. I'd honestly never seen a droid so terrified in my life. I was sure he was about to bust a half dozen gaskets.

"Sympathetic plea! I beg of you, don't shoot!" the little backstabber wailed. "This was all KN-B's idea, I swear!"

The shock I'd experienced immediately gave way to burning hate. My finger twitched against the trigger, and it was all I could do not to blast him apart. "You lied to me!" I yelled. "You lied and all those Kibnali died because of it!"

"I didn't lie! I—" He cut himself off and dropped a few centimeters. "Yes. Much regret. I lied. But I had to!"

I stepped forward. "Shut up! You didn't have to do anything!"

"I did! I did!" he cried. "They all threatened me with such immense suffering, and I'm weak. So very, very weak."

His admission surprised me, and it was probably the only thing that saved his life in that split second. "Give me one good reason I shouldn't kill you," I growled. Before he could answer, I shook my head and amended that statement. "No. Not one. Three. Give me three good reasons why I should let you live."

"Because I'm innocent!" KN-C begged.

"Not in my eyes."

"And I did try and save you, too," he added. "Remember? I said 'this is the part where you run.' I was trying to warn you without them knowing."

Jack appeared at my side. "Dakota," he said. "Those Nodari are still headed this way."

"I know."

"Then stop listening to him," he said. "Blast him. Leave him. I don't care which you do, but we can't stick around."

My eyes narrowed as my weapon's sights crystalized on my target.

"Wait!" he shrieked. "I can help you! The prime mover is inside the main storage!"

My head cocked. "You mean Jakpep?"

"Yes! That's what he likes to call himself now!" he said. "He's locked away here in the Chrono Displacement Labs' vault, but I can teach you how to hack the locks. Then you can take him and fix anything you want. His ability to make portals wherever and whenever you—"

I squeezed the trigger. A single plasma bolt flew from my gun and struck him a hair above his pupil. The shot blew through his fragile body, sending a shower of electronics and bright sparks in all directions. His body crashed to the floor, and flames sputtered out of the entry and exit holes.

CHAPTER TWENTY-THREE: A NEW OLD FRIEND

Cripes, Dakota," Jack said, laughing and shaking his head. "Why did you do that? I mean, I'm glad and all, but I didn't think you would."

"He was lying about helping us," I said, not moving a muscle and trying to rein in my anger. "All the others warned me never to take Jakpep—never to try and fix things with him. Curator. Master of Records. They all said it would lead to disaster, and it almost did. But not him...not him..."

Jack eased in front of me. His face softened and wore a pained look. "You okay?"

His words took me out of whatever hate-induced fog I was in, and I realized my eyes were leaking. A lot. Nose, too.

"Yeah," I said, clearing my eyes and sniffing a couple of times to get things under control. "I just—I just want to make things right, you know?"

"I know," he said. He then slapped my shoulder. "Let's find this part so we can go home."

I nodded, and he took off for the storage room Daphne had said it would be in. I followed, sorta, but I didn't go far. I slowed to a stop, and my eyes drifted back to the giant spire thing in the center of the room.

"Daphne," I said. "Can you hear me?"

"Affirmative," she replied. "I've been listening the entire time."

"Yeah, I assumed," I said. "Is this big spire thing the main vault?"

"Nope."

"What is it then?"

"It stores all the planet's number fours," she said. "Terrible, terrible thing, especially for people like you who can't stand that particular digit. It's so terrible, if I were you, I'd stay far, far away. In fact, I'd stay so far away, I'd forget it even existed."

"Sounds like good advice."

"You're going to look, aren't you?"

I wiped my nose on the back of my arm and grinned. "What do you think?"

"I think Tolby is going to be very upset with you if you do. Even more so if you get eaten."

"He loves me," I said. "He won't stay mad for long."

And he would, I told myself. He would. That said, I did honestly feel a little guilty about abusing the friendship right then and there, but damn, what if it was the vault? What if Jakpep was actually inside the thing? Besides, taking a look wouldn't hurt with Jack going after the dorsal subatomic charm flipper doodad. I mean, it wouldn't take two of us to pop open one measly little storage bin.

I ran over to the only working console. Although it had no obvious signs of outward interface, that didn't bother me since most Progenitor computers seemed to lack them. Using my implants, I made the mental connection with ease and smiled broadly when I heard the pop inside my head.

"All right, baby, show me the Jakpep," I said, bouncing on the balls of my feet. My energy levels dropped considerably when the screen displayed a single line of text before I felt the disconnect in my mind:

Unauthorized Access.

"No, no, I'm very much authorized," I argued. I tried connecting again. And although I was successful in plugging back in—briefly—I was greeted with the same message.

"Come on," I griped. My hands gripped the sides of the monitor, and I kicked the bottom of the spire for good measure.

"I don't mean to second-guess your overall strategy, but we are working against the clock," Daphne said. "Perhaps you would enjoy a sense of wonderment for the rest of your life by not finding out what's inside."

I rolled my eyes and sighed. "No. What I'd like is a hacking routine to get in here. KN-C said I had one. Can you figure out what he was talking about?"

In an instant, my arm tingled, and my eyes darted back toward the screen. The unauthorized access message flickered before giving way to a series of concentric rings, each one having a few little spikey things coming off it.

I cocked my head, unsure what to make of this new development. Operating more out of instinct and curiosity, I reached out with my left hand, fingers splayed so they could touch multiple parts of the outer circle and gave it a spin.

To my delight, it rotated with my hand, and as it did, the ring beneath it spun a little more slowly to the opposite direction. I played with the screen for a few more seconds before I quickly realized that it was possible to have all the spikey things on one ring connect with the spikey things on the rings above and below as long as everything was rotated in the proper manner.

"Oh please, please, please, tell me this is my hacking minigame," I said with a renewed sense of hope. A dozen spins later, I had my answer.

And it was good.

Glory be to the lucky elephant, and may Taz be forever praised across the heavens. The screen flickered, went completely white, and then faded into a typical menu selection I'd seen a thousand times before when playing with the archive cube from the museum and other Progenitor computers.

Jack, panting, appeared at my side. In his hand he held a contraption that looked like the bizarre offspring of a coffeemaker and a cactus. "We can leave now," he said.

"Almost," I said, paging through the current screen I was on.

"What are you looking at?"

"Inventory of this place, or rather, looking for a way to open the vault."

"Leave it," he said. "There's no way that portal device is in there."

"I have to know," I said.

"Do you have to die, too?"

I tore my gaze away from the screen long enough to throw him what I hoped was a reassuring smile. "I know we're short on time, and I know that the portal device has been...problematic, but it's also saved our bacon," I said. "Please, trust me. I've got a good feeling about this."

He said something else, a few somethings actually, but I didn't catch it. I was too focused on what was in front of me. The experiments that they had been conducting here were dizzying, or at least I imagined they would be if I could understand any of them. Hell, their titles alone threatened to put my brain in a tailspin: *Depolarization of Ventral Synthetic Chrono Compressors and Their Effects on Temporal Membrane Alignment. Optimization of Nanowave Entanglers for Spacetime Collapse Engines. Quantum Dark Matter Fluctuations and How They Affect Co-dependence.* So on and so forth.

The worst part of all of it was, however, the inventory list was pretty much filled with the same gobbledygook. I worried that a lot of them were extravagant names for simple tools. For example, deep down I had the feeling that the "small range manual torque device" would end up being a basic wrench, and if I couldn't differentiate the truly awesome from the utterly mundane in short order, I'd use up whatever precious time we had to spare and end up dying on this rock—without my Viking funeral I might add.

"Two minutes, Dakota, before the Nodari arrive," Daphne said.

"And we're done," Jack said, pulling on my arm. "It's a long run back to the transport tubes."

I shrugged him off as I found the submenu that dealt with the contents inside the vault. Only one thing was listed:

Prime Mover (Prototype)

"Oh. My. God," I said. My heart pounded relentlessly in my chest, and no matter how fast I breathed, I never seemed to get enough air. "He was telling the truth. He was actually telling the truth."

"He was? But how? You nuked it."

I shook my head and laughed as I hammered the controls to open the storage area. "I have no idea," I said. "This must be where it was before we got it at the museum. Like, this is the young Jakpep or something."

A loud hiss and pop drew my attention, and off to the side, a single door popped open before sliding to the side. Billowing clouds poured out, like someone had dropped a chunk of dry ice into a hot tub. A metallic tray eased out next, and sitting on a cradle atop it was my portal device. Or, I guess what would be my portal device, come a few million years.

No, check that. I didn't have to wait that long at all. With an impish grin, I snatched the device from its stand. "Oh yeah, come here, you beautiful thing," I said. Goosebumps raised across my body, and thoughts of what this meant for all of us ran rampant through my mind. "We can go home," I said, staring at the device, happy tears running down my cheek. "We can actually go home."

"Not exactly," Daphne said, ruining the mood.

"Why not? It can open a portal anywhere—any*when*—I want."

"Your brain will not survive the calculation," she said. "So, unless you have a spare—no, check that, forgot to carry the one again—unless you have a spare eighty-eight on hand, you won't be able to time hop us back to the future. We'll still need a webway. Besides, Jakpep can't make a portal big enough for our ship, which I'm assuming you'll want."

"Doesn't that just—"

The door leading out opened with a hiss. Jack and I spun around and were greeted with a trio of Nodari scouts, each toting a large blaster in hand. The two of us bolted to either side, guns blazing. I peppered the walls, floors, and even the ceiling with hideous scorch marks that would've made any janitor irate. Jack, on the other hand, drilled the lead scout twice in the chest and once in the leg, causing it to drop. The other two jumped sideways and returned fire.

Tolby's voice suddenly joined the line. "Dakota! What's going on?"

"I'm getting shot at by those damn scouts!" I yelled.

"You can't fight them! Get out of there!"

"I *know,* Tolby! We're cut off!"

"Gah! Why didn't you listen to Daphne and just go?"

I peeked around the hunk of machinery I'd ended up behind and sent a few plasma bolts downrange. I didn't scratch a single Nodari, but at least I was close enough this time they ended up ducking back. "We're holding them off," I said. "I think."

"I'm coming," he said. "Don't play hero. Get somewhere safe and hunker down."

Jack, who was using the doorframe to a storage room as cover, snapped off a half dozen shots before being forced back himself. When the barrage sent his way stopped, he dared a glance and cursed. "Dakota, we're in trouble."

"Par for the course," I said with a bleak grin.

"No, I mean there's more coming," he said. "A lot more. We've got like ten seconds, tops, before this place turns into a Nodari mosh pit."

My mouth dried. There was no way we were blasting out of this. Then again, we didn't have to. I slung my weapon and mentally connected to the portal device. Again, the power of the lucky elephant combined with the ever-awesomeness of Taz made it so I hooked into the device without a single hiccup. It was like putting on an old, familiar glove.

"Tolby," I said, entering my time-hopping state of Zen. "Stay at the ship."

"But—"

"Trust me, Tolby. We'll be fine. I don't need you getting hurt." As I finished, alien symbols appeared in my vision as my mind bathed in the Progenitor formulas needed to create the portals I so desperately desired.

"Dakota!" Jack yelled.

My eyes flickered to the side. Two Nodari scouts barreled toward me. The first dropped when Jack blew apart its head. The second stumbled when follow-up shots knocked its weapon from its hands and drilled into its hip. But the thing kept coming, losing only a stride.

It reared back two of its arms to take my head off with one well-placed strike. In another life, I would've been absolutely petrified—back when I was a slave to time's whims.

Not anymore.

With a half meter separating the Nodari and me, I calmly dropped a portal at my feet and popped out in the storage room by Jack.

"Cripes, I forgot how disorienting that can be," I said, laughing and stumbling into the wall.

Jack fired off a few more shots before darting inside and hammering the controls so the door slid shut and locked. "I'm not sure if I'm elated or terrified you've got that again," he said with a nervous laugh.

Something hit the door with a thunderous clap, knocking Jack off of it and caving in several centimeters. The second blow furthered the dent. And after the third, the door had a sizeable split.

"Dakota get us out of here!" he said, firing madly through the crack.

I nodded, though I was already way ahead of him. I'd been in the process of mentally retracing the entire route we took to get here in order to make as accurate of a blind portal jump as I could. "A few more seconds," I said. Warm fuzzies surrounded me, and I could've sworn I heard the faint sounds of a music box playing in the background. The thought that this was the telltale sign of me about to scramble my brain did come to mind. But when the door exploded in a shower of shrapnel and sparks, it didn't matter.

I threw open a wormhole, and before I could say a word, Jack barreled us through.

CHAPTER TWENTY-FOUR: PICKING UP

A cold, unyielding floor rushed up to greet me, but instead of pancaking on that, my body used Jack's as a giant cushion. So that was nice. The wind flew from my lungs as I crashed into him, and I'm pretty sure I heard a couple of his ribs crack as well.

"Holy snort, that hurt," I said, rolling off him and onto all fours. Regardless of our less-than-stellar landing, I'd never been so glad to see the cockpit of a strange, alien ship. "Hot damn, it worked."

"Dakota!" Daphne exclaimed. "I'm so pleased to see you're alive."

"So am I," I said with welcome relief. "I told you guys Mister Oinker would come through. What do you have to say now, Jack?"

"Never...doubted him...for a second," Jack said, his voice strained.

He had such an unsettling tremor, I had to force myself to turn and look at him. I guess in the back of my mind, I was afraid he'd been impaled by something or caught a stray shot from a Nodari as we escaped and was now missing half a lung.

Thankfully, neither were the case. He lay flat on his back, eyes semi-shut, and one arm thrown across his midsection.

"Are you okay?"

"I'm breathing," he said. "I think."

I ignored the ache spreading across my shoulders and side and offered him a hand up. "Come on, you big baby," I said with a playful tease. "Let me help you up."

His eyes opened fully, and the corners of his mouth drew back. "I bet a kiss would go a long way."

My head went to the side, and I exhaled (though I might have been playing it up a little). "Still?"

"Still what?" he said with a wry grin. "You did land on me. Seems fair."

Tolby and Jainon burst into the cockpit. My big bud's eyes were wide with fright, but when he saw the portal device on the floor nearby, those eyes narrowed with anger. "You brought that *thing* back into our lives?"

"I prefer to think of it as rescued," I said.

"Dakota, you know what kind of trouble it brings! How could you?"

"Because we might need it," I said. "And as much as you hate it, it's the reason we're still alive."

"It's also the reason we've almost died multiple times," he said with a growl. "I say we toss it out the hatch right now. It's not worth the trouble."

"No!" I said, scooping it up and clutching it to my chest. "We might need it to get Empress and Yseri. We certainly can't leave it here where the Nodari could find it."

Tolby growled once more, though this time it was longer and deeper. "I don't like any of this," he finally said. "But perhaps you're right. Perhaps leaving it for the Nodari would end in disaster. Did you at least get what we need from the lab?"

"Here you go," Jack said, offering up the piece. "One dorsal subatomic charm relay chamber. But I hear the warranty on used parts is only five meters or five seconds, whichever comes first."

"Just my kind of bargain," Jainon said, taking it from him. "I've already got the old one out. I'll have this one installed in moments. Get us ready for takeoff."

With that, Jainon zipped out of the cockpit. I climbed into the pilot's seat, and Jack took the one to my left, while Tolby plopped his big furry bulk into a space directly behind me.

"Empress? Yseri?" I called out on the comm. "Can you hear me?"

"Yes," Empress replied. I could still hear the sounds of battle on her end of the line, but at least they didn't sound as if they were only a few meters away. "What is it?"

"Stay on the line," I said. "I'm going to have Daphne pinpoint your position so I can open a portal to you."

"On screen now," the AI replied.

"Here goes nothing," I said, using the display to orient myself to where Empress was in the real world. I then focused my mental energy on my portal device, but before I committed to it fully, I threw a glance to Jack. "Hey, if this liquifies my brain, it's on you to get us out of here."

Jack grinned. "Can I have your stuff, too?"

I grinned back. "You can fight Tolby for it."

I refocused on interfacing with Jakpep and went to work. The wall next to me distorted, and a beautiful wormhole with sharp edges and a faint, blue lining sprang to life. Through it, I saw Empress leaning against a wall. Her eyes lit up when they met mine. "I knew you—"

That's all she got out. The portal collapsed, and my arm felt cold and numb.

"Dakota!" Empress shouted over the comm. "What's going on?"

"I...I don't know," I said, shaking my head. I tried to open another portal, but all I got for my efforts was a massive brain freeze. "I can't get Jakpep to work. It's like he's completely drained."

"How's that possible?" Tolby asked.

"Going through the field notes now," Daphne said. "A moment."

We didn't have to wait even half of that. "I'm afraid to say Jakpep is still equipped with his original dry cell. According to what I'm looking at, they are non-rechargeable, only span five dimensions, and were great for testing purposes but not so much for continual fieldwork. The one you had used at the museum was much better."

"No kidding it was better. I want one those! Where do we get them?"

"Vennonti Fabrication Plant," she said. "Not sure where that is, but that's where they tapped into the peculiar energy-storage characteristics of Gorrianian resonance crystals to make them. Did you know you can jump-start a neutron star with one of those? Very handy if you've got a bag of marshmallows you want to roast."

"What does this mean for them?" asked Jack.

"It means you'll still have to pick us up the old-fashioned way," Empress said. An explosion blasted over the comm. She roared in response, and I heard the re-initiation of a tremendous firefight. "We'll be fine," she finally said after a few tense moments. "Get your ship airborne."

At that point, I realized I had my nails dug into the armrests and had to force them off. "Will do," I said. "Daphne, where's Jainon at with the repairs?"

"Nearly done."

"And how long till we can fly after that?"

"At most, a minute or two," she said. "I'm still having some trouble reconstructing system files and updating the system. Old Yous did a fantastic job destroying AO's ability to govern this ship, but it didn't make my job any easier, that's for certain. In the meantime, do you want to hear something interesting I found in the history files?"

"I'm not sure," I said warily. "Do I?"

"It's about you and your involvement in the Progenitor–Kibnali war."

"Even if she doesn't, I do," Tolby said.

"Lovely!" Daphne said. "Hmm. It's not the most palatable info I dug up, however. Maybe I should find a good way to phrase it."

"Spit it out already," I said.

"I know! I'll tell it like a fairytale," she said with liveliness. "Studies have shown that hearing about gruesome events such as mutilation, infanticide, and genocide in fairytale format can reduce stress levels by up to ninety—"

"Daphne!"

"Right," she said, chuckling. "Once upon an original timeline, the Kibnali invaded the Progenitor homeworld."

"Impossible," Tolby said. "We've never heard of them before."

"You'd see how possible it was if you'd let me finish," she scolded. "Now then, the Kibnali, being the apt warriors they were, had all but conquered the Progenitors a long time ago in a timeline far, far away. Just prior to their total defeat, the Progenitors developed portal technology, and a few hundred managed to escape to the other side of the universe. They ended up in a quaint galaxy regionally known as the Milky Way."

She paused a moment for dramatic effect and then continued. "Once portal technology had been mastered, they modified it to include time travel. Using that, they sent computers and robots through continued time loops to rapidly expand their knowledge about life, the universe, and everything. However, before they could go back and save their species—and wipe out their sworn furry feline enemies—the Big Oops happened."

"Let me guess. They wiped themselves out?" I asked.

"Oh, you've heard this story before?"

"I got the preview."

"Well, one of their researchers dropped a decimal somewhere, and long story short, after a big paradox backlash, the Progenitors were no more," she said. "In fact, they wiped themselves completely out of history, too, so when the timelines settled, the 'new' Kibnali never heard of them before because they were never encountered."

"Where do I come into all of this?" I asked. "This sounds like it could be more of a long story than a short one."

"If you account for all the time loops, it literally spans hundreds of billions of years," she said. "Maybe I should give the ultra-abridged version."

"Let's go with that," I agreed.

"Although the Progenitors disappeared, many of their robots and AI constructs survived who were programmed to finish their work," she said. "Unfortunately for them, they weren't able to actually use the webways due to Progenitor design. Thus, they went searching for unwitting accomplices they could lure and use over the course of many years to do their bidding. Yadda, yadda, yadda, they found you, Dakota, and marched you right into Adrestia and then here, to the Kibnali Empire, where you would open up a portal and let the Nodari fleet in."

"But if the Progenitors, or their robots, or whatever, were trying to kill all the Kibnali, why save some? Why not develop super nukes or super viruses or whatever and kill them before they even became a spacefaring race?"

"I told you, they couldn't use the webways," she explained. "Also, paradoxes precluded them doing anything drastic to the Kibnali until now. As for saving some, apparently, they needed a few Kibnali at the museum to get you to come here. It's all very complicated. Millions of years, tons of timelines. All that good stuff...Point is, in the end, they killed everyone. Oh, wait. That's not how you wanted this to end, is it? We're in fairytale mode." Daphne cleared her throat—well, made it sounded like she was clearing a throat. "And thus, when their work was done, everyone lived happily ever after."

"Screw that ending," I said with disgust.

"You don't want to live happily ever after?" asked Daphne.

"No, I mean screw the 'we're all dying' ending," I said. "We're rewriting that part."

"Damn right, we are," Tolby growled.

"If that's your plan, then I'm pleased to let you know Jainon has successfully installed the new dorsal subatomic charm relay chamber," Daphne said. "Systems are now online."

She'd no sooner finished those words than the consoles all around me sprang to life. Images of the hangar appeared on holographic displays along with a myriad of information about the current ship's status ranging from power levels to heading to engine start-up procedures. I grinned from ear to ear. "Does this mean everything's working?"

"In a sense."

"What you mean in a sense?"

"Jainon has properly installed the dorsal subatomic charm relay chamber, but I might have fudged a few things configuring the startup," she said. "But worry not. I'm reasonably sure we can still fly this thing."

My heart sank into my stomach, and my mind ran rampant with all the ways the Nodari would soon find a way into the hangar and overrun us if we couldn't get off the ground. "You fudged what exactly?"

"Oh, you know, silly things like control libraries and the erasure of a few dozen basic commands that may or may not be required to keep the ship from crashing. It's kind of funny when you think about it."

I shook my head and buried my face in my hands. This couldn't be happening, not when we were so close to escaping. "I fail to see how that's funny."

"As do I," Tolby added.

"Perhaps you two should think about it more."

"I would rather you fix what's wrong so we can be gone."

"Working on it now," she replied. "Please stand by."

"I've been standing by! And for the record, that's something I hate, hate, hate, HATE having to do!"

A massive explosion filled one of the holographic displays. When the smoke cleared, one of the side doors leading into the hangar about a hundred meters away was no more. Most of the wall, two meters in either direction, was gone as well. Then came a massive wave of Nodari swarmlings along with several Nodari scouts toting some impressive weaponry.

"Daphne! We need to get out of here!"

"You're going to have to learn some patience, missy," she said. "I still need to reconstruct some files. Until I do and can gain access to all prelaunch controls and diagnostic procedures, I can't sign off on a safe launch."

"I don't care about the stupid diagnostics! There's going to be a whole hell of a lot more wrong with this ship in about five seconds!"

Two pairs of controls materialized in front of Jack and me. They looked a lot like the control sticks that I used back when I had a ship of my own, although these had triggers built-in for my index and middle fingers.

"Weapon systems online," Daphne said. "Manual targeting is required."

Two targeting reticles appeared on screen, and it didn't take but a half second to realize each was tied to its own joystick. When they were each targeting the front line of the Nodari swarm, I pulled the trigger.

A loud buzz, like the biggest swarm of angriest giant bees you could ever imagine, filled the cockpit. Bright red shots ripped through the Nodari line. As they struck, chunks of swarmlings and scouts vaporized under a shower of sparks. I'd barely begun firing when Jack joined in, and thus between our four streams of Progenitor death, the Nodari fell in moments.

"Holy snort," I said, letting go of the trigger and staring in awe at the massive amounts of devastation we caused. There were body parts everywhere, and the hangar floor as well as the far wall that served as a backstop had a myriad of basketball-sized chunks torn out of them. "What the hell was that we just used?"

"Those were the four ventral, light rotary cannons," Daphne said. "I must say, I'm quite impressed. The data entry I found regarding them does not do their effectiveness justice."

"No kidding," I said.

"That could really turn the tide on the ground war," Tolby said. "We need to get airborne."

From the back of the ship, I could hear a dull thrum. The cockpit brightened considerably before we lifted a couple of meters off the ground. "Engines online. Maneuvering systems online. Flight controls online. Hangar doors now opening. You are cleared for launch."

The joysticks I had used to fight off the Nodari morphed. They lost their triggers, and the one on my left changed into a throttle that looked almost exactly like the one I had on my old Raptor. Pedals to spin the ship left and right even sprang up from the floorboard, but despite all that, I was leery to fly. "This is too weird," I said. "Can't you fly this thing instead? I'm having a hard time believing this is all set up just for me."

"Negative. Both automated and AI controls for piloting are missing from the system library," Daphne said. "This ship was designed to allow a human to return home after her service to the Progenitor scheme for revenge was complete. Said human is specially described as a human female, born on Mars, named

Dakota Adams, who loves exploring and drinking root beer floats, and who has a pathological need to be listened to and an unhealthy reliance on luck. There's also a small addendum that says she occasionally sings to her plants."

"I do not have a pathological need to be listened to," I countered.

"Except for when no one is paying you any attention," Tolby chimed in.

I glanced at Jack, expecting him to throw in his comments as well. The Cheshire grin he wore was all the reason I needed to scowl at him. "Don't."

"I can't believe you sing to your plants."

"Shush."

"Do you sing to them a lot?"

Tolby chuckled. "More than she'll admit."

"Okay, guys, really," I said. "We have more important things to do."

Jack straightened in his chair. "Does she sing them lullabies? Oh, god, tell me she does."

"I suppose they could count as such," Tolby replied with some thought. "They're mostly made up lyrics designed to make them feel better."

"You sing to your plants to make them feel better?"

"They get depressed, okay? And they don't judge me for being off-key unlike some people I know."

"Maybe that's why they're depressed," Jack said, laughing and shaking his head.

"Whatever." I rolled my shoulders and adjusted my grip on the controls. Gingerly, I used them to spin the ship in place, which I successfully did despite what others may say. I did *not* hit the hangar wall with the tip of our wing. That was turbulence, nothing more. And after a few moments, we were pointed squarely at the open hangar doors.

"All right," I said. "Buckle up. Let's go pick up some Kibnali."

Tolby had barely hopped into the third seat before I pushed the throttle all the way forward to its stop. In hindsight, that probably wasn't the best idea. We shot out of the hangar like a bolt on a railgun, and the only thing that kept us alive was the fact that it opened up into clear skies above and calm oceans below. Since we probably covered five klicks before I had a chance to peel my head off the headrest, had we been flying in mountains I'm sure we would've tunneled right through one in the most magnificent of fireballs.

I eased off the throttle and pulled back on the stick. We rocketed into the stratosphere until I jammed a pedal so we rolled over, and I put us into a corkscrew dive before pulling out to skim the water.

"Hot damn this thing can fly!" I yelled. "This is so much better than my old ship."

"It should be," Tolby said. He leaned forward and began using the console at his station. "Intuitive. I like it."

I put the ship into a few barrel rolls before looping around once more for the hell of it. "Man does this ever make me a happy warp bunny," I said, loving every minute. "I give this thing a solid five Super Vortexes."

"Oooh," Tolby said. "The elusive five-vortex rating."

"What can I say? I save it for the best."

Taz popped back into existence a split second later. Or rather, he popped back into our little locale of the universe from wherever he was before. I'm not really sure where he went, as he had something long, wet, and wiggling hanging out of his mouth, but he looked happy enough. And a happy *ashidasashi* meant a super lucky us.

Hell yeah. That's all the good omen I needed to know we'd have Empress and Yseri on board in no time and could put this whole nightmare ordeal far behind us.

"Hey, bud," I said to Tolby. "Can you get a readout on where we are?"

My giant furball flipped through some menus on screen before replying. "We're approximately a hundred kilometers southwest of the city."

"That far? Cripes, how did that happen?"

"Portal technology inside the facility, I suspect."

"As always," I said. "Can you raise the others?"

"Trying," Tolby said, working his comm.

Jack cleared his throat. "Maybe I'm questioning what's already obvious to everyone else here, but seeing how we're about to fly into a massive warzone where the Nodari have clearly established air superiority with their cruisers, what kind of defenses does this thing have?"

"Shield arrays are a mess," Daphne said. "I might be able to restore minimal functionality, but I suspect I will need a lot of time if not additional information on how the systems work in order to restore them to maximum operating capacity, assuming physical repairs aren't required."

I bit down on my lower lip and tried not to let my worry show too much on my face. We needed to stay upbeat and positive since we were going straight back into hell. "Okay, but that's all relative, right? I mean, minimal to the Progenitors has to be still godlike to the rest of us. Or at least demigod."

"I have no data on the shield's effectiveness," she said. "As such, I can only recommend that you avoid incoming fire at all costs."

Tolby put his paw over his ear. "This is Tol'Beahn, captain of the Royal Guard to the House Yari. Is someone on this channel?"

There was some chatter on the other side of the line I couldn't make out, but I had no doubt by the intense expression on Tolby's face that things were critical for whoever happened to be on the line. "Repeat again? Seven klicks south of the city?"

"What's going on?" I asked.

He held up a claw, nodding along. "Copy. Stand fast, brothers, we're on our way."

When the call ended, he looked up at me with fierceness in his eyes. "A few dozen marines are pinned down outside the city. They're requesting fire support."

"Oh we'll give them fire support, all right, and a whole lot more," I said, grinning. "Daphne, get ready with that ramp. We're going to come in hot for a pickup."

"Whoa!" Jack said. "We can't just scoop up Kibnali from battle."

"The hell we can't," I said.

"Have you forgotten we're running minimal shields? For all you know, a scout could sneeze on us and our engines could rupture."

"Then I guess you better be good on the trigger and shoot every last one that has even the slightest case of the sniffles."

"And what about all those issues you kept going on about going back in time to save dead people? You're going to make a paradox and blow us to hell."

I leaned forward and scratched the top of Taz's head, who was currently perched on my console. "See that? We'll be fine. Besides, we didn't go back in time to save these guys. We're here now and reacting to the situation."

"Dakota—" Jack hesitated a moment before throwing Tolby a wary glance and going on. "They're Kibnali. Old Kibnali. Old Kibnali who probably—and in a sense rightfully—blame you for this mess. What do you think is going to happen when they see you at the controls?"

I sucked in a deep breath and blew it out. Believe it or not, his words were precisely the reason why I was so intent on picking them up. They were old Kibnali, and I was responsible for not only the nightmare on this planet but for the genocide that was about to take place. I might not be able to stop it completely, but I sure as hell could save as many of them as possible and take them home. Such a thing might not earn me redemption in any of their eyes— and honestly, how could it—but I figured if there were a heaven and hell, at the very least I might redeem my soul enough to get out of a total eternity of torment.

Of course, that all assumed they even knew what was going on, which was up for debate. Somehow, I doubt each and every one of them got a detailed briefing of everything that had taken place.

The city crested the horizon, and even though we were still a long way away, I could see smoke rising in countless stacks all around. As troubling as that was, nothing quite compared to seeing the gaping wormhole in the sky, or more specifically, the swarm of Nodari ships that appeared to be on the verge of crossing the threshold.

"Jupiter's belts, they're practically knocking on the city door," I said. "Daphne, any chance you can get an ETA on when that fleet will be here?"

"Attempting," she said. "But this Progenitor ship has a few quirks to it, and the spacetime anomaly is making accurate predictions problematic. I will let you know when I do."

"I would like that info before they start shooting at us so I don't lose my mind," I said.

"Then for your mental health, I will avoid sending you the next status update," she replied.

I practically leaped out of my chair. "What?"

"I'm only following instructions," she said.

"Screw the instructions! Who's shooting at us?" My eyes scanned the visual displays but saw nothing other than the ocean below us and a war-ravged city ahead.

"Nodari fighters are speeding toward us at approximately eleven hundred kilometers per hour. They should be firing in five, four—"

A spray of lightning-blue bolts of energy zipped by the ship, a few deflecting off our forward shields.

"Oh," Daphne said with genuine surprise. "Looks like I didn't calibrate this correctly. You keep us from being destroyed. I'll tweak the sensors so we don't have that embarrassing mistake happen again."

A pair of Nodari fighters came at us, and they shot past in a brilliant streak. Jack yelled with devilish delight as he laid into them with the triggers. The buzz of our rotary blasters filled my ears, and streams of cannon fire leaped from our guns. Sadly, as much firepower as Jack leveled at the Nodari fighters, he didn't hit a single one of them. The two fighters broke away from the attack, each going wide to either side and curving back around toward us.

"Don't let them get on our tail," Tolby said.

"I know!" I said, pulling back on the stick and sending us rocketing upward once more.

Our ship lurched to the side after another spray of Nodari fire went by, harmlessly at first, but then the last several found our port stabilizer and punched a few neat holes into it. I only know the exact location because as soon as we were hit, the damage report flipped on screen.

"I hope we didn't need that too much," I said with a grimace.

"It will only be necessary to keep from crashing if the starboard stabilizer is destroyed," Daphne replied. "But since it isn't, you should be fine. So go, you, keeping that starboard area protected."

"I need you to bring us back around, Dakota," Jack said. "These guns have a limited arc."

I kicked the pedals so that we rolled completely over before pulling on the stick once again. My eyeballs pressed into their sockets, and I could feel the blood leaving my brain, making me feel lightheaded and woozy. The Nodari fighters were following us, at least as best they could. It was clear that although they were incredibly maneuverable, especially compared to what the Kibnali fielded for an air force, they couldn't match us in either speed or agility.

I picked out the fighter on the left arbitrarily and went after it. It dove back toward the ocean, and while I figured it was trying to bait us into following so that the other could get a shot, I decided to rely on our speed to bring it down before the others could catch up and followed.

My gamble paid off, much to my delight. Within a few heartbeats we could practically roast marshmallows on its exhaust.

"Eat it!" Jack yelled, squeezing the triggers again.

We were so close that there was no possible way he could have missed. Our shots struck the Nodari fighter's tail and then ran up the entire fuselage. Large chunks of metal and internals went flying, and sections of the ship exploded. A heartbeat later, what was left of the fighter spun out of control in a flaming wreck. I pulled into a gentle, climbing bank and watched it fall until it disappeared into the ocean.

"You would make any wing commander proud," Tolby said to the two of us, flashing an approving smile.

"Where's the other?"

"Struggling to keep up," Daphne said. "I'm starting to feel bad for it. This is clearly going to be a slaughter, provided you don't let it shoot at us again.

"No, I won't," I replied.

Now, I'll be the first to admit that I'm not an ace pilot, especially when it comes to dogfighting skills. But since I was strapped into literally the most advanced warship I'd ever dreamed of, I didn't have to be an ace. I didn't have to be good. I just had to not suck, and that was something I could do.

It took a couple of attempts, but I soon managed to bring our ship around and latched onto the Nodari's six. It weaved and rolled in all directions to try to throw us off its tail, but it didn't have a prayer. I eased off the throttle so we didn't overshoot, but instead made slow gains. When we were within no more than a hundred meters, Jack opened up on the craft. His shots sawed through its left wing, and like the first one, it went out of control and crashed into the ocean.

"I think we found your calling," Tolby said, laughing. "Now let's go get the others."

"On the way," I said.

One moment we were racing across the ocean, and the next we were over the rolling, grassy hills that lay just south of the city. It didn't take long to find the Kibnali who were calling for fire support. There were three or four dozen of them hunkered down in a slew of stone ruins. A laser light show went on between them and the hundreds of Nodari who had taken up positions on hilltops on three of the four sides.

I eased the throttle and slid our craft sideways until it had a magnificent view of one of the Nodari assault points. It was worse than I thought. While the hilltop had scores of Nodari grunts and a couple of summoners, there were hundreds of swarmlings gathering.

"Jack! Get them before it's too late!"

"I see them!" he called back.

Once again, Jack pulled his triggers and our rotary cannons sprang to life. The devastation he caused in the Nodari line was unbelievable. Their bodies vaporized under his withering fire, and what Nodari weren't immediately destroyed had their bodies shattered or limbs melted. They tried to fire back, but we were high enough, and I guess our shields were strong enough, that it didn't matter.

"Dakota, I am pleased to announce that I have recalibrated the sensors," Daphne said. "Isn't that exciting?"

"Yes, but we're a little busy shooting fish in a barrel," I said as I side-slipped the ship to the right and turned so Jack could get a better angle on the now-fleeing Nodari line.

"Well unless you pick up those Kibnali soon, it's going to be us who are the fish in a barrel," she said.

I tore my eyes away from the carnage that was happening below and checked the monitor that had been set to keep watch over the wormhole. Whereas before the Nodari hive fleet looked like a swarm of insects far away, now it looked like a seething mass of actual warships with one particularly large and nasty-looking one in the lead. "Oh damn," I said. "How long do we have?"

"Only a few minutes until the battleship gets here," Daphne said. "Scanners are reading it is at least three times as large as the two cruisers currently engaged in combat."

"Is there any good news?"

"Yes. It has enough firepower that we will be granted an instantaneous death should it bring its guns to bear on us."

CHAPTER TWENTY-FIVE: YSERI & THE EMPRESS

Tolby! Get ready to get your guys in here, ASAP!" I said, pushing the stick forward and plummeting us toward the ground.

Jack continued to fire as best he could, but given our rapid descent and our continued shifting angle, most of his shots went wide or high. That said, it seemed to be enough to keep the Nodari from moving in on the Kibnali forces.

We touched down about thirty meters south of the Kibnali position. My bones rattled with the impact, and I hope whatever shock absorbers and struts this thing had were more than enough to take the abuse I was throwing at it. "I really hope there wasn't anybody under us," I said with a cringe.

"Thankfully, Kibnali are more aware of their surroundings than you are," Tolby said, staggering out of his seat. "Daphne, open the ramp."

"Opening now."

Tolby raced out of the bridge, rifle in hand. I kept my hands on the controls, ready to get us the hell out of there. With my stomach in knots, I watched the outside monitors. At first, the Kibnali soldiers kept engaged with the Nodari. But then I saw a few of them lob a number of large canisters through the air. They hit the ground, and within seconds, thick, blue smoke poured out, completely obscuring anything and everything. As the smoke billowed in all directions and began to envelop the Kibnali hiding in the ruins, the warriors began a fighting retreat for our ship.

"Portside!" I yelled, pointing to the monitor as a Nodari captain crested the rise.

He lifted a massive bio cannon with two limbs and fired. The shell flew from the elongated barrel in a shallow arc and struck the ruins dead center. Stone and earth vanished in a dazzling explosion. I'm not sure how many Kibnali were killed because there was nothing left but a hollow crater with chunks of glowing debris.

What Kibnali I could see directed all of their combined fire onto the Nodari captain. Their shots skipped off an invisible shield and only served to draw his attention to them. It brought its cannon to bear, but Jack managed to fire first.

A heavy stream of rotary cannon fire poured into the monstrosity. Its personal shields flared a moment, sending arcs of lightning all around, and then collapsed altogether. Jack ripped apart its left side at the shoulder, sending it staggering back.

A high-pitched alarm blared in the cockpit, and Jack cursed several times over before slamming the bottom of his fist into the armrest. "Guns are overheated," he said, looking at me apologetically.

"That's not your fault," I said.

"No, but they've been overheated for a while," he said. "I might have hit the override."

"You hit the override? Why the hell did you do that?"

"Because they were shooting at us. Why else?"

"No, I mean...gah! We better not be touting around slag for barrels."

"Damage unknown," Daphne said. "Complete system reboot is in effect."

I opened a comm to Tolby. "Bud, what's the sitrep down there? Weapons are offline."

"Soldiers are loading now," he said. He paused for a moment as he rattled off a few shots and chuckled darkly. "Heh. Stupid scout."

I'm not sure if it was bad luck, or that the Nodari sensed our weakness. As soon as Tolby had finished, I glanced at the hilltops to see hundreds upon hundreds of swarmlings charging our position.

"Holy snort, that's a lot," I gasped.

Jack drummed his hands on his legs. "I think they're going to get here before our guns come back."

Nodari scouts and grunts followed the charge, and since the ruins were completely obscured by smoke and we were not, we were the ones that took the brunt of their fire. At first, our shields flickered white, but it wasn't long before that white started to take on more and more of a redshift.

"Daphne? Are our shields coming down?"

"I prefer to think of it as increasing airflow potential," she replied. "Very important for comfort and general well-being, you know."

"How is that increasing airflow potential?"

"With all the new holes in the ship that will undoubtedly soon follow, I would think the answer to be obvious."

I groaned. "Tolby, we're about to be Swiss cheese, bud. Tell me we can dust off."

"Two left," he replied.

I flipped the monitor to display a view looking out of the ramp. My bud was at the bottom along with a few others, and they were relentlessly firing at the incoming Nodari horde. They were clearly waiting for the other two, but with all the smoke, I couldn't see where they were.

The Nodari captain crested the hill once again. Apparently being half-dead meant that he was still half as deadly and more than capable of using his super cannon. He brought it to bear on our ship and fired. As before, the shot made a shallow arc, but thankfully, it didn't hit. It sailed wide and impacted somewhere behind us. Though we didn't suffer any damage, it was close enough that I saw Tolby and the other Kibnali security force reflexively duck for cover and bits of debris hit their backs and necks.

"Tolby, we can't wait much longer! Where are they?"

"I don't know, Dakota," he said. "I can't see through the smoke any better than you can."

"Punch it, Dakota," Jack said. "For all we know, they could be dead already."

The incoming Nodari fire seemed to intensify, and our shields seemed to be in a perpetual state of red. A couple of heartbeats later, large holes formed in the shell and then the shots began to rip into our fuselage and wings. Going by the readouts, the damage was negligible, but I knew it wouldn't take long for that to change, especially if the captain, who was readying his cannon once again, landed a shot on us.

"We've got to go, Tolby," I said. "Get in!"

"There's still—" He cut himself off, and in the display, I could see him shaking his head. I don't know what he said, but he shouted to the others and waved them in. The moment the last one's feet hit the ramp, I raised it up and swung the ship around. Hopefully, like most ships I'd ever known, the shield generators had at least been designed to handle forward and backward arcs separately, and thus I'd give our foes a relatively fresh section to shoot up.

The ship rocked forward with a tremendous explosion from the rear. Instinctively, I slammed the throttle as far as it would go and somehow managed to keep us from driving through the ground at the same time. As the ground raced beneath us, a new damage report came through with a single glaring red line:

Aft shields offline.

"At least it wasn't engines," I said with a nervous laugh. "Do we have guns yet?"

"Negative," Jack said.

I eased off the throttle and banked the ship into a gentle turn so that we would soon be headed back toward the city.

"Nodari battleship has crossed the threshold of the wormhole," Daphne announced. "According to onboard ship data, it should be within firing range of its main cannons in four minutes, assuming it takes note of us."

"Then I suggest everyone rub their lucky elephants so it doesn't take notice of us."

"Onboard ship libraries are without virtual pachyderms," Daphne said.

Tolby raced onto the bridge. His brow dropped, and his pupils had narrowed. It was a look I was unfamiliar with, despite how much time we spent together since we'd met.

"I had to go," I said, swallowing hard.

"I know," he replied before jumping into the last seat. "We need to get Empress and Yseri."

"Where are they?"

"Trying to raise them now," he said.

I kept the ship low and fast along the ground and in its sweeping arc, tensely waiting for him to raise them on his comm. I kept us deliberately a good way away from the city, thinking it was an excellent idea to let our shields rest as much as possible from any sort of fire and build back their strength. As I sat there waiting for Tolby to find Empress and Yseri, Jack shouted in triumph. "Guns back online," he said with an enthusiastic fist pump.

"All of them?" I dared to hope.

"Yeah," he said. "Looks like it."

"Good, try not to fry them again," I said with a grin. "I'm fond of having them around."

"...ota? Can you hear me?"

Yseri's voice was weak, and static crackled on the line, but hearing her speak lit a fire in my soul.

"We can hear you," Tolby said. "Where are you? A battleship has crossed into Kibnali space. We can't stay much more than a few minutes."

"The prefab plant on the north side," she replied. "But Empress isn't with me."

"Where is she?"

The answer to Tolby's question came swift and from the Empress herself. The transmission was stronger, but like Yseri, she, too, was clearly embroiled in the fighting. "Barracks, south side," she said.

A pair of triangles suddenly appeared on my HUD, one at each end of the city. "Locations marked accordingly," Daphne said. "These should be accurate within two meters."

"Outstanding," I said. I sucked in a breath before exhaling sharply and adjusting my grip on the controls. "Sit tight, you two. We can grab you both in less than a minute."

I banked hard, and then the display to my right flipped from showing system status readouts to a pixelated view of the battleship. From its belly, several triangular objects shot out, leaving bright orange streaks as they headed toward the planet.

"Multiple warheads detected," Daphne said.

"Warheads? What kind of warheads?"

"The kind that shatters continents," she replied. "Everyone who values the integrity of their bodies should take appropriate action. Estimated time to impact, two minutes, two seconds."

I shook my head in disbelief. "They're going to nuke everything?"

"Not everything," Daphne replied. "Their fleet will be safe from any mushroom clouds and associated blast waves."

"Why the hell would they do that? Aren't their own people or constructs or whatever the hell they are down there?"

"Goshun must be putting up enough of a fight that they want to end it quickly," Tolby said. "This wouldn't be the first time they nuked everything to end the battle."

"I thought you guys were the ones that did that, not them," Jack said.

"We only made the Last Act of Defiance when we were cornered on our homeworld and wanted retribution," Jainon explained. "The Nodari don't care if they blow themselves up. The fallen will rebuild and come back eventually, and far quicker than you would think possible."

"I was at Adrestia, remember?" Jack countered. "Not much can surprise me anymore when it comes to their regeneration capabilities."

Tolby growled, and I cursed under my breath, as I knew whatever he was going to say was going to be anything but good news. "Those warheads will never hit the ground," he said. "They will be air bursts to maximize the devastation."

"That would explain some of the readouts I'm getting," Daphne said. "Adjusting estimations to reflect time remaining until an escape must be made."

The countdown she had on screen flipped from a little under two minutes to less than thirty seconds. "What?" I said, leaning forward. "We've got thirty seconds to bug out?"

"Correct," she said. "This ship will not be able to accelerate fast enough to avoid the blast. Correction, you will not be able to withstand the acceleration that the ship is capable of that would be necessary to avoid the blast. Further correction, you will also not survive the sudden acceleration induced by the blast wave when it hits this ship, nor the immense transfer of energy."

"Get Empress," Yseri said, cutting into the conversation. "If one of us has to die, it will be me."

"Belay that order!" Empress shot back. "Dakota, you will pick up Yseri and save our Empire, do you understand?"

"Your Most High! I cannot allow that," Yseri said.

"It is not your decision!" Empress barked over the line. "Dakota, you've pledged yourself to the Kibnali Empire and to me. Do not abandon your oaths."

My mouth dried as my gaze fixed on the timer. I flew on autopilot, unable to decide. I heard Tolby and Jainon express their desires as well, or at least weigh in on the situation, but I was so detached trying to figure out what to do, their words passed through my ears. All I could think about was that stupid countdown and how unfair the positions was I was put in.

CHAPTER TWENTY-SIX: TO ORBIT

Dakota!" Tolby roared.

I snapped back into my seat. I didn't know what the right thing was to do, still, but I knew what I was being told by the one who I pledged my service to. All I could do was hope and pray Yseri would understand—that the others would, too. Maybe then after all that, I could come to peace with it myself.

Gah! Why couldn't I have been tasked with a more straightforward choice? Anything would've been better, except for trying to figure out why I'll keep checking the fridge as if food I want will magically appear.

"Stand by for extraction, Yseri," I said, my voice sounding unnaturally calm in my head. "On you in ten seconds."

"No!" she shouted. "I'll shoot myself if I must! Get Empress!"

"Then your death will be for nothing because I'm coming to you on her orders," I replied. "I am her fang and claw."

I threw a glance at Tolby, who nodded at me approvingly. Even Jainon, who wore a pained expression on her face, gave a slight nod as well. I pulled back on the throttle as we got to the south edge of town. The Nodari saturated the area and poured out of the buildings. Below, swarmlings ran through the streets, but they fell in great numbers to pockets of Kibnali resistance.

"On those guns, Jack!" I ordered as I brought the craft down and dropped the ramp.

The words weren't needed, and he relentlessly fired into any Nodari group he could see. Swarmlings and scouts vaporized under his fire, and chunks of buildings blew apart as he raked his stream of cannon fire into the Nodari taking cover in the Kibnali structures.

"Yseri, get in here, now!" Jainon yelled.

I glanced to the monitor and saw her dart out from one of the buildings. She ran with a limp and instead of the rifle she had had before, all she was armed with was a pistol that she used to pop shots off to both sides. A few of the Kibnali soldiers who we'd rescued earlier ran out and provided covering fire. I wasn't sure who or what they were shooting at given the plethora of targets, but the return fire from the Nodari was minimal, so they must've been effective.

As soon as Yseri and the other Kibnali started up the ramp, I had it raised. They were probably barely inside the belly of the ship when I pulled the nose up and started to go.

"You guys strapped in yet?" I called back.

The reply took several painful seconds. "We're good."

Those were all the words I needed to hear before pushing the throttle all the way to the stop. True, we had about three seconds to spare, but since Daphne had fudged calculations before, I wasn't about to trust it was completely accurate.

"We've got her, Empress," I said, knowing the matriarch would want to know. "Do you have any other wishes?"

Those last words put a lump in my throat, and as a monitor flipped to the rear display and showed the city shrinking behind us, I had a hard time focusing due to the tears in my eyes.

"No, Dakota," she said. "I am honored to have been a part of your life. You are my proudest *Ralakai*."

"May Inaja bless you with good fortune, Empress," Jainon said, her voice cracking.

"May her luck be your luck," the matriarch replied.

Jainon tried to eke out the rest, but her voice caught in her throat. All she got out was, "We will—"

And then the sky turned white.

Like a rowboat tossed at sea by an angry storm, our craft bounced through the air as the shockwave battered us around. I fought with the controls to keep us from crashing, and three times I overcorrected so much that we nearly drove through the planet's crust and ended up getting a tour of the mantle.

"God, that was too close," I said once I'd stabilized our flight.

"Maybe it's too early to be asking, but how are we getting home?" Jack said. "There's no way the webway survived that."

"This ship is equipped with hyperspace drives that operate on similar principals to our own, albeit much more efficiently," Daphne said. "Using them, we could travel to another Progenitor planet and—oh, will you look at that. Now that's something unexpected."

"There had better not be a fire in the engine room," I said.

"No, look," she replied as the status screen to my left switched. Whereas it had once been displaying ship information, it now had a chart of the immediate area for the solar system. The planet was clearly labeled, as were icons for the wormhole and the three Nodari ships, which were in low orbit. Beyond that were the two moons, which was expected, but on the far side of the outer one, four green triangles were on display, and said triangles were slowly closing in on the planet.

"More Nodari?" I said.

Jainon, who had a similar display showing at her station, manipulated the controls. "No. That's 39th Flotilla. The reinforcements Goshun sent for."

"Can they do anything?"

Jainon's ears went flat. "Doubtful. Originally, they were sent here to investigate when contact had been lost with the planet. They were never heard from again."

"But that was then," I said. "This is now. Like, a different now."

"They'll still be torn apart if they engage," Tolby said.

"When they engage," Jainon corrected. "They won't abandon those on the surface, especially since this is the first contact the Empire will have had with the Nodari. They won't know any better."

Frustrated, I gripped the controls. "But there's no one left on the surface!"

"Something, sadly, they are unaware of," Jainon replied.

"Can't we do something?" I asked, but deep in my gut, I had the dreadful feeling I already knew the answer.

"Yeah, Dakota, we can leave," Jack said, jumping in. When Tolby and Jainon shot him a glare, he didn't back down. "Look, I get it. I really do. Those are your kin. But let's be real. There's a massive Nodari fleet about to pop into this sector, and this isn't a hill I want to die on."

"We can't do nothing," I said. "Can we at least tell them to turn around? Put you onscreen to testify? Or all the other Kibnali marines for that matter we're toting around?"

"I'm happy to report that I should be able to fine-tune the comm system in approximately four minutes and forty-two seconds, give or take a few nanoseconds," Daphne replied.

Jainon checked the screen in front of her and hit a few of the controls to bring up more data on the situation. "They'll be in combat by then," she said. "Which means they won't last much longer than that, especially when the rest of the Nodari fleet comes through that wormhole."

"They won't warp out?" I asked. "Surely it won't take them long to realize the colony is nothing more than a crater."

"Nodari battleships have interdictor generators on them. Anyone caught in their field will be stuck in real space until the ship or those generators are destroyed," Tolby said.

"Can't they take down the battleship?" I asked. "I thought you guys had a kickass navy."

"We do," Tolby replied. "But it took several battles for us to make adjustments to our weapons for them to be effective."

"Look on the bright side," Daphne said. "You'll be able to have one last chat with your Kibnali friends before they die a glorious death worthy of any fleet. You can assure them their tale lives on for future generations to come."

Jainon pressed her lips together and growled. At first, I thought her reaction was directed at Daphne's accidentally insulting, cheerful tune, but I soon realized where it was really aimed. The Nodari. "Those generations are numbered," she said.

"As much as it pains me to say so, Jack is right," Tolby replied. "For whatever reason, the gods have set this upon us, and the flotilla will be lost. Furthermore, after having personally witnessed Dakota's gigantic mess she created at the museum trying to rewrite history, we're best to leave while we can."

"Hey! That wasn't my fault!"

Tolby raised an eyebrow.

"Okay, some of it was my fault," I said. "But you can't blame me for wanting to hop around time when a portal device literally ended up in my lap. It's not like it came with a warning label that said, 'do not hop spacetime.'"

"Curator warned you," Tolby replied.

"He wanted to die anyway," I said. "He doesn't count."

"Tour Guide also said not to."

"Okay, one guy did."

"And Master of Records," Tolby added.

"Yeah, well, he doesn't count either. He talked funny."

"Dakota, literally everyone we met who knew anything about that artifact said not to use it," Tolby said. "Regardless, saving the 39th Flotilla, even if we could, would be pointless in the war. It's an extreme risk with no gain."

For the next few moments, I stared at the scanners and watched the Kibnali ships approach the planet, clueless as to what they were about to get themselves into. My throat tightened. As much as I wanted to change the outcome of what happened here, I knew Tolby was ultimately correct. Even if our intervention didn't create a massive paradox backlash that sent our atoms scattering across the universe, saving those few ships that had been sent to investigate would never tip the balance of the war. The Nodari were legion.

"What if..." My voice trailed as my vague thoughts began to gel. I gnawed on my lower lip as my hands readjusted themselves on the controls.

"I know that look," Tolby said, sounding both wary and amused.

"As do I," Jainon said. "You have the warrior's spirit."

"Well someone fill me in, because apparently, I'm just a guy that doesn't know what everyone else is thinking," Jack said, throwing up his hands. "I'm not a mind reader."

"What if we save the fleet here and take them with us?" I asked. "History would still say they're lost, but they'd be safe with us in the future, back in the Milky Way."

Jack looked at me with more shock than if I'd hit him with a cattle prod hooked up to a fusion reactor. "Take them through the webway with us?"

"Why not?"

"Because they're Kibnali, Dakota!" he said, drawing looks of ire from both Tolby and Jainon. "Look, I'm not trying to rain on anyone's parade, and no offense to our reformed furry brethren, but you're talking about bringing warships crewed by the old guard, the Kibnali who sought to subjugate any and everyone, and that's assuming we even survive."

Nervously, I drummed my fingers on my leg. He did have a point. Then again, we were already toting around a platoon of elite Kibnali soldiers. I glanced at the monitors again, unsure of what to do. The only thing that was crystal clear was the fact that we were running out of time. "Future us will just have to deal with that later," I said. "Daphne, how long till we have comms?"

"Two minutes," she said. "They will be engaging the Nodari in half that."

I nodded and pushed the flight stick to the side, bringing our ship around. "Then I guess we better get to work," I said. "Tolby. Jainon. How do we take this battleship out?"

"With the rotary guns on this ship? I don't think we do," Tolby said. "Not before the rest of the hive fleet gets here, at least."

Hoping he was wrong, I looked to our bubbly AI for confirmation. "Any insights from ship records or the archive cube, Daphne?"

"Yes, I am pleased to report that Tolby's assessment is indeed accurate, but I'm also pleased to report that you have two other things at your disposal that may help."

"An antimatter cannon capable of vaporizing a small moon?"

"Oh, do they make those?" she replied. "That would be handy. Let me check. Hmm...that's not it. No...wait... Oh, never mind. Wait...wait...Yes! Score!"

"We do?"

"No, but I found something else that you're going to love," she said. "I would've noticed it sooner, but the code in here is a mess. Toilets look like radar arrays. Weapon controls look like the thermostat. And by the Planck—if I may steal some of Tolby's euphemisms—and I'm still not sure what this one thing does, other than it's definitely not the food replicator. Or the night light. Or the—"

"Out with it!"

"I'm pleased to say that the Progenitors who previously owned this ship had purchased an extended warranty," she replied. "Isn't that great?"

"That's not great, Daphne! That's stupid!" I shouted. "We don't have time for nonsense."

"You only think it's stupid," she said. "Do you know why they purchased it? Well, I'll tell you. They wanted extra coverage for the onboard portal device. Apparently, they were worried the lattice matrix might shatter and wanted the ability to bring it back to any pre-approved Progenitor repair shop and have it swapped out for free."

I perked. "We have a portal device built into the ship?"

"We do! Isn't that wonderful? I thought that would improve your mood."

"Why the hell didn't you tell me that before?"

"I told you, I'm still figuring out what everything does, and this was the first opportunity I had," she said. "The device has limited functionality, I'm afraid, compared to your handheld version. I believe the tech installed here was a precursor to Pakjep."

"You mean Jakpep," I corrected. "That was the name of the artifact at the museum."

"No, the records definitely say Pakjep," she said. Daphne chuckled. "Or maybe I'm dyslexic."

"Hey!" I said perking. "The one on this ship must've been the one I used before back in the facility!"

"When?" asked Jack.

"Right when the Nodari attacked," I said. "That stupid little drone said I should portal out of there, which didn't exactly make a lot of sense—even when I ended up teleporting back to the apartment. I must've tapped into the one here on the ship and bam! Of course, that doesn't explain why I wasn't able to use it again..."

"A combination of low batteries and range, I imagine," Daphne explained. "Also, according to the notes here, the onboard portal device can only form small wormholes capable of traversing limited amounts of real space."

I tilted my head. "Which means what, exactly?"

"It means you can effectively teleport about a thousand kilometers. Anything beyond that will be wildly inaccurate," she said.

"Well that's not too bad," I said. "Better than nothing."

"And there's no time traveling, either."

"Which is probably for the best," I replied.

Tolby grunted. "Definitely for the best."

"Also, the ship batteries only have enough stored power for three jumps. After that, they will take some time to recharge, which is why I suspect you weren't able to hop around like you were before," she added. "But combined with the other thing you have at your disposal, namely an entire platoon of Kibnali warriors, I estimate you have a decent chance at disabling the Nodari battleship's interdictor systems, thereby allowing the escape of all Kibnali ships."

"A boarding action?" Tolby asked, his face full of angst. "Even our most elite commandos rightly feared to do such things against their ships."

"Well, have fun with that," I said.

"I'm so glad you think it will be an enjoyable experience, Dakota, since you'll be the one making it," Daphne said.

"What? Me?" I said, sticking my index finger into my chest. "I've already done my space marine duty for my lifetime. Aside from the fact that I'll be way more of a liability than an asset, someone has to fly the ship."

"That someone can be Jack, as I've mirrored the controls as closely as I can to ships you two are familiar with," Daphne replied. "But unless you go with the party, I'm afraid we won't be able to use the portal device to extract the team since their location will be unknown."

I flopped back in the chair and blew out a puff of air. "Of course."

"We could ask for volunteers, Dakota," Jainon said. "No one would expect you to undertake such a high-risk assault, especially after all you've done."

I blanked out for a few seconds, but eventually, my eyes drifted over to Tolby. Oddly, or maybe not so much, he looked neither worried nor fearful. "You will always have my respect and admiration, no matter what you choose," he said. "But if you do go and do not return, know that I'll make sure the entire Universe never forgets the woman you've become."

I probably should've been more serious at that moment. But hey, if you've heard my story up until this point, you'd know that would never happen. "No, bud," I said, a grin slowly forming on my face. "If I don't make it out, what I want is a Viking funeral."

CHAPTER TWENTY-SEVEN: NAVAL BATTLE

Full steel ahead!" I said with a dramatic wave of my hand.

Jack, who recently acquired control of our ship, threw me a puzzled look. "I think you mean full steam ahead."

"No, full steel ahead," I replied. "You know, like you're driving your ship made of steel forward into battle."

"No, that's full steam ahead."

"It is not! What the hell kind of sense does full steam ahead make, anyway."

Jack smirked. "Pretty sure it's full steam ahead, as in the old steam engines."

"Pfft, show's what you know," I said with a dismissive wave of my hand. "They never used steam engines out in space. That's ridiculous. It wouldn't even work."

"Not in space, Dakota, on the water," he explained. "As in what they used after they progressed from sails."

My mouth twisted. My brow furrowed. My brain tried to come up with some sort of rebuttal. "Yeah, well..." I stammered. "We have more important things to do than fact-check your hypothesis."

"Mm-hmm," Jack replied, looking ever so smug. At that moment, I probably should've been more irked at his attitude, but I'll be damned if I couldn't help but laugh like a schoolgirl. Guess the guy was starting to rub off on me again. Did I just say that? Let's pretend I didn't.

I directed my attention back to the short-range scanners. The Kibnali flotilla had engaged the Nodari battleship. It was hard to tell what was going on, but there was a slew of tiny dots flying between the bigger dots on the display.

"Daphne, now that we're going along with this insane suggestion of yours, any chance you can expand upon what exactly we're going to do once we beam over there?"

"Displaying general battleship schematics now," Daphne replied. A moment later, a wireframe representation of what we were going up against popped on my view, and honestly, even on the computer screen as a tiny little model, the thing looked downright terrifying. It easily spanned two kilometers, bristling with cannons, and if I was reading the schematics right, which unfortunately I was, its armor was as thick as any planet's mantle. "I should point out that the layout I'm displaying is an estimation at best. According to records, no two Nodari battleships are the same."

"Your records are accurate," Jainon replied. "This is more due to the fact that they are just as organic as they are metallic. After every battle, they adapt to what they fought, especially as repairs are made."

"Cripes," I said, taking it all in. "We're going inside that thing? How many Nodari are running around in there?"

"Forty-one thousand two hundred, if memory serves," Jainon said.

My eyes went so wide, it was a wonder they didn't burst from their sockets. How I hated that number! I mean, I've already said how much I detest the number four, but forty-one thousand two hundred is even worse! As I said way back when, four sounds like a faster-than-light drive when it's about to go supercritical, but forty thousand feels like...well, like forty thousand nails being dragged across a blackboard. Just thinking about the number is almost enough to send me into permanent seizures.

"Could we please agree never to use that number again?" I asked, gripping my sides and practically falling out of my chair.

"I would also recommend not using that number," Daphne replied.

"Oh, good."

"Because the number for this particular Nodari ship is probably closer to fifty thousand."

"Fifty?"

"The lower bounds of the estimation, yes."

"Now it's the lower bounds?" I buried my face in my hands and said a silent prayer. I still was far from the religious type, but hey, it couldn't hurt. "What's the upper bounds?"

"Eighty thousand. Give or take twenty thousand," she said. "On the bright side, I've almost finished adapting the Progenitor array subroutines. We should be able to hail the Kibnali flotilla in thirty seconds."

"Well that's a plus," I said.

"Provided they don't blast us apart before that," Daphne added. "We will be within firing range of their ships in ten seconds."

My face blanked. Surely I'd heard wrong. "Say again?"

As soon as the words left my mouth, our ship lurched to the side, and from that point on, it felt like we were in a tiny prop plane caught in a Cat 5 hurricane. "Oops, forgot to move that pesky decimal again," Daphne said. "We are within firing range. I have initiated appropriate evasive auto-maneuvers."

"Gah!" I yelled, gripping the armrests. "Why are they shooting at us? We're the good guys!"

"They don't know that," Tolby said. "We're just a blip on their scanners headed straight into battle."

"A blip, no doubt, that's not responding to any IFF systems," Jainon added. "So if they can't identify us as friend—"

"We're foe," I finished.

A brilliant flash of orange exploded on the bow of our ship. Our ship jolted and then took a nosedive. Thank god I was strapped in, because I lifted so hard against my restraints, that if they hadn't been there, I'd surely have punched a hole through the ceiling.

"Incoming flak. Shields are currently holding," Daphne said. "I doubt they will take another direct hit and stay operational, however."

"I vote we don't get hit again," I said.

"I second such a course," Tolby said.

I threw Jack a glance. "Got that?"

"Aye, aye," he said.

Another flurry of explosions erupted around us, and once again our ship violently shifted side to side before entering a tight corkscrew. I was pretty sure we pulled enough Gs that my brain took up temporary residence in my gut.

"Hailing Kibnali flotilla now," Daphne said once our flight leveled out to more tolerable levels.

Jainon practically leaped out of her seat to handle the call. "Ceasefire, 39th Flotilla! This is Jainon Makabe aboard the *Empress's Fang*," she said. "We are not the enemy!"

Much to my utter delight, the withering fire directed toward us suddenly shifted back to the Nodari battleship. A crystal-clear reply came through the comm a moment later. "*Empress's Fang*, this is Rear Admiral Misumo of the 39th Flotilla," he said. Though we had no visual, his voice sounded rough and deep, and I pictured an old, salty Kibnali with muscles as big as tree trunks and more battle scars than I had birthdays. "What is the status of Nagakuro? Sensors are jammed, and there's not much we can see."

"That's because there's not much left to see," Tolby said. "The Nodari have obliterated everything down there."

"Huh, that's strange," Daphne interjected.

"What's strange?" I asked.

"I'm detecting a massive power spike coming from the Nodari battleship," she said. "If it continues on its projected climb for the next five seconds, the ship will blow itself apart."

"Misumo! Full overload on your shields! Now!" Jainon yelled.

Her warning came too late. A half dozen yellow beams leaped from the belly of the battleship and converged before shooting forward and slamming into the lead Kibnali cruiser. Shields flared, and even as far away as we were, I had to shield my eyes from the blinding light. The damn thing might as well have doubled as a supernova.

"What the holy hell," I said, turning back around. "It's got a mega death laser thingy?"

"Yes," Jainon said, blowing out a tense puff of air. Somehow, she managed to crack a smile. I guess when you've seen that much death, dark humor comes naturally. "Though we have a slightly more technical name for it than 'thingy.'"

"*Empress's Fang*, this is Commander Ito," came a new voice on the comm. "What the gods' names was that?"

"A mega death laser thingy," Jainon said, still holding her forced grin. She sucked in another breath before recomposing herself. "Apologies, Commander, we're a little shocked."

"Unless you have a better idea, *Empress's Fang*, I'm ordering a full retreat," Ito said. "We can't repel firepower of that magnitude."

"Negative, 39th," she said. "A retreat is not possible. That ship is running an interdictor field. You'll never make warp."

Ito growled. "Then we fight to the death and make them rue the day they thought they could attack the Kibnali Empire."

At this point, I snapped. I'm not sure why, maybe just the idea of sitting around waiting for us all to be blasted apart didn't sit well with me. "Daphne, pipe whatever plans you've got cooked up for us into my helmet," I said, undoing my buckles and popping off the seat. "Jack, keep flying and keep us alive. Jainon on the guns. Regardless of how ineffective Kibnali weapons are right now, it seems the Progenitors were anything but helpless. So maybe we'll get lucky and knock out that superweapon mega laser thingy before it has a chance to fire again."

"Is that the tailless giving orders?" Ito said, sounding as shocked as ever.

"Yes, and this tailless is going to save your collective fury butts," I said.

"By doing what?"

"Boarding that massive hulk and detonating the storage batteries with some well-placed explosives," I replied, reading

Daphne's plan off my HUD. I then gave Taz a quick belly rub before grabbing my rifle off the back of my seat and rushing for the exit. "That'll take out half of their weapons as well as their interdictor generator."

"You're not boarding anything without me," Tolby said, chasing after me.

"We'll take Yseri, too," I said. "She'll probably want payback."

"I will need Yseri here," Daphne said.

"Why?"

"Someone has to build the bomb," Daphne explained. "I have located the appropriate components inside the ship, including how to fashion a crude timer and detonator, but I am unable to put it together myself."

"Fine," I said. "Being the one who gets to blow them all to hell will probably sit best with her anyway."

We were nearly out of the door when Jainon called out to me. "Dakota!"

"Yes?"

"May Inaja bless you with good fortune."

I smiled. "May her luck be your luck."

I raced down the hall to the portal room. As it turned out, the portal room was the area near the aft of the ship with the large raised platform in the middle. Along the way, I opened a comm to Yseri and filled her in. I probably could've told her all the details better and faster if Jack hadn't had to take evasive maneuvers again, thereby slamming me into the wall once, twice, and then three times again.

"Wormhole creation will be available shortly," Daphne said. "I hope you're at the portal room."

"I'm about to be," I said, hitting the button on the wall that opened the last door between me and it. When the door slid open, my eyes took in three dozen heavily armed, armored and determined Kibnali with Yseri standing front and center.

"A tailless is leading us into battle?" one of the Kibnali scoffed.

I was about to say something when Tolby, who was borrowing a chest piece off a wounded soldier on account of his having been melted previously, beat me to the punch. "Leading, no? That is your duty. But she is the Empress's fang and claw, Major," he said, eyes fiercer than I'd ever seen before. "I assure you, she will not disappoint the honors bestowed upon her."

"A bold claim," the major said. "I hope you're right."

"I know I am," Tolby replied. "Get her to the ship's batteries, and we'll blow them back to the deepest parts of the void."

The Kibnali gave a short nod of approval. "So be it," he said before spinning around to face his troops. "Black Talons, on the ready!"

A chorus of thirty-eight roars went up, which was immediately proceeded by a slap of rifles against armored chests.

I hit the button for my faceplate, and it slid and locked with a loud click. The screen flickered a moment as the self-diagnostic systems ran.

Once it was finished, Daphne spoke into my ear. "I'm locked on to your suit. Ready? Ten seconds until the device is charged."

"Relatively speaking," I said. "I'd rather be in a hot tub."

"So would I," she replied. "Or I think I would. Never really been in one, you know? Electrical systems and all."

I threw a nervous glance at Tolby. "We're going to make this, right?"

"Damn right we are," he replied, slapping me on the back.

A round, hazy blue portal sprang to life in the center of the platform. "Time's up! Go before it closes!" Daphne ordered.

Before I knew it, Tolby and I were charging through with our rifles at the ready, surrounded by a slew of Kibnali warriors.

CHAPTER TWENTY-EIGHT: BOARDING PARTY

The inside of the Nodari battleship was nothing like I had expected. Instead of unyielding floors made from nano-fiber metallic weaves, typical of any spacefaring vessel, what we stood on was an amalgam of flesh and metal. The countless ribs ran up the walls to the top of a peaked roof. Tendrils hung from the ceiling, each with a bulbous sack on the end and dotted with flecks of glowing orange light, and clouds of vapor hung in the air. Side passages came from all sides, as well as the top and floor, making it feel much more like an organic network of blood vessels and organs than anything else.

"Hotter than a furnace in here," one of the Kibnali remarked.

"No kidding," I said as the group fanned out across the hall. For the moment, we were alone, but there were four nearby hatches—oblong, iris-looking things—as well as two directions the hall stretched in. Trouble could come from anywhere, fast, and from multiple directions. "Daphne, can you still hear me?" I asked. "We're in."

"Still reading you loud—" Her voice cut off when there was a loud explosion. Everyone in the platoon instinctively ducked, and I happened to plaster myself on the floor.

"Daphne? Daphne! What's going on?"

"That's not good," she said. "Hope we didn't lose anything important."

"Cripes, what are you on FaceSpace, getting your jollies vague booking? Tell me what happened!"

"Hull breach in the forward cargo bay," she replied flatly. "Some of the supplies kept therein have escaped into the vacuum. Tell you what, whoever didn't tie those down per protocol is going to be in big trouble."

"Dammit, Daphne, I thought you were going to say the engine was on fire," I said, shaking my head. "You scared me half to death."

"What if there was a hot tub in those crates? I bet you'd be sad then."

I growled, and glancing around, it looked as if my frustration with the eccentric AI was shared by the Kibnali marines accompanying me. "Daphne, we don't have time for this. What are we looking for?"

"Right," she said. You need to find a long, glowing yellow thingy that's encased in dark purple thingies, and sort of looks like an old sewer pipe with tiny handlebars every five meters."

My brow arched. "Thingies?"

"I don't have a direct Progenitor translation, and the transliteration as best I can tell is about one hundred and thirty-three characters long. I thought you'd appreciate me saying thingies more. It'll either be on the wall near the ground or somewhere overhead."

I relayed her description to the others, and we found her yellow pipe thingy near the floor, and it was precisely as she described. To my reluctant admittance, it was so oddly shaped that 'thingy' was probably the best descriptor. Unless you wanted to be morbid, because it did have a spine-like quality to it as well.

"Got it," I said.

"Perfect, follow it aft of your position. It should lead you right to the battery room."

"What's the sitrep on the bomb Yseri's building?"

"Should be done in a few minutes," Daphne said. "You'll need to hurry. I wouldn't call it stable. Unless you think an active volcano is stable. Then it's quite so."

"Trust me. We're moving as fast as we can."

A spurting sound came from behind. I spun around as four Nodari scouts entered the hall from the other end. For a split second, they stopped and gawked at us, which was nice because that meant they could be startled like anyone else.

My Kibnali buddies drilled each one a dozen times over with a hail of plasma fire. Their smoldering bodies had yet to hit the ground when Tolby gave his orders. "Move like you've got a purpose, Black Talons," he barked.

Our squad pressed forward. Tolby took the lead, flanked by two other Kibnali. I trailed behind with five others while the rest provided rear security. Following the yellow-purple conduit (which is what I started calling it, as I just couldn't say "thingy" in my head anymore), we went through a hatch that automatically opened when we drew near. Once through, the hall split left and right while at the same time descending down a pair of small ramps covered in some sort of pink membrane covered in pus.

"This is going to make me sick," I said after my second squishy step. I could feel the bile rise in my throat, and I think the only thing that kept me from spewing was the thought of how rancid the inside of my suit would become.

"For once in my life, I wish I had your nose," Tolby said. "The stories from our assault marines do not do the stench of this place justice."

I shuttered, realizing how bad it must be for my best bud. At the same time, my awe for how tough he was grew tenfold.

We followed the conduit, which took us down the passage on the left, but it ended up meeting the other passage anyway. Apparently, the layout had been an elongated donut. There, we continued to follow it for another fifty meters before we hit a T-junction. Before we reached said T-junction, our world erupted in chaos.

Scouts rounded both corners from above, but unlike our previous encounter, they were expecting a battle. I dove to the right, finding scant cover behind some weird-looking organic support that ran from floor to ceiling.

Streams of acid-filled darts flew from the Nodari weapons. Though their fire was met with our own, the Nodari scouts did not falter. They stood there and took the hits in order to land their own shots.

The Nodari fell, heads exploding, torsos shattering, but so did the Kibnali. Roars of defiance blasted in my ears, and the Kibnali marines who hadn't been outright killed struggled to pull off pieces of armor before the acid ate through.

"Incoming rear!" one of the Kibnali yelled.

I twisted so my back was against the beam, figuring I'd best deal with whatever was coming that I didn't have cover from.

Tunnelers, four of them, barreled down the hall, jaws open and ready to snap shut. The first two made it about ten meters before succumbing to the Kibnali fire. The third a few paces more. The fourth, however, thanks to a combination of luck and speed, closed the distance and struck our rearmost guard. It's scissor-like jaws sheared through the Kibnali's rifle as well as his left arm.

To the Kibnali's credit, he didn't falter. Instead, he spun with the momentum of the charging monster and used a kick to get himself clear. A half second later, the rest of our rear guard finished it off.

"Grenade out!" Tolby yelled. I glanced over my shoulder to see him lob one off his belt. It landed in the middle of the T-junction and exploded. A storm of organic-metal shrapnel blew in all directions, and flames licked the sides of the beam I was behind. Despite the fierceness of the blast, we seemed to suffer no other casualties. I couldn't say the same for the scouts.

"Well, if the entire ship didn't know we were here before, they all do now," I said.

A deep rumble came from all around.

We gathered ourselves together in a flash. A few Kibnali went to aid the injured, which amounted to nothing more than slapping some sort of cauterizing gel on the wounds and then sticking the warriors with combat stims.

"Dakota, I hope you're almost there," Jack said into my headset. "The fleet out here is taking a beating."

"Working on it," I said as we all ran down the hall, again following the conduit.

"Work on it faster!"

"We're kind of taking a beating here, too, Jack," I said. "You think we're playing tourist?"

He huffed something, but I didn't catch it. Probably just as well. We didn't need to be jabbing each other, especially as the Kibnali and I were racing through the battleship's tunnels once again.

Our path twisted, and the entire time we ran, I swear I could feel the walls watching us, directing the Nodari to our position. The distant, but closing, howls of multiple Nodari hordes closing in on us from every direction only solidified that belief.

The door ahead unfolded. It didn't want to at first, but after Tolby put a few shots through it, the damn thing unfolded, slinging yellow goo from the wounds my bud gave it.

On the other side, we were met with the most glorious of sights. Seriously, I could've broken into the Hallelujah chorus at this point. True, we hadn't been in the ship long, but it was long enough that all I wanted at this point was to be at our target, which we were.

The chamber before us was almost exactly what Daphne had displayed on screen. It was a cavernous thing that looked like it could swallow a small starship, and given the teeth-like protrusions all around, it would probably devour one just the same. Countless emerald-green bulbous sacks lined the walls, and near them were these large, semi-clear chutes in which a thick, mucusy fluid dripped. The conduit we followed ran to the center of the room where a giant pedestal stood. A dozen spines sprouted from said pedestal, many curling upward to form a loose, wire cage around a pulsating sack.

"We're here," I said. "I can't believe it."

"Perfect," Daphne replied. "We're on our way back to pick you up. Be there soon."

"Back? Back from where?"

"I was going to tell you earlier, but I didn't want to be the bearer of bad news," Daphne said. "You know how you get."

"How I get? What—"

"Watch it! Left flank!" Tolby yelled.

I dropped to the ground and crawled for cover as acidic darts filled the air. Off to our side, some fifty meters away and coming down three separate passages, were scores upon scores of Nodari scouts. Within moments, we were pinned. A few more after that, Kibnali started to fall.

A Kibnali marine a few meters away darted out of his position to get to a better vantage point. Along the way, he fired a short burst from his rifle that took out a couple of scouts. Despite such skill, Fate did not smile on him. Before he reached cover again, his head vaporized, and his body toppled over.

Five seconds later, another two Kibnali died, and then a third when we were suddenly caught in a crossfire as more Nodari came from yet another passage, this one to our right.

"Damn it, Daphne, where are you?" I said, firing like a madwoman. I think I hit a few, but as far as this fight went, a few were nowhere near enough. What we needed was the angry fist of God to smite these abominations.

"As I was saying, we had to take evasive maneuvers and flew out of range of the portal device," she said. "We're back now."

"Send the bomb! Send it right now!"

"Are you sure?" Daphne asked. "It sounds like a lot of fighting is going on. A stray shot and the bomb might detonate. And wouldn't that be a dreadful mess if that detonation occurred in here."

"I'm sure, damn it! We're getting chewed to pieces!"

"Okay, but if we go nuclear, I'm blaming you."

I ducked behind the sack I was using for cover as more Nodari fire zipped by, threatening to melt my face off. "I'm going to open two portals back to back, got it?" I said, peeking around the corner at the battery array we needed to take out. "Set the timer to thirty seconds."

"Say again? Twenty seconds? That's not a lot of time."

"I know, Daphne! If we're not out of here by then, we're all dead!" I pulled a grenade off my belt, and with a little boost from my telekinetic awesomeness, I landed it directly into the Nodari line. Scout bodies vaporized, giving us a few precious seconds of reprieve. "Soon as the bomb is here, shut the first one down, and I'll open a second by us."

"I hope you know what you're doing," Daphne said.

I sucked in a breath. "So do I."

I shot out my hand and focused on the battery array. As troublesome as Daphne was being, she was right about a stray shot ending things quickly. Not to mention, if I opened a portal facing the Nodari, they'd have free access to shoot up our ship. Now, I don't know how you feel about people—or ravenous aliens for that matter—playing target practice with the interior of your ship, but I for one, am not a fan.

A beautiful portal sprang to life on the far side of the battery array, safely tucked behind it. A warhead as tall as I was and easily as thick fell out and landed inside the chamber with a heavy thud. I cringed reflexively, half expecting my world to end right there. The portal closed a split second later, and after launching my last grenade, I dropped a portal near the entrance we'd come through, about twenty meters away. I would've liked to have made it closer, but it was the nearest spot that wasn't facing a Nodari firing line.

"Black Talons, we are leaving!" Tolby bellowed. The intensity of fire from the Kibnali went up tenfold, and no doubt their power packs would be spent, and their weapons would overheat in a matter of seconds, but that's all they needed.

The remaining Kibnali bolted through the portal with the wounded being either carried or dragged through. Even the dead weren't left behind. Tolby was one of the first to the portal, but he didn't go through. Instead, he took up position using an alcove for cover and kept the Nodari at bay as much as he could.

I raced for the exit with everything I had. Less than a few meters away, out of the corner of my eye I caught sight of a Nodari captain charging through the scouts. Before I could get another stride in, he raised his weapon and fired. Dozens of bolts of lightning shot out of the funnel-shaped barrel, electrifying everything they hit.

Three Kibnali caught most of the blast, and as their charred bodies fell, secondary bolts leaped off them, one striking my arm. The jolt through my body was more than enough to send me to the ground, screaming in pain.

"No! God, no," I groaned. I tucked my knees up under me, but I couldn't get up.

Something rammed into my side, rolling me over. Tolby, my furry knight in battle-hardened armor, kept me pinned. "Stay down," he ordered as he tossed a grenade.

As soon as it went off, he yanked me up. We started for the portal, but to my utter horror, it distorted for a split second before disappearing altogether.

CHAPTER TWENTY-NINE: RUNNING AMOK IN MUCK

Stop the detonation!" I yelled. I tried reopening the portal, but all I was successful at doing was sending a stab of pain up my arm and through my neck.

"Why?" Daphne asked.

"We're not aboard!" I said as I slammed into the wall full tilt. For Frapgar's sake, why couldn't that stupid portal have de-stabilized two seconds later? "Now stop the damn bomb from going off!"

"I can't, failsafe settings and all," Daphne said.

"Get us a portal open then!"

"Power levels are still too low," she replied, actually sounding sad for a brief moment before going back to her plucky self. "You'll be pleased to know, however, that in twenty seconds, you should cease to feel any sort of terror. Unless those hellfire and brimstone types are right, then you'll feel a lot of terror. And pain. And suffering. For eternity, of course."

"You're not helping!"

"I did try to help, remember? I tried giving you the Word right after we went through that wormhole after the museum. You wanted nothing of it."

Tolby peeked out from the cover he was using long enough to explode a scout's head with a well-placed shot. "Everyone is safe. That's what matters."

As he spoke, I was barely listening. The hell I was going to die coming this far. My eyes darted around the chamber a hundred times in less than a second, scouring for something—anything— that might save us.

"There!" I said, directing Tolby to a nearby drainage chute. I snapped up my rifle, and with a short burst, I blasted the casing apart. "In! Now!"

I dove headfirst into the tube. Tolby followed right behind. The thing was like a bumpy, mucus-filled waterslide designed explicitly to terrorize anyone foolish enough to shoot down it. The only thing that would've made it worse was the detonation of a small-yield nuclear device and the subsequent chain reaction of energy cells rupturing throughout the entire Nodari ship.

Oh, wait...

My world shook worse than if I'd been trapped in a giant hamster ball and tossed into a tornado. Tolby slammed into my ass as we fell when the blast wave caught up to us. Thank god for Kibnali armor. That stuff is tough. Even if I'd been in a Martian Mk IX battle tank, I bet I would've been torn to pieces. Thankfully, I was wearing the best tech any spacefaring race had ever developed, Progenitors aside, and survived the hit.

The shockwave accelerated us to speeds beyond compre-hension. We probably flew a half a klick before shooting out of the tube like a wayward champagne cork. Now don't get me wrong. I was thrilled to still be alive and nearly as ecstatic to be out of that slimy, dark tunnel of putrid crap, but where we ended up wasn't much better. I might even go as far as to say that it was even worse.

We landed inside an oblong sack, for lack of a better word, that probably stretched thirty meters from where we ended up. Numerous other tubes entered this area from above, each one dripping a thick, yellow mucus that made me gag just thinking about it. And because said mucus was dripping in from numerous other places, that meant that the entire room was covered in it. In fact, it was so covered in it the floor was drowned in the substance by almost a meter. So when we bounced off the wall and fell back down, we were each treated to a full bath.

"I almost wish we died," I said, finding my footing. I tried to get Daphne on the comm but stopped after being greeted with a lot of static, which was then followed by me noticing a flashing icon on the bottom left of my HUD. The connection was lost. Damn.

"This might be the grossest thing you've led me through," Tolby said. "And that includes chasing that firetoad through that malfunctioning septic system."

"That was not my fault!" I said. "How was I supposed to know he was going to eat my keys?"

"Because he ate your flashlight before that."

"So?"

"And your laser pointer. And your socks. And your—"

"Okay, okay. Sheesh," I said.

Tolby smiled, and that smile turned to a nervous one when another explosion rocked the ship. "At least this is just like old times, huh?"

I wrinkled my nose as the sickly sweet smell of the god-awful room we were in started to seep through my armor. Apparently, my armor wasn't completely sealed from atmo anymore. "Old times? Gah, I don't ever want this to be considered old times to look forward to."

"If the past week is any indicator of our future, seems like we're in store for this a lot," he said. "After all, what's this, the third ship now that's started to disintegrate with us in it?"

"To be fair, the museum took two out at once," I said. "But if we wind up on another abandoned planet with some long-forgotten Progenitor facility with aliens trying to make us a snack, I'm calling shenanigans on life." The comm link indicator on my HUD suddenly lit up, and I seized the moment. "Daphne? Are you there?"

"Dakota! How delightful that you lived!" she said. "Well, mostly delightful. I'm out twenty credits."

"You're out...wait, you bet against us?" I said, filling in the details. "How could you do that?"

"Oh, very simple," she said. "After calculating the odds of your survival, the bet was a no-brainer. Have you ever thought that you might have some feline DNA? By my estimations, you used at least a few lives up these last few days. I don't suppose you've found a shuttle bay that you could escape out of?"

I shook my head and sighed. "If only. I have no idea where we are."

"That does add a certain challenge to things."

"You think?"

"Especially since the Nodari reinforcements will be here in less than seven minutes. Maybe six. But if I were you, I'd be out of there in five at the most. Their cruisers are a lot quicker than I'd anticipated. On the flip side, you did manage to knock out their shields. You should see the fireworks from here. The Kibnali are tearing the ship you're in to pieces. Perhaps you could escape through one of the many breaches in the hull."

I stumbled as the battleship rocked with a series of explosions, and thankfully Tolby kept me upright before I was swimming in mucus again. Actually, I should correct that. He caught me from swimming in the mucus for about two seconds. After that, the bottom of the sac fell out, and we were treated to a nice sticky bath of putrid goo.

Tolby and I tumbled down a slanted wall and ended up in the middle of a large, egg-shaped room. Banks of bio-mechanical contraptions lined both sides of the room, each one manned by a separate Nodari scout, probably three dozen in total. Each scout had a slew of tubes attached to its head and body, wiring it directly into whatever contraption it was seated in front of. Of those three dozen Nodari, maybe six were still alive. The rest were slumped over or sprawled on the floor, many of them being nothing more than charred husks. The ones who still lived didn't seem as if they fared much better. They barely moved in their seats, offering little more than a twitch at our arrival.

At the far end, the floor ramped up to what I can only describe as a perverse throne built on flesh, resin, and mechanical equipment that seemed more at home in an old steampunk thriller than out here in space. Atop said throne sat a monster who was plugged into the ship like the others, and he, no doubt, was what the boogeyman checked for under his bed, especially since he was far from dead.

The damn thing was over four meters tall, and it stared at us with four milky eyes that were set into a bulbous head. And if the number four hadn't been used enough in its creation to torment me, it had four arms sprouting from its side, along with a beard of four tentacles hanging from its chin. Four fours. Cripes. Could it get worse? Oh yes. Yes, it could.

Its chitinous armor looked white as bone, though it had some dark purple highlights where the ridges were. And for whatever reason, I suspected that nothing short of a naval railgun would punch through said armor. The look in Tolby's eyes confirmed that feeling.

"He does not like carrots, does he?" I said, easing back.

"That is a Nodari monarch," Tolby said, making me immediately wish that he hadn't. "He doesn't like anything."

The monarch stood, and with one sweep of his powerful hands, he tore himself free from his throne and bellowed.

"I suggest we run," I said.

"I agree."

I whipped my rifle up and pulled the trigger. My shot zipped through the air and struck it square between the eyes. Under any other circumstances, I would've been elated. How often do actually hit what I want with my first shot? Or my tenth, for that matter. Actually, don't answer that. Anyway, instead of the plasma bolt installing new ventilation in the monarch's head, it struck a force field that flared momentarily before dissipating harmlessly.

Refusing to believe it, I fired off several more rounds. All of those missed wildly thanks to my typical shooting abilities, but one landed with similar results.

"You're not punching through that shield, Dakota!" Tolby said. He grabbed my arm and pulled right as the monarch brought up a pair of heavy blasters.

"Look out!" I yelled.

The monarch fired. Two superheated beams of plasma shot forward, one driving for each of us. Tolby bolted behind a console without being hit. I went the other direction but wasn't quite as lucky. Even though I got behind a console as well, the beam hit my rifle, punched through it, and then took a nice chunk of armor out of my hip. Globs of molten metal went everywhere. Most of it flew away from me, some, however, seared my skin, and it was all I could do not to curl up into a little ball of agony.

"Dakota! Great news!" Daphne said into my earpiece. "I know where you are!"

"Please tell me you can get us out," I said, trying my best to scamper away while using the consoles for cover.

"Easily!" she replied. "I see you are in the throne room! Did you know it doubles as the bridge? You have to respect that kind of ingenuity."

Stupidly, I peeked over the edge of the console to see where the monarch was, and he was so close, we practically bumped noses. Well, I assumed it was a nose. He had this stumpy thing in the middle of his face with four pits on each side, like the heat pits on a viper. (And there's that stupid number four again). He whipped his blasters up, and reflexively I dove to the side while at the same time, telekinetically punching one of them.

Thank my lucky stars my brain went with that plan. He fired a split second later with both weapons and the one I hit sideways ended up frying the other. Damn, I'm good sometimes. Course, the subsequent explosion wasn't very pleasant, especially the part where I ended up getting peppered with shrapnel. Thankfully, the Kibnali armor I sported deflected most of it.

Unfortunately, whatever super shield the monarch carried deflected all of what hit him. So while I got away with a few minor wounds, he came out completely unscathed.

I staggered backward as the monarch roared. I took that time to put as much distance between myself and it as I could by sprinting for the only exit I saw, which happened to be where Tolby was headed as well.

Long before we got there, a dozen Nodari scouts came pouring in from that precise location.

"Cripes! How many of these guys are we going to run across?" I yelled, vaulting over a console in order not to take the half dozen shots that headed my way a moment later.

"My current estimations of surviving Nodari put the number at thirty-nine thousand, seven hundred," Daphne replied.

"Is that all?" Tolby said with a sneer. Like me, he was taking cover behind a console, but he still had his rifle, and he put it to good use. In the span of a few seconds, the dozen Nodari numbered nine. A few seconds after that, he brought that down to eight when an overly zealous scout tried to rush his position and had his face melted.

"I don't care about their numbers, Daphne! Get us out of here!" I yelled.

"Of course," she said. "We can pick you up about five hundred meters from your position. There's a sizeable breach in the hull there."

The room shuddered, and then the walls, ceiling, and floor crumpled together like a giant hand from the outside gave it a friendly squeeze.

"What the hell was that?"

"Didn't I tell you?" Daphne asked. "The destruction of the interdictor generator has left a peculiar vortex in spacetime that's currently swallowing the ship. I suggest leaving."

"We're trying!"

The monarch leaped over the console, closing the distance between him and me. As he flew through the air, a blade suddenly appeared in one of his hands, and he brought it down in an overhead chop. A combination of luck from Taz's belly rubs and a telekinetic punch from yours truly kept me from being cut in half.

"Dakota, we've got to leave!" Tolby said.

I threw a glance at my buddy, ready to rip him a new one for stating the obvious. My words got stuck in my mouth when I saw the hordes of Nodari that were racing down the corridor and into the bridge. I didn't need a calculator to know no matter what we did, we'd be swimming in Nodari in a dozen seconds at most.

"Why aren't they abandoning ship?" I asked, dodging yet another attack by the monarch.

"They don't abandon anything!" Tolby said. He popped off a few more shots, taking down two scouts in the process. He was forced back when a hail of acidic darts threatened to turn him into a smoldering puddle. He tried to return a few more shots of his own, but they had him locked down under enough suppression fire that even an entire platoon of Kibnali would be lucky to sneeze and not be ripped to shreds. It was a small wonder that the consoles even remained semi-intact.

"Daphne, we'll never make it out! You've got to open up a wormhole for us!" I yelled, feeling my throat tighten and eyes water. God, I was so close to getting out, getting home. I couldn't believe I was going to buy it here in some stupid alien ship a bajillion years before I was even born. How do you write that tombstone anyway? I mean, those dates would give anyone a double take.

"Power reserves for the portal will not be at high enough levels for operation for another ten minutes," she said.

"Gah!"

The monarch threw his blade. The thing whipped by, missing my neck by a Planck length. The weapon embedded itself in the wall behind. The attack, however, was still enough to get me off balance. The monarch pounced, striking me dead center.

I hit the ground square on my back as the thing towered over me like a bear. I managed to get my hand up in time before the monarch drove his full weight through my chest and stopped it with a telekinetic punch. To my dismay, it wasn't enough to knock him aside thanks to his stupid super shield. So what ended up happening was that he staggered a second before renewing his attack, which was then met with more of a constant telekinetic push from my implants than a strike. Worse, I could feel my arm getting cold, and my energy would be depleted in moments. I tried to pull energy from the air as I had with the water using my left arm, but I don't think I got much, if any.

"Daphne! Where's the flotilla?"

"Escaping. Why?"

"I need a full salvo on the bridge!"

"Aren't you in it?"

"Not for much longer! Do it!"

"Okay, but if you cost me another twenty credits, I'm not going to be happy."

CHAPTER THIRTY:
TWENTY CREDITS

Everything exploded.

And I mean everything. The first thing that went was a twenty-meter-wide portion of the wall across from me. It vaporized in a flash, and from the edges white-hot globs of metal went flying. The monarch shielded me from most of it, and in turn, his shields shielded him, too. I did catch a rather large chunk in my forearm, which while painful, wasn't the most pressing matter. What followed next was.

The next things that exploded were threescore of Nodari as a missile flew through the breach in the hull, sailed past my head, and detonated in the middle of them all. Immediately following said blast was the disintegration of pretty much everything in the bridge. The only things spared were me, thanks to the monarch; the monarch, thanks to his super annoying shields of you'll-never-kill-me-no-matter-what-you-do (note to self, put in an order for those ASAP); and Tolby, who had four consoles, two bulwarks, and the body of a Nodari scout to keep him safe.

With hull integrity being exactly zero for our location, physics took over and whisked us out into space with a rush of escaping air.

End over end I tumbled, and my head erupted in pain and confusion. I tried to see who was where and what the hell was going on, but everything was spinning so fast I didn't have a prayer. I tried to scream for Tolby, and then again to Daphne so she could come pick us before we were lost and frozen to the void, but thanks to the vacuum we were in and the fact that my armor was compromised, I had no air. And because I had no air, I wasn't saying a damn thing.

That said, trying to scream was probably the only thing that kept me from having an embolism since the rapidly expanding air in my lungs could get out. The next few seconds stretched for eternity as consciousness slipped away. My world went cloudy, then dark, then ceased to exist.

The next thing I knew, something large, wet, and scratchy smeared across my face. I open my eyes and found Tolby hunched over me. I was flat on my back in the loading bay of the *Empress's Fang*.

Yseri stood next to him, and once I came to, he threw the handmaiden a wry grin. "I told you that would wake her up."

I brushed a hand against my cheek and made a face as it came back with slobber. I love my bud and all, but seriously, I didn't need a deluge of giant cat slobber on my face.

"That's twice now I've had to do that," he said. "Think we could avoid suffocating in space from here on out?"

"I'd be okay with that," I replied. "What happened? Are we safe?"

"For the moment," he said. The ship rocked. "And that moment's over."

Tolby hoisted me to my feet as I tried to get my bearings. "What's going on?"

"We're still in the middle of a Nodari invasion," he said.

Before I could reply, Daphne spoke over the comm. "Did she live? If so, I could use her help on the bridge. And I could also use another twenty credits, too, due to an unforeseen incurring of debt."

"Yes, I'm alive thank you! And thanks a lot for betting against me!" I shouted as I ran through the ship. I bounced off a few walls along the way thanks to more shaking, more rumbling, and what I presumed were evasive maneuvers that were keeping us from being annihilated. So I guess I can't complain that much, but there was no way I wasn't coming out covered in more bruises than the loser of a twelve-round MMA bout.

When I got to the bridge, both Jack and Jainon were still at their stations. Jack was intensely focused on his screen, flying and working the guns on Nodari drones that were still swarming the area. Jainon, on the other hand, stared at the floor, a hand over one of her ears, as she coordinated chatter between herself and all the other Kibnali ships in the flotilla.

"They're clear and jumping in ten seconds," she said, looking up.

"Why aren't we?" I asked as I staggered sideways thanks to another evasive maneuver.

"Our ship is caught in that spacetime vortex caused by the ruptured interdictor generator," Daphne said. "Destroying the battleship's main reactor ought to destabilize its pull long enough for us to escape."

"What can we do about that?"

"You can get over here and help me shoot," Jack cut in.

I jumped into my seat, and he transferred some of the gun control to my station. Targeting computers brought to view what was left of the Nodari battleship. Even though we were spinning around it at high speed, I could still see exactly what they were talking about.

The battleship had a massive hole blown out one side, presumably where the bomb we detonated went off. However, the rest of the ship had collapsed in on itself, like it was a submarine far too deep and crumpling from overpressure. In the couple of brief seconds I was watching, the starboard bow folded in on itself and massive gouts of flame shot forth.

"How long do we have?" I asked, grabbing the controls.

"Less than a minute," Daphne said. "Putting the approximate location of the main reactor on screen now."

A triangle flashed on to the display, and immediately I went to work swiveling the antimatter cannons around and letting them rip. It didn't take me long to realize that our target was buried in so much ship, we were going to be sucked in long before we shot our way free. "This is never going to work."

"Do you have any other ideas?" Jack asked.

"Yeah. Hit the nitro button."

"This ship is not equipped with nitrous oxide," Daphne said. "Besides, that only works with combustion engines."

I smacked my forehead. "It was a figure of speech, Daphne."

"Oh good," she said. "Because you'd need a lot more than nitrous oxide to see any sizeable gains in the catalytic matter convertor. Anything short of a finely tuned packet of antimatter or a maybe a Gorrianian resonance crystal won't produce enough energy."

"A what?"

"A Gorrianian resonance crystal," she said. "They are highly prized gems—"

"I know what they are!" I said. In a panic, I ripped off my armor and found the crystal I had stashed away. "Jainon, you're the Progenitor engineer around here. Catch! Daphne, walk her through the process over the comms! Jack and I will keep shooting."

I tossed the little red gem, and she snatched it out of the air. "On it," she said, racing out of the bridge.

"How clever of you to have one lying around," Daphne said.

"I've had it for days!"

"You have? Hmm. Looks like my inventory database isn't working too well," she said. "Regardless, perhaps we should stock up on more for just this sort of occasion."

"I'd love to stock up on more, Daphne. I really would," I said as I tried not to think about how much money I was about to lose.

Jack and I continued to blast apart the Nodari ship. Tolby strapped himself into his spot in the bridge. I think he was chanting some sort of battle hymn, or maybe it was a final recital their warriors did when they were about to die. Not really sure. Seconds ticked by and the Nodari battleship grew bigger and more prominent on the view screen.

"We're about to make out with this thing, Jainon," I called out. "Need that crystal injected!"

"I'm trying!" she called back. It's not like throwing a log in the furnace!" she yelled back over the comm.

A klaxon blared. If I hadn't already had a death grip on the controls, I'd probably have rocketed through the ceiling.

"That sounds like a very bad noise," Jack said.

"Incoming Nodari assault pods," Daphne said.

"Assault pods? For us? Don't they land on planets or something?"

"They land on—or through in our case—anything they want," Tolby said.

I swiveled my guns around to meet the new threat, and my jaw dropped. It wasn't just a few assault pods coming. It was a swarm of them, thicker and scarier than any pissed-off hive of killer veloci-wasps. And if you're wondering, yes, those are the freakish velociraptor/wasp hybrids that got loose on...on...well, whatever the official name of Planet Don't-Ever-Land-Here is.

I gritted my teeth and blasted away, but for each one I vaporized, two more drew closer. It was like trying to defeat a flamethrower with a garden hose.

"Jainon!" I yelled. "We're out of time!"

The interior of the cockpit suddenly flared with light, and the guns I was on seemed more responsive and deadlier than ever.

"Power injection successful," Daphne said.

I didn't even have time to suck in a breath. Our ship tore free of the tractor beam as the pinpoint stars in the distance stretched into long lines across our view.

CHAPTER THIRTY-ONE: FIN

A thousand light-years from Kumet, I sat on the bridge of the *Empress's Fang*, having one last talk with Commander Ito over the comms while Tolby and his handmaidens were satiating their carnal desires, *again*.

The surviving ships of the flotilla had made necessary repairs over the last two days, and we'd transferred all but ten members of the Black Talon company over to their ships as well.

"I wish you'd reconsider, Commander," I said, feeling saddened at their upcoming departure. "We can't change the past, well, the future for you guys."

"I understand your concern," he said, "but it seems you've already changed our past. None of us could live with ourselves should we not try and defend our home."

"If you saw what I had in the museum..."

"Perhaps. But should we still fail, you have ten of my finest male and female Kibnali to see to the rebuilding of our race. That is more than enough to sprout a new empire, gods willing."

I sighed heavily and fell back into my chair. There was no arguing it. Not now, at least.

"You could still come with us, as long as we're talking about decisions," he said. "The tech you have could be capitalized before the war swings out of our control."

I shook my head. "I can't," I said as I threw a glance to Jack. He gave an approving nod but said nothing. He and I had already had our talk. "I've made a promise I have to keep."

"You are as noble as you are fierce," he said with a chuckle. "My apologies for ever doubting you."

I smiled at the compliment. "No worries."

"Then this where we say farewell," he said.

Before he could say anything else, the unease that had been building in my heart the last couple hours gave birth to a magnificent idea. "Wait," I said, quickly bringing up a list of Kibnali worlds deep in their empire. I wanted one that wouldn't be decimated too quickly, but not so close that we'd instantly be blown apart if we showed up out of the blue. "The planet Nuro, do you know it?"

Ito smiled. "There's not a Kibnali alive who doesn't. Famous throughout the Empire for its rich spices and unparalleled shipyards. Not to mention it is the birthplace of warrior-poet Nakamu Se."

"Perfect," I said, tapping the screen to drill the planet's name into my memory. "Tell your Empress that we'll be there in thirty years, on the nose."

"It has no nose," he said, brow dropping.

I laughed and shook my head. "Figure of speech where I come from. I mean we'll be there exactly thirty years from now."

"Because?"

"To check in," I said. "That'll be long enough for you guys to see if the war is winnable, but hopefully not so long we can't at least do something if things haven't changed from my view. Should be easy to pop on over there no matter where or when we are once we're zipping through the webway network like old pros."

Ito gave a slight bow. "You are an honor to your species. Empress will look forward to meeting you, especially after she hears of all your exploits."

"Be sure to remind her to tell everyone else not to blast us out of the sky when we show up," I said. "I'd appreciate that."

"Of course," he said. He then touched the top of his head and bowed once more. "May Inaja bless you with good fortune."

I repeated the gesture. "May her luck be your luck."

Once the call ended, Jack spoke. "Thanks. I'll be honest, I had my reservations you'd hold up your end of our deal."

I grinned. "Well, your brother is the cute one of you two. Is he seeing anyone?"

"Ha. Ha. Very funny."

My smile faded, and I raised an eyebrow.

"You are joking, right?"

I turned back to the nav panel. "Daphne, did you get us a lead on another webway?"

"Affirmative," she said. "Sending you the most promising location now."

"Awesome sauce. Plot us a course, then. Second star to the right. Straight on till morning."

"It's actually fifth star to our eight o'clock low."

"Whatever," I said, laughing.

Jack cleared his throat. "Dakota?"

"Yes?"

"You were joking...right?"

I shrugged, slipped on some headphones that were piping in my favorite tunes, and sank back in my chair. Maybe I'd give him an answer in a few hours.

Maybe.

(PAGE LEFT INTENTIONALLY BLANK)

(EXCEPT FOR THAT LINE; AND THIS ONE, TOO)

ONE STEP BEHIND
(DAKOTA ADAMS BOOK IV)

Dear Little Miss Doppelganger,

I know you think you're clever, stealing my life and my best friend.

And you might've succeeded if I'd died after you marooned me.

But guess what? I found a way off this god-forsaken rock, and now I'm coming for you.

So, if you value your existence, I suggest you leave my ship, friends, and family alone this instant. I promise if you do, that'll be the end of it.

I'd rather be plotting my next dig while sipping root beer anyway. But if you insist on pretending to be me...

Well, all bets are off, and you won't even get a Viking funeral.

Love,
The *Real* Dakota Adams

ACKNOWLEDGMENTS

As always, I have the usual crew to thank: My wife for putting up with a lot of bad writing over the years, my wonderful editor Crystal for turning slop into something decent, Katrina for proofing it one last time, and my kids for giving me endless ideas on what's fun and adventurous.

I'm also forever grateful to Katherine Littrell who breathed wonderful life into the characters and gave Dakota the voice she needs.

Of course, none of this would be possible without all my brilliant readers, new and old; so here's to hoping you enjoyed book three and are off to see what book four has in store.

ABOUT THE AUTHOR

When not writing, Galen Surlak-Ramsey has been known to throw himself out of an airplane, teach others how to throw themselves out of an airplane, take pictures of the deep space, and wrangle his four children somewhere in Southwest Florida.

He also manages to pay the bills as a chaplain for a local hospice.

Be sure to drop by his website https://galensurlak.com/and sign up for his newsletter for free goodies, contests, and plenty of other fun stuff

ABOUT THE PUBLISHER

Tiny Fox Press LLC
5020 Kingsley Road
North Port, FL 34287

www.tinyfoxpress.com